THE EYRIE

WEIRD TALES was the first and most famous of all the fantasy-fiction pulp magazines. It featured tales of the strange, the marvelous, and the supernatural by the finest authors of the macabre and the fantastic, old and new, from its first issue in 1923 until its 279th and last consecutive issue in 1954.

Now it is back, with all new stories—and even such an exciting find as *Scarlet Tears,* a recently discovered and never before published novelette by Robert E. Howard.

Over the years many great writers were published in the pages of WEIRD TALES, and now a great tradition is being continued into its second half-century.

MORE FANTASTIC READING!

Weird Tales #1

Edited by Lin Carter

ZEBRA BOOKS

KENSINGTON PUBLISHING CORP.

ZEBRA BOOKS

are published by

KENSINGTON PUBLISHING CORP.
21 East 40th Street
New York, N.Y. 10016

Welcome to the new *Weird Tales*! With this first issue — in an exciting new format — the first and most famous of all the fantasy fiction pulp magazines returns to thrill you again with new stories of the strange, the marvelous and the supernatural, by the finest authors of the macabre and the fantastic, old and new.

It was in the earlier issues of this magazine that so many of the immortal stories of H. P. Lovecraft, Robert E. Howard, Clark Ashton Smith and others first appeared. Through these pages first stalked the grim figures of Solomon Kane, King Kull and Conan the Cimmerian; herein Jules de Grandin, merriest and most inimitable of all the ghost-chasers, pursued evil monsters in many a memorable tale; and here the dark shadows of Cthulhu, Nyarlathotep and Tsathoggua first brooded ominously. For it was in *Weird Tales* that today's popular genre of "sword and sorcery" began and the fascinating and eerie "Cthulhu Mythos" was born.

continued on page 255.

Weird Tales

Spring, 1981   Vol. 48, No. 1

LIN CARTER, EDITOR
Associates: Roy Torgeson, and Robert Weinberg

What was in the jade box that was worth the lives of so many men?

Scarlet Tears

By Robert E. Howard

A recently discovered, previously un-published complete novelette by the late master of weird heroic fantasy

Robert E. Howard first appeared in the pages of this magazine with a short story called "Spear and Fang," which was published in our issue of July, 1925. From then until now, his superlatively evocative verse and vigorous fiction graced no fewer than one hundred and eight issues of the Unique Magazine. So forceful were the characters he created—Conan the Cimmerian, King Kull, Bran Mak Morn, Solomon Kane—so enthralling were the adventures he spun for them, that they have gone on into books and paperbacks, comic magazines and even the movies, winning for themselves and for their creator an immortality richly deserved. We are fortunate indeed that one last story could be found to adorn this first issue of the newly-revived *Weird Tales*!

1. A Cry in the Night

Kirby swore, twisting the wheel of the little roadster as tires skidded in the loose dirt of the country road. Beside him the girl gasped and clutched his arm. Moments later he had regained control of the machine and they both breathed easier.

"We should be getting close to your uncle's estate," the burly detective muttered as he guided the car through the foggy night, its headlights slashing twin cones of brilliance through the eerie mist. The dark girl shivered, nodding.

"It's not much farther now," she said. "Soon you'll see for yourself, and stop doubting my story!"

Kirby grinned; it was a crazy yarn the dark-haired girl had spun back in his dusty cubbyhole of an office—sinister Oriental cultists skulking in the bushes around a country estate, trying to get their swarthy hands on *something* brought back from the East—she didn't even know what! According to her, dark, foreign men had been glimpsed in the underbrush, there had been several attempts at burglary, and her uncle's watchdogs, huge fierce mastiffs, four of them, killed with poisoned darts.

The worse thing about the girl's story was that

her uncle was—*frightened*. Frightened nearly to death. And from everything Kirby had read in the newspapers about Richard Corwell, the explorer and adventurer, he didn't sound like the sort of man anyone could easily frighten.

A road sign swam into the glow of the headlights. It bore the name of a nearby town called Baskerton.

"The side road leading to Uncle Richard's estate should be next," the girl murmured. Not taking his eyes from the road, the detective nodded grimly. Under one arm he felt the reassuring bulge of his automatic in its worn holster, under the other the flat weight of a Bowie knife. Both had served him well in tight spots before. And if there was anything at all to the girl's wild tale, they would soon come in handy.

"You've no idea what these people are after?" he inquired.

Gloria Corwell shook her head reluctantly, dark curls tousling. "Something that's in a carven jade box, that's all I know, Mr. Kirby. Uncle will tell me nothing at all! But surely—"

"Surely it must be valuable enough, for people to kill dogs and try to break into houses," he finished for her, with a sideways glance. Her dark eyes were troubled, the pale oval of her face serious.

"I told you about the veiled threats over the phone," she said, "and how the servants were frightened off, all save Farnum, Uncle Richard's valet, and Daley, an old retainer who's been with the family as far back as I can remember—" She broke off; the side road had appeared so suddenly

11

in the headlights' glare that Kirby almost missed it. Brakes squealed as he whipped the roadster into the dark mouth of a lane framed with rows of ancient elms. Gravel crunched under spinning wheels.

"It's not far now," she whispered as the car followed twists and turns in the road. Unbroken darkness closed about the car; despite himself, Kirby felt a chill touch of uneasiness. He didn't like the way clammy coils of mist glided between the dark trees, luminous shapes in the glare of the lights, and he growled something under his breath. All the fighting Irish in his blood awoke when he came close to fear — or as close as the rugged, two-fisted detective *could* come!

It was almost midnight when they came within sight of the huge shape of Corwell Manor crouching behind its walls. To the southeast a few lights indicated the nearest town, but no other sources of illumination broke the thick darkness. The moon was hidden behind a veil of clouds and, evidently, no other houses were near enough to relieve the solitude of the wooded countryside. The master of Corwell Manor was obviously not gregarious.

"If they haven't gotten over the walls of the estate yet," Kirby muttered, "we may have a chance. They'll know we're reinforcements, when we turn in at the gate. We'll have to take a chance of being shot at, and work fast—"

"You can park here and we can use a side-door," Gloria said nervously, trying to peer into the shadows between the trees. "I slipped out that way.

I haven't got the keys for the front gate, and besides, most of them will be there."

He nodded, easing the car to a standstill, dousing the lights. The wall loomed before them, tall as the battlements of a castle. It was easy to see why the cultists hadn't gotten through or over it. Gloria touched his arm, pointing at the little door, half-hidden by bushes. He slid out of the car, shoulders instinctively hunched, momentarily expecting a blast of hot lead from the shadows, but none came. Now it was touch and go! Gloria was fumbling at the small, iron-braced door in the wall, and Kirby's flesh crawled at the thought of poison darts in the night. Gun in hand he crouched, straining his eyes, alert for the least flicker of movement in the gloom, shielding the girl with his own body. In the utter stillness he heard her quick breathing, and the scrape of her key in the lock. The silence was oppressive, stifling. Somewhere, far off in the woods, he heard a strange quavering cry that might have been a night bird. But no bird's cry ever sent chills up his spine like that!

Then the key turned in the lock, and an instant later they were on the other side of the wall, and Gloria was locking the door behind them and fixing the bolt back into place, trembling with relief.

The old house bulked huge and dark above a wide lawn, thickly shadowed by trees and shrubs. Not a light showed in the barred and shuttered windows. They followed a narrow walk among thick bushes to a side-door, and there Gloria beat a quick tattoo with her slim knuckles. There came no other sound, and no reply. Her face turned questioningly towards him, a pallid oval in the wan starlight that shone through rents in the clouded skies.

"There's no answer!" she whispered, clutching at his hand; he could almost feel the wild throbbing of her heart. "It's so still—oh, I'm afraid something's happened!"

Away off in the woods there rose again that weird, ululating cry, and Kirby knew it came from no bird's throat. He scanned the rugged stony walls of the house, the barred and shuttered windows, the wisps of fog that clutched like vaporous tentacles seeking entry.

"Let's try the front," he suggested. They hurried around the somber, silent house which was like a brooding citadel of mystery. They reached a wide, pillared veranda—

A low cry burst from Gloria's lips. The front door gaped open, sagging on broken hinges. Within, the darkness was Stygian, impenetrable, but Kirby thought he heard something stirring, like a stealthy footfall. Taking a desperate chance, he flashed the beam of his electric torch through the door. Gloria screamed—

"*Uncle Richard!* They've killed him!"

2. *Shadowy Intruders*

Just within the front hall a man lay with a great bloody welt on his brow. The dark girl broke from Kirby's restraining hand and threw herself beside the prostrate form, sobbing convulsively. He

14

followed, his flesh creeping at what the darkness might conceal, flashing his beam in all directions—it halted on another body sprawled in a pool of blood. The man's throat had been cut from ear to ear.

"Farnum or Daley?" Kirby asked, dreading to show the girl this new horror, but urgently needing information. She looked, shuddered sickly, but kept her head. "It's the other servant, Daley," she moaned.

Kirby played his torch about, illuminating a broad stair that wound upwards into inky gloom, panelled walls, a fireplace, doors that led into outer halls. The house seemed silent, deserted, but Kirby wondered what might be crouching in the darkness beyond the range of his faculties.

"Let's get him into a chair," rapped Kirby, for the older man was breathing raggedly but seemed more stunned than hurt. As Kirby worked over the senseless man, he was listening with fierce intensity for sounds from the interior of the house. For all he knew, the gloomy mansion was full of stealthy murderers . . .

Richard Corwell was beginning to groan and stir. Kirby pressed a flask to his lips. Presently the master of the manor blinked dazedly in the light of the torch. He was a lean, aristocratic man of middle age but worn and shrunken and quite changed from the newspaper photographs Kirby had seen. His face seemed haggard, his eyes haunted.

"Kill me if you will," he groaned like one in a dream. "But take the cursed box and go . . ."

"It's Gloria, Uncle Richard!" cried the girl,

throwing her arms about his neck, sobbing. "Don't you know me? What's happened here?"

"Gloria?" he mumbled. "Thank God you're safe! When I found your note I didn't think I'd ever see you alive again—"

"But what happened?"

"They got in—somehow. The alarms didn't work. They were breaking through the door before we knew it—lean, dark-skinned devils with eyes like mad dogs!" He shuddered. "I think Farnum killed one of them with the fire poker. Then another one struck me on the head . . ." His vague, wandering gaze caught sight of the corpse and his face went grey. "Poor Daley! Oh, the murderous swine!" Then his gaze became fixed on the burly stranger at his niece's side, and he demanded suspiciously: "Who is this man?"

"A private detective," she answered. "Here to help us—"

"Who did this? What do you know about them?" rapped Kirby, wasting no time on social amenities. The older man shook his head feebly.

"I never saw them before they burst in here— shadowy intruders—strangers," he murmured. Then, as his attention wandered, his face crumpled wearily, and an expression of horrible recollection blanched his features. "Farnum!" he exclaimed. "They've got Farnum, the fiends! God—they'll torture him mercilessly, and he knows nothing! We can't leave poor Farnum in their cruel clutches!"

"Who are 'they'?" demanded Kirby in a roar that made the other blink and regain control of himself. When the answer came, faltering, his nape-hairs tingled and the flesh crept on his forearms. For the truth was even more menacing than the girl's crazy story suggested . . .

"Hindu madmen!" whispered Richard Corwell in hollow tones. "Devilish votaries of the death-goddess, Kali."

"You mean—?" murmured Kirby through stiff lips. Richard Corwell nodded hopelessly.

"Yes . . . *Thuggee.*"

The ugly syllables of that ancient, dreaded name seemed to rustle in sinister echoes through the black gloom of the hall like the dry scales of a deadly serpent slithering over dead men's bones.

3. Blood on Cold Steel

Kirby lit a small lamp on a side-table; its faint gleam could hardly be visible through the shuttered and curtained windows. He pushed the broken front door shut, wedging it tight with the back of a chair. The dim light made shadows lurk eerily in the corners, glinted on antique swords and the horns of mounted trophies adorning the walls.

"Stay here," the detective snapped. "I'm going to search the house; I doubt if anybody's hiding here, but we've got to be sure."

Corwell nodded shakily. Kirby went through the nearer door and moved cautiously down a hall, his torch lighting the gloom ahead. He looked briefly into each room opening off the hall, but saw no one, alive or dead. As he approached the kitchens in the rear, he found a door which led out onto the lawn. It was open and unlocked; snapping off his light he checked and found the door had neither been broken nor forced from the outside. Had the murderers left by this door? Perhaps . . .

Outside, he crept into the cover of bushes to look around. The clouds had parted and a full moon floated like a silver skull in the dark heavens. The clammy mist had vanished and the night was still. Suddenly, he froze, for out on the lawn the moonlight disclosed a skulking figure moving in the shadows of the trees. Like a bodiless shadow it glided towards the side of the house. Tensing for action, Kirby fisted his gun and waited.

There came the slap of running feet, the labored breathing of a man. Then a second figure burst from the shrubs near the wall and raced for the house, not furtively like the first, but openly and in desperate haste. As he passed the shrubbery into which the other shape had vanished, it reappeared without warning—leaping full onto his back, crushing him to earth with the speed of a striking panther. The two merged into a writhing tangle, and Kirby, abandoning caution, sprang from his place of concealment and entered the fray. His beam revealed two figures locked in battle. One man, the second, was white. The other might have sprung from a nightmare—a lithe, muscular, dark-skinned figure, naked but for a loin-cloth and a turban, a horrific scarlet symbol painted on his swarthy brow. His eyes burned red as a panther's, and greasy black hair fell long on his powerful shoulders. His strong hands tightened a knotted silken cord about the white man's throat, the strands sinking deeper into the flesh. The victim clawed at his assailant vainly, face purpling. Kirby swung the barrel of his automatic against the skull of the strangler with a meaty thud, and the Oriental fell sprawling. His victim staggered to his feet, tearing the cord from his throat, gasping.

An instant later, the man in the loin-cloth was on his feet again. Evidently, the thick turban wrapped about his head had absorbed most of the impact of the blow. Now his dark hand flickered to his waist and emerged into the moonlight grasping a glittering knife. Before Kirby could make a move the knife flashed in the moonglow, its bright glitter quenched in a sudden gush of hot blood!

Kirby's gun slammed a slug through the half-naked strangler which wrung a mewling cry from him. Then he whirled and leapt into the bushes. The foliage swallowed him and he was gone in an instant, as if he had never been. Kirby swore, scalp tingling—had the mysterious Thug *really* been there, or was he a figment of the imagination, a trick of moonlight and shadow, an illusion caused by over-strained nerves and no sleep? True, he had melted out of existence like a phantom. But moonlight displayed stark evidence that the Thug had been no apparition.

For there lay the victim of that flashing stroke, gasping with pain as blood flowed, dark and wet upon the grass. And there beside him lay the weapon—a cruel, hooked blade of weirdly Oriental design. And there was blood on the cold steel!

4. The Jade Box

Kirby pillowed the injured man's head against his thigh, striving to staunch the wound. Farnum—for it could only be he—was sinking fast. Every ragged breath he drew forced the dark blood to pump from the ghastly wound above his heart. Ripping the man's shirt open, Kirby tried to halt the bleeding, but a glance told him the valet was beyond help. He clutched at the lapels of Kirby's coat. Dry lips moved in a hoarse whisper.

"Heard them talking while they carried me off—Khemsa is—the old Warburton house," panted Farnum, but what he said made no sense to Kirby, who let it pass from his mind.

"Take it easy, old-timer," Kirby grunted. The other would not listen.

"There's no help for me, sir," Farnum whispered. "The box—the jade box—they will spare no horror, no atrocity, to regain it—"

"What's in the box?" growled Kirby. Vague horror shone in the eyes of the dying man.

"Scarlet tears," he said dully, then sagged back dead in the arms of the detective.

The Irishman's lips tightened grimly. It was not the first time he had seen a man die by violence, but it was never a pretty sight. Rising to his feet and shouldering the body, he strode back to the house. Entering by the side-door, which he slammed and locked after him, he went through the hall into the drawing-room. Corwell sat in a chair, sipping from a brandy glass, his niece at his side. They stared in shock at the grisly burden Kirby bore.

"Farnum!" exclaimed Corwell, his face crumpling in dismay. Laying his burden on a sofa, Kirby briefly related all that had transpired. He fixed the other man with a hard, riveting gaze.

"Look here," he snapped. "Up to now, I've been fumbling around in the dark—in more ways than one! Now I've seen a man killed—butchered in front of my eyes. This has become a matter for the police—"

Corwell raised a trembling hand. "No police," he breathed. "I cannot have private matters brought to the public attention."

"We have two corpses on our hands already," Kirby growled, tense with anger. "If we don't get some help, any one of us could be next! I can't fight an enemy I can't see and can't find. And I want to know exactly what this is all about. I'll be damned if I'm going to get my throat cut without at least knowing why!"

Gloria Corwell added her voice to his. "Yes, Uncle! It's time to tell us everything. We're in this, too, and have a right to know."

Too shaken to resist further, Corwell sagged back into the embrace of his chair, setting down the brandy glass. "Perhaps you're right. I kept the truth from you, my dear, hoping you would not become involved in this horror. But you're in it now, I fear, nearly as much as I am." His voice was a weak whisper, his features drawn and pale, as the master of the manor began a strange story.

"Two years ago I was in India," he related. "I heard rumors of a rare treasure hidden in the time of Akbar, emperor of India in the sixteenth century. It was guarded by a weird cult, and even the Grand Moghul was powerless to fight them, for they struck from the shadows, like the Assassins of old. The clue I needed was in the hands of a renegade Brahman who had lost caste for some nameless crime. His name was Ditta Ram, and he needed money, but feared for some reason to steal the treasure himself. When I asked him why, he muttered some native legend or other. At the time I paid no attention, dismissing his tale as mere superstition—but there's a world of truth behind some of those queer old myths, things even science cannot explain."

"Get on with it," urged Kirby impatiently. "The Thuggee could be creeping up on the house this very minute." The old man nodded soberly and resumed his narrative.

"I combined forces with Ditta Ram, agreed to split the treasure evenly. It was concealed in abandoned crypts beneath an old temple ruin near Agra, guarded by fanatic Moslem priests. Well, we got in, but we had to kill two men to open the way. And found something unexpected—"

"The treasure was gone?" Kirby hazarded a guess. The other smiled bitterly.

"Or had never existed, in the first place! Ditta Ram had duped me, I found. There was nothing but a small jade box with a necklace of odd gems. *This* was what Ditta Ram had been after all along, I now realize . . . well, we got out of there somehow, with half a hundred howling Moslems at our heels. During the first night, Ditta Ram tried to knife me and make off with the gems. I was stronger then than I am now; I struck him flat, bound him securely, left with the jade box. By his treachery, it seemed to me that Ditta Ram had forfeited all claim to the jewels."

His eyes haunted by a nameless fear, Corwell stared into shadows. "I soon realized someone was following me. From a police commissioner in Calcutta I learned that Ditta Ram was no Brahman, renegade or not, but a member of the Thuggee—the murder cult, believed crushed long ago by the British, had flourished in secrecy, led by a man of mystery called Khemsa—"

"Khemsa!" Kirby barked, startled. Suddenly, the nonsensical words Farnum had whispered with his dying breath came to his recollection. He scowled, chewing on his lower lip.

"Yes, Khemsa. What can the name mean to you?" demanded Corwell. Briefly the Irishman reported what he could remember of the valet's last words. The other man paled to the hue of wax.

"Centuries ago," he whispered, "Khemsa was a black magician who perverted the worship of the death-goddess into a murder cult styled on the Assassins, in a fiendish attempt to seize power over all of India through terror and poison and the knife. His power resided in a necklace of curious gems called 'the Scarlet Tears' or the Tears of Kali. Moslem loyalists invaded his sanctuary, crushed his followers, slew him before making off with the mystic gems. The cult persisted in secret, though, guarding the tomb which holds his mummified body, searching for the gems—"

Kirby scratched his jaw. Farnum had mumbled

something about Scarlet Tears, too; the pieces of this nightmare puzzle were beginning to fall into place. "Which Moslem priests have guarded all these centuries—until you stole "the Tears" from their descendants?" he observed keenly. Corwell flushed guiltily, forced a wan smile.

"Yes, until I stole them, at the behest of Ditta Ram—no Brahman, but a member of the Kali cult! Moslem curses guarded the jade box from theft by the Thugs, but the curse couldn't harm a white man who knew nothing of it. That's why the rogue solicited my help!"

Crossing the room, the older man opened a wall-safe concealed behind a worn Persian tapestry. He withdrew a strangely-carven box of lambent green jade, stared at it moodily. "Would that I had never heard of the treasure," he sighed. "Or that I had let Ditta Ram carry it to his lord, Khemsa, self-named in obvious imitation of the ancient magician. But I smuggled the gems out of India. I smuggled them into the States. But the Thuggee followed me across India and halfway across the world—they were not far behind the very night I opened Corwell Manor again. From that night to this, we have been under seige—and I have hardly drawn a peaceful breath! Now you can understand why I can't risk bringing the police into this, for I would be a self-confessed thief, smuggler and murderer," he finished bitterly.

"*What was that!*" cried Gloria, jumping up. Kirby sprang to his feet, grabbing for his automatic. For the heavy silence of the night broke before that eerie, ululating cry he had heard twice before

—and the jangling crash of shattering glass!

"They're breaking into the house!" Corwell shrilled.

5. *Thuggee Knives*

Kirby's reaction was instinctive. Ordering the two to stay where they were, he left the house by the side-door to investigate. The moon was hidden again, as scurrying clouds obscured its luminance; cursing the dark, he raced across the lawn and into the bushes. Broken glass crunched underfoot; looking up he saw that two windows leading into the dining room had been shattered. They were still barred, however, and afforded no means of entry. The breaking of the windows, he guessed, was a try at shaking the nerve of the inmates of the house, part of a lengthy war of nerves.

No one seemed to be about and the bushes were empty of skulking Orientals, he decided to make his rounds before returning indoors. He felt confident of their ability to resist a siege, for the house was built like a fortress and the pantry was probably full. But the restless instincts of his Celtic foresires were astir in his blood, uneasy.

He checked one side of the house, moving as soundlessly as a hunting panther, and was rounding the southwestern corner when he heard the faint rasp of a bolt being drawn. Dropping flat, peering around the corner, he saw a door partly open. A shadowy hand rested upon the jamb and a dark face peered out. He caught the gleam of the whites of the man's eyes in the wan starlight. Kirby rose lithely into a half-crouch, glided into the bushes. The man coming from the house might easily be armed, and there might be others with him.

Just as he was beginning to lose patience, the dark figure emerged from the dark doorway: a large man, heavily-built, broad shouldered. He came out noiselessly, closing the door behind him, and moved stealthily toward the south, heading for the estate wall. As he reached the corner, Kirby launched himself from the bushes, lashing out for his jaw.

The stranger was quick, for all his bulk. With a startled cry he recoiled and Kirby's fist missed his chin by the fraction of an inch. Then, before the detective could recover his balance, the man was at his throat, stabbing and slashing like a madman. The very frenzy of his attack robbed it of any accuracy. The knife ripped Kirby's coat and drew blood from a shallow cut on his neck, then Kirby caught his wrist with his left and sunk his right fist into the man's midriff. Gagging, he paled, sagged to his knees, sprawled on the grass in a tangle of robes. As he did so something tumbled from his garments which burst open on the ground and disgorged a glittering thing which shone in the starlight like gobs of frozen blood.

"Judas!" muttered Kirby, absently dabbing at the cut on his neck. He bent, scooped up the jewels, replaced them in the curiously carved jade box, stuck it in his pocket. There was the sound of footsteps within the house and he straightened, his hand going to the hilt of the long knife under his coat. The sting of steel had roused the Irishman's hot blood and he was about through with fist-work for the night. Then the side-door opened and the dark-haired girl peered out cautiously.

"Is that you, Mr. Kirby?" she faltered. "Oh! You're hurt—bleeding!"

His savage laugh reassured her. "Only a scratch. And I took a prisoner, too—" He paused, noticing the fear in her wide eyes. "What's up?"

"Come quickly! We've been attacked by an unknown assailant."

Hauling his groaning captive to his feet and shoving him ahead, Kirby steered the robed man through the door and waited while the girl barricaded it behind him. "I told you to stay inside with your uncle," he snapped. "Now what's happened?" The girl shivered, hugging her arms. With a timid glance at the groggy Thug, she whispered, "Just a little while after you left to investigate, the—the light went out. My Uncle yelled something and I heard the thud of a falling body, the floor creaked under rapid footsteps. When I got the lamp re-lit—but come, and see for yourself!"

Entering the drawing room they found Corwell downing gulps of brandy, pale and shaken. A second purplish bruise adorned his brow and his eyes were wild with fear. "Kirby!" he cried, they are in the house—God knows how!—I was struck from behind, thrown to the floor—*and the jewels are missing!*"

Kirby grinned tigerishly, while teeth flashing in

his dark face. "Is that all!" he laughed. Thrusting the robed Hindu into the circle of light, he said, "See what I found on the lawn—"

"*Ditta Ram!*" cried Corwell shakily. Looking thoughtful, Kirby nodded. "Yep, I guessed it might be him," he growled. Then, plucking something from his pocket, he tossed it clattering on the table. A second object of identical design he snatched from the sleeve of the heavy man's robe and threw it down on the table beside the other. The lamplight glittered on two cruelly-hooked daggers of evil Oriental design.

"Those are Thuggee knives," Corwell whispered in fear-haunted tones. Kirby said nothing. The girl put her hands to her cheeks and stared at the barbaric weapons in fascinated dread.

6. The Tears of Kalli

It occurred to Kirby that, by making the ringleader his captive, their chances of living through the rest of the night were considerably improved. Without Ditta Ram, the gang of Thugs might hesitate to attack in force, fearing thereby to cause his death. Murderous fanatics themselves, they doubtless imputed similar ways of thought and action to their foes.

He dragged the bulky man to a chair and heaved him into it. Ditta Ram made no resistance, bent double, clutching at his belly; Kirby's sledgehammer fist had taken a lot of the fight out of him, it seemed. But he was getting his breath back by now and his groaning subsided. The detective looked him over. Ditta Ram was a portly, broad-shouldered man, his skin not much darker than Kirby's own tanned and weather-beaten hide, though unhealthily sallow. His features were degraded by dissipation and excess, but lacked the utterly inhuman quality stamped into the visage of the Thug he had fought earlier. He had been bestial, a demon: Ditta Ram, however brutalized by vice, yet retained some semblance of humanity, for all that he was a criminal devoid of scruples. There was a suggestion of a mirthless smile at the corners of his thin lips as he regarded Corwell; the white man stared back with haunted eyes.

"So you have taken the gems at last," Corwell murmured. The Hindu shrugged. "I knew they would be hidden somewhere within the house," he admitted in perfect English. "I was spying from concealment as you removed them from the safe to show your friend. While others drew him away with a ruse, I turned off the lamp and snatched them from the table under cover of darkness. I was about to take my departure, when Kismet—in the person of a human tiger!—intervened." This last was said with an ironic, almost admiring, glance at Kirby.

"You mean to say—" gasped Corwell, turning a wondering gaze on the detective. Kirby grinned, plucked the box from his pocket, dumped the gems out on the table. They were cut from an unknown, mysterious fragile-seemingly crystal unfamiliar to Western science, with archaic worksmanship, in the shape of elongated teardrops. The small ends

29

of the jewels had been pierced and were threaded upon a loop of fine gold wire, kept apart by smaller beads of the same weird crystalline substance. In the lamplight they glimmered like liquid clots of freshly-spilled human blood!

"The Scarlet Tears!" Corwell whispered with dry lips. The girl drew her breath in sharply. Kirby said nothing, his features hard and grim. Many human lives had been spent in the pursuit of these red stones—too many!

The insatiable hunger of a famished wolf blazed in the slitted eyes of Ditta Ram. "The Tears of Kali," he muttered, putting his palms together in a mystical gesture.

"The Devil's Tears, you mean!" Kirby retorted. "We've got 'em and we're keeping 'em, just like we're going to keep you." Ditta Ram glared at him, cold menace flaming luridly in his narrow eyes. "On the contrary," he said cooly, "It is I that have you."

"The devil you say," Kirby laughed. "Your men won't dare attack, so long as you're under our thumb. You're our hostage. If they attack the house, we'll shoot you like a dog."

"I doubt it," replied the Hindu. "It would only infuriate them. I am not their leader, merely their chieftain. Khemsa is our master; I am expendible. But think of your position: you are isolated here, cut off from help. Your house is surrounded by armed men, the telephone lines are cut and you cannot summon help. With the two remaining servants slain, only you three are left to defend the house. Do you really think you can stay here forever, holding me prisoner, fighting off seventy men?"

Kirby did not reply. Ditta Ram was their prisoner, but they were imprisoned, too, being surrounded by his men. At that moment from the woods outside came that weird, quavering call Kirby had heard before.

"Listen!" Ditta Ram lifted a hand. "They are there. I am your only hope. They lust for your lives, like blood-mad beasts. But I can control them. Slay me, and you remove their last restraint. But I am able to reason and to compromise."

Kirby caught him up at that word. "What's your idea of a compromise?"

"The men outside are savages, they delight in murder. The lord Khemsa and I desire only to regain the Scarlet Tears, which rightfully belong to our Order. Give them to me, and go free!"

"They're the only bargaining card we have," Kirby admitted grudgingly.

"Be reasonable," urged the Hindu. "We are at a deadlock. You surround me, my men surround you. If you kill me, they will kill you. On the other hand, if they attack, you might slay me in reprisal. I do not wish to be a martyr. You might threaten to kill me, and they might make promises, but they would not keep them. They obey no code of honor, like civilized men. But you can trust me. Give me the Tears, release me, and I will lead the Thugs away." Kirby did not at once reply.

"And what of me?" inquired Corwell. Ditta Ram shrugged.

"To have withheld the Tears from us was

31

sacrilege. But Khemsa will let that pass. So long as you stay out of India, you will not be molested. But if ever you return, you will pay the price of your sacrilege. You will die . . . *slowly,* very slowly. His cold eyes held Corwell's gaze like the hypnotic eyes of a serpent. Suddenly the other man, goaded to the limit, went wild. His control snapped.

"It's you who'll die, Hindu dog!" he shrieked. Tearing a rapier from the wall he lunged at the unarmed Thug. Kirby struck the blow aside with a burly forearm; growling an oath, he tore the hilt from Corwell's grasp and flung it aside. "One more move like that," Kirby gritted between his teeth, "and I'll tie you up." Their eyes clashed murderously, then Corwell sagged limply.

"You're a fool to trust that brown devil," he groaned.

"How do we know you'd keep your word?" Kirby demanded of the Thug. Ditta Ram met his eyes squarely. Rogue though he was, a vestige of manly honor yet clung to his soul. "You do not. You have only my word. If I give my promise freely, I will keep it."

Kirby turned to Corwell. "You have a claim to half of these gems. Are you willing to give them to this man, in exchange for life and freedom?"

"Willing?" exclaimed Corwell bitterly. "I am eager to see the last of the accursed stones!" Nodding, Kirby closed the jade box, put it back in his pocket.

"I'm going to trust you halfway, Ditta Ram," he said. "You and I are going out of here together, to talk with the Thuggee."

"What?" It was a cry from Gloria and Corwell. The girl stared at him as if he had taken leave of his senses.

"Don't worry," he advised. "We'll go to the gate and Ditta Ram will call to his men that I am not to be harmed. Then he will tell them—in English—to go. When I'm sure they're gone, we'll return to the house and wait till morning. Then, if nothing occurs, I'll give him the Tears and let him go."

"Have you gone mad?" cried Corwell. "What's to prevent them from murdering you and rescuing Ditta Ram? Or seizing you for a hostage?"

"At the slightest hint of treachery, I'll crush the jewels underfoot. They'll be destroyed instantly."

Corwell groaned, eyes wild. "Don't trust him—remember how he betrayed me! Destroy them now, and cut his throat!" Growing madness seemed to possess the older man. The long, unendurable strain was telling on him; Kirby could see he was cracking beneath the pressure.

He made no reply. Instead, he showed his gun to Ditta Ram, then replaced it under his coat. "I trust you about as far as you trust me," he grunted. "Go ahead—walk!"

The Curse of Khemsa

They advanced out on the verandah; starlight was not yet paling, but a hint of dawn was in the fresh breeze. Silence brooded on all sides, tense, enormous, heavy. It was as if the monstrous gods of India crouched among the trees, ready to leap and crush. Kirby forced such vain thoughts from his mind, lest they demoralize him. He did not look back at the door, where, despite orders to close and bar the portal, he knew the girl watched, unspeaking.

As they went down the wall towards the great iron gate, Kirby felt the pressure of unseen eyes. Ditta Ram began calling his men in a deep voice that carried far. There was no reply. He called again, warning the watchers that the white man with him was not to be harmed, telling of the bargain he had struck. There was no response. Just before they reached the gate, Ditta Ram halted, turning a tense face to Kirby.

"They don't reply because they think it's a trap! They think you are forcing me to say these things! I must go forward alone to speak with them—trust me!"

"Do you take me for a fool?" demanded Kirby.

"Listen to me, *sahib!* You are in terrible danger! I understand their minds. They do not believe I have made a bargain. They think I am being compelled to lie to them. At any moment a blowdart may strike you down. They might try to kill you, but you may manage to destroy the Tears!" Sweat beaded the Thug's face, and he was trembling. Kirby believed the man; after all, it was the gems, not the pistol in his pocket that held Ditta Ram in bondage to his bargain.

"Go back!" begged the Hindu. "Before they kill you! I will keep my promise to you. I would not keep a promise to Corwell, but you are a man of honor, and I will not lie to you. I will talk to them and send them away, then I will return to you and remain your prisoner till day-break. You can trust me! In a moment they will loose death upon you."

Kirby made a quick decision, based on a deep knowledge of human nature. "Alright," he grunted. "But remember! If you don't come back in ten minutes, the jewels are gone for ever."

"I will keep my word, *sahib,*" intoned the Hindu. Lifting his voice he called to the silent wall, the dark woods: "Do not harm the white man! He is returning to the house. I am coming to talk with you alone."

The detective went back along the walk towards the house, unable, in spite of himself, to enjoy turning his back on those that lurked in the shadows. When he had covered half the distance, Ditta Ram opened the gate and stepped into the utter darkness beyond.

Kirby halted, assailed by black doubts. Could he trust the Hindu, or had he been fooled? He could feel the tense silence that gripped the house. Outside the wall there sounded an unintelligible muttering of voices too low to be made out. Then, suddenly, shockingly, there arose a blood-freezing scream! Kirby swore, ran for the gate. A dim figure reeled drunkenly through it, slamming it behind him. It was Ditta Ram! He staggered towards Kirby, streaming blood. Dark, half-naked figures clustered at the gate, which had locked automatically. Kirby triggered his gun, hot lead stabbed through the darkness. The figures scattered, ducking, and he reached the Hindu just as the man collapsed, turning an agonized, blood-dripping face to him.

"Khemsa!" he moaned. "He has turned upon me—"

Kirby grabbed his robe and dragged him back up the walk. Dark shapes appeared momentarily atop the wall, red fire stabbed the gloom as his automatic blazed. "Gloria!" he yelled urgently.

The girl appeared in the open doorway. "They've knifed Ditta Ram," he snarled. "And they're coming over the wall! Help me get him into the house!" He stooped, gripped the bleeding Hindu and slung him over his shoulder like a sack of wheat. Then he ran to the veranda, carrying with ease a weight at least equal to his own. Suddenly he noticed a strange expression on the girl's face. She was staring at something behind him. Some impulse or premonition made him glance over his shoulder.

A tall figure stood motionlessly behind the locked gate. Entirely grey, it was like a shadow devoid of substance. And it seemed to have no face! Kirby's blood thrilled as all the superstitious nightfears of his Irish ancestry rose within him—

Then the moon emerged from its shroud, bathing the immobile figure in stark radiance. It was a man gaunt to the point of being skeletal, wrapped from head to foot in a misty web of some kind of grey, gauzy robes. Though the thin fabric blurred and obscured his features, two eyes burned, red and febrile, bright as the "Scarlet Tears" themselves, through the veil.

"Lord Khemsa," hissed Ditta Ram.

A voice dry and thin as a crisp, dead leaf drifted

36

to Kirby in a penetrating whisper. "He who betrays the Order, betrays himself. And the penalty is death!"

Kirby tore his eyes away from that burning gaze, looked down at the thing the veiled man clenched in one bony hand. It was a Thuggee knife, drenched in gore, and doubtless the same blade that had drunk the life of Ditta Ram. Growling an oath, he raised his gun, then blinked. For the thin figure vanished instantly, as if it had never been there at all!

"Inside!" he rapped, shoving the girl before him and following with his burden, which he dumped on a divan, then slammed the broken door and jammed the chair in place to secure it.

Returning to the divan, he examined Ditta Ram, then hesitated. For there was nothing he could do; indeed, it was a miracle the Thug still breathed. Some vagrant whim made him slide the box from his pocket and lay it near the Hindu's hand.

"The Tears of Kali," sighed the dying man, fondling the carven jade with his fingertips. Then his head fell to one side and his gaze became sightless. Retrieving the box, Kirby tossed a coverlet over the corpse, then turned to face the girl and her uncle, tensely.

8. *The Fight in the Dark*

"What now?" whispered Gloria.

"Fight," said Kirby, briefly. "Are there any guns in the house?" She shook her head. "They took them all when they ramsacked the manor earlier," she said. He checked his revolver with a grimace.

"One gun between us, and I'm down to my last cartridge!" Kirby said. "They'll be over the wall in no time, so we'd better douse the lights before they start shooting through the shutters—"

"They can't see through the shutters," said Corwell. "And we'll need the lights if they break in. They see like cats in the dark, but they're poor shots and won't use guns unless they have to."

"What will they use, Uncle?" the girl asked.

"Knives, strangling cords, blowguns—that's their way."

"Well," advised Kirby, "let's look to our defenses. All the doors downstairs are locked and bolted, except the broken one. They'll probably try to get in that way again. Gloria, go upstairs and see if you can find a stout corner we can defend up there. If they break in down here, we ought to have another refuge to fall back on."

The girl nodded. He followed her out into the hall.

"It's so still!" she whispered. Her features were pale but there was no hysteria in the dark eyes she lifted to his. Her hand went out instinctively to cling to his own.

"You're a brave kid," he said seriously. "I wish I had half your guts! Take care now." She nodded and mounted the stair while Kirby re-entered the drawing room. He was not perturbed for himself, for he had been in tough spots before, and felt the comforting weight of the hidden knife and gun under his jacket. But Corwell was long past his

adventuresome days, and there was the girl to consider—

Suddenly a shrill scream of terror ripped the
heavy silence. Kirby and the older man whirled.

"Gloria!" the detective cried.

Corwell yelled, "Look out! *They're in the house!*"
And then the lights went out!

From the floor above sounded a sudden rush of
feet, the impact of heavy bodies, a shrill cry. Kirby
sprang to the foot of the stairs up which Gloria
Corwell had disappeared, gun ready in his fist.
And then the shadows disgorged a frenzied rush of
hurtling, half-naked, dark-skinned bodies, long
black hair sweeping their muscular shoulders,
knives in their hands and murder in their gleaming
eyes.

It was red fury and madness, an end to plot and
counter-plot, stealth and intrigue. It was a crimson
climax of hand-to-hand slaughter, bestial and
primitive. He fired his last bullet point-blank, and
the foremost of the attackers went down, face a
ghastly smear of red ruin. He heard Corwell cry
out something as he parried with the revolver barrel and slashing knife of a rabid-eyed fanatic. They
were all about him; he dodged and struck instinctively with hard fist and steel barrel. By the dim
starlight that seeped through the shutters, he saw
Corwell rip an epée from the wall and run a
frothing devil through the body, as the gun in his
hand crashed down on a Thug's skull.

And then, as swiftly as it had begun, it was all
over. He and Corwell stared at each other, panting
heavily, amid the heaped bodies. "I guess only a

small advance party got in upstairs somewhere," he said.

The girl's uncle gave him a wild-eyed look. "And—Gloria?" he gasped. Kirby growled an oath, whipped up the stair. He prowled rapidly through a succession of empty rooms, finding nothing but a broken and unbarred window, with a long length of knotted rope trailing down the outer wall. That was how the devils had gotten in, all right, and how they had escaped with the captured girl, however few survived. Jaw-muscles knotted with tension, he went back down the stair to give Corwell the bad news.

The older man met him at the foot of the stairs, a scrap of torn paper in one shaking hand. "They will give us Gloria—alive—in return for the Tears!" Corwell panted, showing him the scrawled note.

Hot anger blazed in Kirby's eyes. "The hell they will!" he said roughly. "After the way they betrayed Ditta Ram, we can't trust them to hold to any other bargains. I'm going after them! Where could they possibly be holed up? Quick! Think, man! They must have some place to stay during the daylight hours!"

"The nearest house to mine is the old Warburton place," said the other in a trembling voice. "But it's been closed for years—" The detective smote his brow, growling a lurid oath. *That* was the other thing Farnum had mentioned before dying; Kirby had racked his brains till now to recall it. Clattering down the stair, he snapped, "Which way is it—and how far?"

The bushes closed around Kirby the moment he left the house. Surely, the place was closely watched, but Kirby felt certain he could elude the watchers in the underbrush. He wormed under bushes, crept between the dark boles of trees, crossed the lawn where the shadows were thickest and slipped out the little half-concealed door in the wall by which he and the girl had gotten in.

Dawn was paling the east, but stars still clustered in the clouded skies. By them the detective guided himself through the woods in the direction indicated by Corwell, wary that every bole might be hiding a lurking Thug. He went as quietly as he could, making as little noise as possible, alert and quivering in every sense; but he encountered no skulking Orientals, and soon the dark bulk of the Warburton house loomed up blackly against the paling skies.

Keeping to the bushes, Kirby crept around the house, seeking entry. No lights shone in the tall windows, seemingly the place was empty and had been untenanted for years, but Farnum must have meant *something* by his dying words. Before long, Kirby found and pried open an unlocked basement window; the glass was obscured by grime but a flicker of lurid radiance could be glimpsed. He wormed through it, fell lightly to a stone floor, gun clenched in one fist, shoulders hunched to meet a sudden assault. Something crunched underfoot and Kirby guessed he was in the coal-room. He glided through the darkness, found a damp wall, searched along it with seeking fingers, found a wooden door. Opening it a mere slit, he peered through—to view an astounding scene!

The stone-walled basement room was huge and shadowy as an ancient crypt. Torches flared in iron brackets along the walls, orange light gleaming on the naked backs and shoulders of a kneeling throng of Thugs. Beyond them, Kirby saw a huge, throne-like chair of black wood; seated thereon was the lean, veiled figure of Khemsa! Feral fires blazed in Kirby's eyes at the sight of his enemy, a growl rose unbidden deep within his breast. Then he paused, a chill shooting through him.

Directly before the enthroned cult-leader, Gloria struggled in the grasp of two muscular men. Her slim figure writhed as she fought to be free. Black curls tousled across slender, bare shoulders; fighting down an oath, Kirby saw they were tearing away the filmy fabric of her soft blouse—stripping the white girl naked before the gloating eyes of the merciless Thuggee gang!

Throwing caution to the winds, Kirby slammed the door open and sprang into the room, brandishing his empty revolver. "Hold it right there!" he grated harshly, fanning the gun so all could see it. "Get your hands off that girl, you devils!" Gloria cast him a wide-eyed, uncomprehending look over her shoulder; he glimpsed the white rondures of her bare breasts as she half-turned.

The Thugs rose to crouching positions, growling, ready to launch a wave of muscular human flesh upon him. The veiled figure halted them with a swift gesture; they eyed the unwavering gun in his fist, licking their lips uncertainly. It was like a tableau from some melodrama, frozen in time by the photographer's camera. For a long, breathless instant he held the horde at bay.

Then Kirby broke the tense stillness with a reckless laugh! He pulled the jade box from his pocket, held it high.

"Take you Scarlet Tears," he demanded. "Give me the girl, and we'll go!" Without waiting for a reply, he strode confidently forward until he had almost reached the forefront of the foe.

"Let the white man pass," commanded Khemsa in a thin but penetrating whisper. The human wave parted before the Irishman as the Red Sea had opened to the Israelites. Not deigning to glance to right or left, he strode boldly to the foot of the thronelike chair and stood there, looking into the red glare of those burning eyes with cool, level gaze. The master of the Thuggee extended a bone-thin arm.

"Give me the jewels!"

"Not so fast," snapped Kirby. "How do I know you'll keep your end of the bargain?"

Khemsa turned his lurid eyes upon the two Thugs who held Gloria. "Release the woman," he hissed. Reluctantly, the burly Thugs removed their hands from her, and Gloria fled to Kirby's side. He wrapped a protective arm about her trembling shoulders.

"Now we're going out of here by the front door," said Kirby in tones that brooked no opposition. "Your men can follow us—at a distance! When we are at the gate of Corwell Manor, I'll put down the jade box in the roadway; we'll go inside, and your people can reclaim "the Tears". Take it or leave it!"

"Very well, I agree to your terms," said the veiled figure tonelessly. Kirby turned on his heel, half-supporting Gloria's weight.

"Keep your chin up," he whispered to her. She gave a wan smile. Then—

"Seize him!" said Khemsa, and the Thugs threw themselves upon the two! Growling a furious oath, Kirby kicked one full in the face, smote another across the brows with the gun-barrel. Then iron fingers wrenched it from his grasp and the girl screamed! Tearing free—and leaving shreds of his torn jacket in their clutches—he sprang to where the veiled master of the cult sat motionless, and, whipping his Bowie knife from its scabbard under his arm, set the sharp blade against Khemsa's throat.

"Hold it, you brown devils!" he roared. "Hold it right there or your boss gets it!" The half-naked horde froze, growling uncertainly.

"Thought you'd try a dirty trick or two," snarled Kirby. Khemsa said nothing, his scarlet gaze coldly inscrutable. Suddenly impatient, the detective ripped away the veils that concealed Khemsa's features laying bare a visage of such grisly horror that the very sight wrung a gasp of astonishment from his lips and a shrill cry of terror from Gloria.

What they saw before them was not the living features of a human being, but the shrunken, withered horror of a skull! The flesh had dried and cracked like old leather, revealing patches of

44

scabrous naked bone; the lips were peeled back to bare discolored fangs; the throat was so thin they could actually *see* the bones of the spine.

In all that mask of grisly, undead horror only the eyes lived. And Kirby, in that instant of shock and dread, realized the final truth: the master of the cult was the same Khemsa that had ruled centuries ago! In his unholy lust to regain the gems that were the keys to his power, the black magician had somehow transcended death itself!

The living mummy fixed its lurid gaze upon him.

"You have looked upon that which no white man may ever see—and live!" it whispered sibhilantly. Then, to his motionless throng of followers, "Capture him now! For how can his blade slay one that already died centuries ago—"

10. Scarlet Tears

Kirby threw his Bowie, and the knife sank to the hilt in the throat of the first Thug who launched himself forward. Sprawling backward in a gush of blood, the fellow tripped up those behind them; they went down in a tangle of dark, naked limbs. Taking advantage of his momentary respite, the Irishman backed against the further wall, sheltering the shrinking girl with his brawny body. It was all or nothing now, and he had but one card left to play.

He ripped open the jade box with an oath, dashed the gems to the stone pave. They glimmered in the torchlight like fresh-spilled blood. Khemsa rose from his tall chair and turned to confront him, his snarling Thugs gathering about him, ready to launch the final assault.

Kirby stepped forward and ground the Scarlet Tears to dust under his heel!

A mournful, quavering cry rose from the dry lips of the mummy. It raised bony arms skywards, trembling in the grip of some inhuman passion unnamable and unknown to mortal men. In the next instant, the gaunt figure collapsed in a sprawl of shadowy gauze robes. And even the brutal Thugs shrank back fearfully from the horrible sight that met their eyes: for even as they watched the undead thing crumbled into dry powder, the bones falling apart with a clatter, the skull rolling across the floor as the unnatural forces that had revitalized the long-dead sorcerer ebbed and died with the destruction of the talisman that held his power.

Shrilling forth sobbing, moaning cries in an Eastern tongue, the horde came apart, a scattered mass of furtive, fleeing figures, deserting the unhallowed spot upon which their ancient master and his uncanny powers had perished. In a twinkling the basement room was empty, save for Kirby, the girl, and the crumbling remains of the mummy.

He put his arms about her shoulders, comfortingly. "It's all over now," he said wearily. "Buck up! Let's get back to your uncle. And I could sure use some breakfast!"

When they left the house, the sun was up and the voices of birds were greeting the morning of a new day.

A chilling tale by a modern master . . .

Down There
by Ramsey Campbell

"Hurry along there," Steve called as the girls trooped down the office. "Last one tonight. Mind the doors."

The girls smiled at Elaine as they passed her desk, but their smiles meant different things: just like you to make things more difficult for the rest of us, looks like you've been kept in after school, suppose you've nothing better to do, fancy having to put up with him by yourself. She didn't give a damn what they thought of her. No doubt they earned enough without working overtime, since all they did with their money was squander it on makeup and new clothes.

She only wished Steve wouldn't make a joke of everything: even the lifts, one of which had broken down entirely after sinking uncontrollably to the bottom of the shaft all day. She was glad that

47

hadn't happened to her, even though she gathered the sub-basement was no longer so disgusting. Still, the surviving lift had rid her of everyone now, including Mr. Williams the union representative, who'd tried the longest to persuade her not to stay. He still hadn't forgiven the union for accepting a temporary move to this building; perhaps he was taking it out on her. Well, he'd gone now, into the November night and rain.

It has been raining all day. The warehouses outside the windows looked like melting chocolate; the river and the canals were opaque with tangled ripples. Cottages and terraces, some of them derelict, crowded up the steep hills toward the disused mines. Through the skeins of water on the glass their infrequent lights looked shaky as candleflames.

She was safe from all that, in the long office above five untenanted floors and two basements. Ranks of filing cabinets stuffed with blue Inland Revenue files divided the office down the middle; smells of dust and old paper hung in the air. Beneath a fluttering fluorescent tube protruding files drowsed, jerked awake. Through the steamy window above an unquenchable radiator, she could just make out the frame where the top section of the fire escape should be.

"Are you feeling exploited?" Steve said.

He'd heard Mr. Williams' parting shot, calling her the employers' weapon against solidarity. "No, certainly not." She wished he would let her be quiet for a while. "I'm feeling hot," she said.

"Yes, it is a bit much." He stood up, mopping

48

his forehead theatrically. "I'll go and sort out Mr. Tuttle."

She doubted that he would find the caretaker, who was no doubt hidden somewhere with a bottle of cheap rum. At least he tried to hide his drinking, which was more than one could say for the obese half-chewed sandwiches he left on windowsills, in the room where tea was brewed, even once on someone's desk.

She turned idly to the window behind her chair and watched the indicator in the lobby counting down. Steve had reached the basement now. The letter B flickered, then brightened: he'd gone down to the sub-basement, which had been meant to be kept secret from the indicator and from everyone except the holder of the key. Perhaps the finding of the cache down there had encouraged Mr. Tuttle to be careless with food.

She couldn't help growing angry. If the man who had built these offices had had so much money, why hadn't he put it to better use? The offices had been merely a disguise for the sub-basement, which was to have been his refuge. What had he feared? War, revolution, a nuclear disaster? All anyone knew was that he'd spent the months before he had been certified insane in smuggling food down there. He'd wasted all that food, left it there to rot, and he'd had no thought for the people who would have to work in the offices: no staircases, a fire escape that fell apart when someone tried to paint it — but she was beginning to sound like Mr. Williams, and there was no point in brooding.

The numbers were counting upward, slow as a

child's first sum. Eventually Steve appeared, the solution. "No sign of him," he said. "He's somewhere communing with alcohol, I expect. Most of the lights are off, which doesn't help."

That sounded like one of Mr. Tuttle's ruses. "Did you go right down?" she said. "What's it like down there?"

"Huge. They say it's much bigger than any of the floors. You could play two football games at once in there." Was he exaggerating? His face was bland as a silent comedian's except for raised eyebrows. "They left the big doors open when they cleaned it up. If there were any lights I reckon you could see for miles. I'm only surprised it didn't cut into one of the sewers."

"I shouldn't think it could be any more smelly."

"It still pongs a bit, that's true. Do you want a look? Shall I take you down?" When he dodged toward her, as though to carry her away, she sat forward rigidly and held the arms of her chair against the desk. "No thank you," she said, though she'd felt a start of delicious apprehension.

"Did you ever hear what was supposed to have happened while they were cleaning up all the food? Tuttle told me, if you can believe him." She didn't want to hear; Mr. Tuttle had annoyed her enough for one day. She leafed determinedly through a file, until Steve went up the office to his desk.

For a while she was able to concentrate. The sounds of the office merged into a background discreet as muzak: the rustle of papers, the rushes of the wind, the buzz of the defective fluorescent like an insect trying to bumble its way out of the tube. She maneuvered files across her desk. This man was going to be happy, since they owed him money. This fellow wasn't, since he owed them some.

But the thought of the food had settled on her like the heat. Only this morning, in the room where the tea-urn stood, she'd found an ancient packet of Mr. Tuttle's sandwiches in the waste-bin. No doubt the packet was still there, since the cleaners were refusing to work until the building was made safe. She seemed unable to rid herself of the memory.

No, it wasn't a memory she was smelling. As she glanced up, wrinkling her nostrils, she saw that Steve was doing so too. "Tuttle," he said, grimacing.

As though he'd given a cue, they heard movement on the floor below. Someone was dragging a wet cloth across linoleum. Was the caretaker doing the cleaners' job? More likely he'd spilled a bottle and was trying to wipe away the evidence. "I'll get him this time," Steve said, and ran toward the lobby.

Was he making too much noise? The soft moist dragging on the floor below had ceased. The air seemed thick with heat and dust and the stench of food; when she lit a cigarette, the smoke loomed reprovingly above her. She opened the thin louvres at the top of the nearest window, but that brought no relief. There was nothing else for it; she opened the window that gave onto the space where the fire escape should be.

It was almost too much for her. A gust of rain

51

dashed in, drenching her face while she clung to the handle. The window felt capable of smashing wide, of snatching her out into the storm. She managed to anchor the bar to the sill, and leaned out into the night to let the rain wash away the smell.

Nine feet below her she could see the fifth-floor platform of the fire escape, its iron mesh slippery and streaming. The iron stairs that hung from it, poised to swing down to the next platform, seemed to dangle into a deep pit of rain whose sides were incessantly collapsing. The thought of having to jump to the platform made her flinch back; she could imagine herself losing her footing, slithering off into space.

She was about to close the window, for the flock of papers on her desk had begun to flap, when she glimpsed movement in the unlit warehouse opposite and just below her. She was reminded of a maggot, writhing in food. Of course, that was because she was glimpsing it through the warehouse windows, small dark holes. It was reflected from her building, which was why it looked so large and puffily vague. It must be Mr. Tuttle, for as it moved, she heard a scuffling below her, retreating from the lifts.

She'd closed the window by the time Steve returned. "You didn't find him, did you? Never mind," she said, for he was frowning.

Did he feel she was spying on him? At once his face grew blank. Perhaps he resented her knowing, first that he'd gone down to the sub-basement, now that he'd been outwitted. When he sat at his desk at the far end of the office, the emptiness between them felt like a rebuff. "Do you fancy some tea?" she said, to placate him.

"I'll make it. A special treat." He jumped up at once and strode to the lobby.

Why was he so eager? Five minutes later, as she leafed through someone's private life, she wondered if he meant to creep up on her, if that was the joke he had been planning behind his mask. Her father had used to pounce on her to make her shriek when she was little—when he had still been able to. She turned sharply, but Steve had pulled open the doors of the out-of-work life-shaft and was peering down, apparently listening. Perhaps it was Mr. Tuttle he meant to surprise, not her.

The tea was hot and fawn, but little else. Why did it seem to taste of the lingering stench? Of course, Steve hadn't closed the door of the room off the lobby, where Mr. Tuttle's sandwiches must still be festering. She hurried out and slammed the door with the hand that wasn't covering her mouth.

On impulse she went to the doors of the lift-shaft where Steve had been listening. They opened easily as curtains; for a moment she was teetering on the edge. The shock blurred her vision, but she knew it wasn't Mr. Tuttle who was climbing the lift-cord like a fat pale monkey on a stick. When she screwed up her eyes and peered into the dim well, of course there was nothing.

Steve was watching her when she returned to her desk. His face was absolutely non-committal. Was he keeping something from her—a special joke, perhaps? Here it came; he was about to speak. "How's your father?" he said.

It sounded momentarily like a comedian's catch-phrase. "Oh, he's happier now," she blurted. "They've got a new stock of large print books in the library."

"Is there someone who can sit with him?"

"Sometimes." The community spirit had faded once the mine owners had moved on, leaving the area honeycombed with mines, burdened with unemployment. People seemed locked into themselves, afraid of being robbed of the little they had left.

"I was wondering if he's all right on his own."

"He'll have to be, won't he." She was growing angry; he was as bad as Mr. Williams, reminding her of things it was no use remembering.

"I was just thinking that if you want to slope off home, I won't tell anyone. You've already done more work than some of the rest of them would do in an evening."

She clenched her fists beneath the desk to hold onto her temper. He must want to leave early himself and so was trying to persuade her. No doubt he had problems of his own—perhaps they were the secret behind his face—but he mustn't try to make her act dishonestly. Or was he testing her? She knew so little about him. "He'll be perfectly safe," she said. "He can always knock on the wall if he needs anyone."

Though his face stayed blank his eyes, frustrated now, gave him away. Five minutes later he was craning out of the window over the fire escape, while Elaine pinned flapping files down with both hands. Did he really expect his date, if that was his problem, to come out on a night like this? It would be just like a man to expect her to wait outside.

The worst of it was that Elaine felt disappointed, which was absurd and infuriating. She knew perfectly well that the only reason he was working tonight was that one of the seniors had to do so. Good God, what had she expected to come of an evening alone with him? They were both in their forties—they knew what they wanted by now, which in his case was bound to be someone younger than Elaine. She hoped he and his girl friend would be very happy. Her hands on the files were tight fists.

When he slammed the window she saw that his face was glistening. Of course it wasn't sweat, only rain. He hurried away without looking at her, and vanished into the lift. Perhaps the girl was waiting in the doorway, unable to rouse Mr. Tuttle to let her in. Elaine hoped Steve wouldn't bring her upstairs. She would be a distraction, that was why. Elaine was here to work.

And she wasn't about to be distracted by Steve and his attempts at jokes. She refused to turn when she heard the soft sounds by the lift. No doubt he was peering through the lobby window at her, waiting for her to turn and jump. Or was it his girl friend? As Elaine reached across her desk for a file she thought that the face was pale and very fat. Elaine was damned if she would give her the satisfaction of being noticed—but when she tried to work she couldn't concentrate. She turned angrily. The lobby was deserted.

In a minute she would lose her temper. She could see where he was hiding, or they were: the door of the room off the lobby was ajar. She turned away, determined to work, but the deserted office wouldn't let her; each alley between the filing cabinets was a hiding-place, the buzz of the defective light and the fusillade of rain could hide the sound of soft footsteps. It was no longer at all funny. He was going too far.

At last he came in from the lobby, with no attempt at stealth. Perhaps he had tired of the joke. He must have been to the street door, for his forehead was wet, though it didn't look like rain. Would he go back to work now, and pretend that the urn's room was empty? No, he must have thought of a new ruse, for he began pacing from cabinet to cabinet, glancing at files, stuffing them back into place. Was he trying to make her as impatient as he appeared to be? His quick sharp footsteps seemed to grow louder and more nerve-racking, like the ticking of the clock when she was lying awake, afraid to doze off in case her father needed her. "Steve, for heaven's sake what's wrong?"

He stopped in the act of pulling a file from its cabinet. He looked abashed, at a loss for words, like a schoolboy caught stealing. She couldn't help taking pity on him; her resentment had been presumptuous. "You didn't go down to find Mr. Tuttle just now, did you?" she said, to make it easier for him.

But he looked even less at ease. "No, I didn't. I

don't think he's here at all. I think he left hours ago."

Why must he lie? They had both heard the caretaker on the floor below. Steve seemed determined to go on. "As a matter of fact," he said, "I'm beginning to suspect that he sneaks off home as soon as he can once the building's empty."

He was speaking low, which annoyed her: didn't he want his girl friend to hear? "But there's someone else in the building," he said.

"Oh yes," she retorted, "I'm sure there is." Why did he have to dawdle instead of coming out with the truth? He was worse than her father when he groped among his memories.

He frowned, obviously not sure how much she knew. "Whoever it is, they're up to no good. I'll tell you the rest once we're out of the building. We mustn't waste any more time."

His struggles to avoid the truth amused and irritated her. The moisture on his forehead wasn't rain at all. "If they're up to no good," she said innocently, "we ought to wait until the police arrive."

"No, we'll call the police once we're out." He seemed to be saying anything that came into his head. How much longer could he keep his face blank? "Listen," he said, his fist crumpling the file, "I'll tell you why Mr. Tuttle doesn't stay here at night. The cleaners too, I think he told them. When the men were cleaning out the sub-basement, some of the food disappeared overnight. You understand what that means? Someone stole a hundredweight of rotten food. The men couldn't have cared less, they treated it as a joke, and there was no sign how anyone could have got in. But as he says, that could mean that whatever it was was clever enough to conceal the way in. Of course I thought he was drunk or joking, but now . . ."

His words hung like dust in the air. She didn't trust herself to speak. How dare he expect her to swallow such rubbish, as if she were too stupid to know what was going on? Her reaction must have shown in her face; she had never heard him speak coldly before. "We must go immediately," he said.

Her face was blazing. "Is that an order?"

"Yes, it is. I'll make sure you don't lose by it." His voice grew authoritative. "I'll call the lift while you fetch your coat."

Blind with anger, she marched to the cloakroom at the far end of the office from the lobby. As she grabbed her coat the hangers clashed together, a shrill violent sound which went some way toward expressing her feelings. Since Steve had no coat, he would be soaked. Though that gave her no pleasure, she couldn't help smiling.

The windows were shaking with rain. In the deserted office her footsteps sounded high-pitched, nervous. No, she wasn't on edge, only furious. She didn't mind passing the alleys between the cabinets, she wouldn't deign to look, not even at the alley where a vague shadow was lurching forward; it was only the shadow of a cabinet, jerked by the defective light. She didn't falter until she came in sight of the lobby, where there was no sign of Steve.

Had he gone without her? Was he smuggling out his girl friend? They weren't in the room off the

58

lobby, which was open and empty; the overturned waste-bin seemed to demonstrate their haste. The doors of the disused lift-shaft were open too. They must have opened when Steve had called the other lift. Everything could be explained; there was no reason for her to feel that something was wrong.

But something was. Between the two lift-shafts, the call-button was glowing. That could mean only one thing: the working lift hadn't yet answered the call. There was no other exit from the lobby—but there was no sign of Steve.

When she made herself go to the disused lift-shaft, it was only in order to confirm that her thought was absurd. Clinging to the edges of the doorway, she leaned out. The lift was stranded in the sub-basement, where it was very dim. At first all she could distinguish was that the trapdoor in its roof was open, though the opening was largely covered by a sack. Could anything except a sack be draped so limply? Yes, for it was Steve, his eyes like glass that was forcing their lids wide, his mouth gagged with what appeared to be a torn-off wad of dough—except that the dough had fingers and a thumb.

She was reeling, perhaps over the edge of the shaft. No, she was stumbling back into the foyer, and already less sure what she'd glimpsed. Steve was dead, and she must get out of the building; she could think of nothing else. Thank God, she need not think, for the working lift had arrived. Was there soft movement in the disused shaft, a chorus of sucking like the mouthing of a crowd of babies? Nothing could have made her look. She staggered away, between the opening doors—into total darkness.

For a moment she thought she'd stepped out into an empty well. But there was a floor underfoot; the lift's bulb must have blown. As the doors clamped shut behind her, the utter darkness closed in.

She was scrabbling at the metal wall in a frantic bid to locate the buttons—to open the door, to let in some light—before she controlled herself. Which was worse: a quick descent in the darkness, or to be trapped alone on the sixth floor? In any case, she needn't suffer the dark. Hurriedly she groped in her handbag for her lighter.

She flicked the lighter uselessly once, twice, as the lift reached the fifth floor. The sudden plunge in her guts wasn't only shock; the lift had juddered to a halt. She flicked the lighter desperately. It had just lit when the doors hobbled open.

The fifth floor was unlit. Beyond the lobby she could see the windows of the untenanted office, swarming with rain and specks of light. The bare floor looked like a carpet of dim fog, interrupted by angular patches of greater dimness, blurred rugs of shadow. There was no sign of Mr. Tuttle or whoever she'd heard from above. The doors were closing, but she wasn't reassured: if the lift had begun to misbehave, the least it could do would be to stop at every floor.

The doors closed her in with her tiny light. Vague reflections of the flame hung on the walls and tinged the greyish metal yellow; the roof was a hovering blotch. All the lighter had achieved was to remind her how cramped the lift was. She stared

60

at the doors, which were trembling. Was there a movement beyond them other than the outbursts of rain?

When the doors parted, she retreated a step. The fourth floor was a replica of the fifth—bare floors colourless with dimness, windows that looked shattered by rain—but the shuffling was closer. Was the floor of the lobby glistening in patches, as though from moist footsteps? The doors were hesitating, she was brandishing her tiny flame as though it might defend her—then the doors closed reluctantly, the lift faltered downward.

She'd had no time to sigh with relief, if indeed she had meant to, when she heard the lobby doors open above her. A moment later the lift shook. Something had plumped down on its roof.

At once, with a shock that felt as though it would tear out her guts, she knew what perhaps she had known, deep down, for a while: Steve hadn't been trying to frighten her—he had been trying not to. She hadn't heard Mr. Tuttle on the fifth floor, nor any imaginary girl friend of Steve's. Whatever she had heard was above her now, fumbling softly at the trapdoor.

It couldn't get in. She could hear that it couldn't, not before the lift reached the third—oh God, make the lift be quick! Then she could run for the fire escape, which wasn't damaged except on the sixth. She was thinking quickly now, almost in a trance that carried her above her fear, aware of nothing except the clarity of her plan—and it was no use.

The doors were only beginning to open as they

reached the third when the lift continued downward without stopping. Either the weight on its roof, or the tampering, was sending it down. As the doors gaped to display the brick wall of the shaft, then closed again, the trapdoor clanged back and something like a hand came reaching down toward her.

It was very large. If it found her, it would engulf her face. It was the colour of ancient dough, and looked puffed up as if by decay; patches of flesh were torn and ragged, but there seemed to be no blood, only greyness. She clamped her left hand over her mouth, which was twitching uncontrollably, and thrust the lighter at the swollen groping fingers.

They hissed in the flame and recoiled, squirming. Whitish beads had broken out on them. In a way the worst thing was the absence of a cry. The hand retreated through the opening, scrapping the edge, and a huge vague face peered down with eyes like blobs of dough. She felt a surge of hysterical mirth at the way the hand had fled — but she choked it back, for she had no reason to feel triumphant. Her skirmish had distracted her from the progress of the lift, which had reached the bottom of the shaft.

Ought she to struggle with the doors, try to prevent them from opening? It was too late. They were creeping back, they were open now, and she could see the sub-basement.

At least, she could see darkness which her light couldn't even reach. She had an impression of an enormous doorway, beyond which the darkness, if it was in proportion, might extend for hundreds of yards; she thought of the mouth of a sewer or a mine. The stench of putrid food was overwhelming, parts of the dark looked restless and puffy. But when she heard scuttling, and a dim shape came darting toward her, it proved to be a large rat.

Though that was bad enough, it mustn't distract her from the thing above her, on the lift. It had no chance to do so. The rat was yards away from her, and darting aside from her light, when she heard a spongy rush and the rat was overwhelmed by a whitish flood like a gushing of effluent. She backed away until the wall of the lift arrested her. She could still see too much—but how could she make herself put out the flame, trap herself in the dark?

For the flood was composed of obese bodies which clambered over one another, clutching for the trapped rat. The rat was tearing at the pudgy hands, ripping pieces from the doughy flesh, but that seemed not to affect them at all. Huge toothless mouths gaped in the puffy faces, collapsed inward like senile lips, sucking loudly, hungrily. Three of the bloated heads fell on the rat, and she heard its squeals above their sucking.

Then the others that were clambering over them, out of the dark, turned toward her. Great moist nostrils were dilating and vanishing in their noseless faces. Could they see her light with their blobs of eyes, or were they smelling her terror? Perhaps they'd had only soft rotten things to eat down here, but they were learning fast. Hunger was their only motive, ruthless, all-consuming.

They came jostling toward the lift. Once, delirious, she'd heard all the sounds around her grow stealthily padded, but this softness was far worse. She was trying both to stand back and to jab the lift-button, quite uselessly; the doors refused to budge. The doughy shapes would pile in like tripe, suffocating her, putting out the flame, gorging themselves on her in the dark. The one that had ridden the lift was slithering down the outside to join them.

Perhaps its movement unburdened the lift, or jarred a connection into place, for all at once the doors were closing. Swollen hands were thumping them, soft fingers like grubs were trying to squeeze between them, but already the lift was sailing upward. Oh God, suppose it went straight up to the sixth floor! But she'd found the ground-floor button, though it twitched away from her, shaken by the flame, and the lift was slowing. Through the slit between the doors, beyond the glass doors to the street, a streetlamp blazed like the sun.

The lift's doors opened, and the doughy face lurched in, its fat white blind eyes bulging, its avid mouth huge as a fist. It took her a moment prolonged as a nightmare to realize that it had been crushed between lift and shaft—for as the doors struggled open, the face began to tear. Screaming, she dragged the doors open, tearing the body in half. As she ran through it she heard it plump at the foot of the shaft, to be met by a soft eager rush—but she was fleeing blindly into the torrent of rain, toward the steep maze of unlit streets, her father at the fireside, his quiet vulnerable demand to know all that she'd done today.

Icy terror strikes from Beyond, in . . .

The Light from the Pole
by Clark Ashton Smith*

Mr. Smith first appeared in the fifth issue of this magazine, and his role in its rise to greatness dates, therefore, to the very first year of its publication. It was not until the early 1930's, however, that he began to hit his stride as far as fiction went: from then until some period in 1936 or '37 his gorgeously-written fables appeared in almost every issue; at that point, unaccountably, his story-production dwindled to a mere trickle. After his death in 1961, there were discovered among the papers of Clark Ashton Smith various fragments of unpublished prose, notes and outlines for unwritten stories, and lists of unused titles

*Completed by Lin Carter.

and coined names, as well as drafts of unfinished stories. Your editor has been at work for some years now, completing these unfinished tales, the first of which appeared in *Weird Tales*, the issue of Fall, 1973. This is the fifth in the series, and, like all of its predecessors, is to be thought of as a chapter from the *Book of Eibon*, Smith's answer to the *Necronomicon* of the Mad Arab, Abdul Alhazred: it is, in fact, Chapter Ten. "The Light From the Pole" is unique, however, in that it incorporates within its text some 3000 words of previously unpublished prose by Clark Ashton Smith, taken from the abandoned first draft of one of his later stories, "The Coming of the White Worm."

Pharazyn the prophet abode in a tall house of granite built on the cliffy heights above a small fishing-village on the northernmost coasts of Zabdamar, whose rock-bestrewn shores are unceasingly washed by the cold black waters of the polar main. It was quite early in the reign of the Emperor Charnametros, in that year known to the chroniclers as the Year of the Green Spider, that Pharazyn first became aware of the imminence of his singular and ineluctable doom by certain small signs and presagings. His dreams were perturbed by malign and shadowy shapes, which ever remained half-glimpsed; cold auroras flamed and flickered unseasonably in the nocturnal heavens, although the season was midsummer; and always, in the loud wind and crying surf, it seemed to Pharazyn that he harkened to the weird whisper of voices from realms of perennial winter.

Now, from atop the granite towers of his high house, it was the wont of Pharazyn to observe the wheeling constellations overhead and to persue those starry omens which appertain to events yet unborn in the dark womb of time. Of late, these nocturnal portents had been strangely ominous, as well, and yet imprecise: it was as if they prefigured the encroachment of some curious manner of doom so unique as to stand without precedent in the annals of the astrologic science, which could thus be only *hinted* at in vague, ambiguous terms. This, as well, was troubling to the serenity of Pharazyn.

As to the relevance of the approaching event, it seemed in some wise to bear upon the destiny of the prophet himself; for the stellar omens were occultly consonant to his own natal house, wherein Fomalhaut was ascendant; and also to that zodiacal sign the astromancers of this epoch termed The Basilisk. But in no degree could the prophet discern with precision or clarity the lineaments of the impending event which would seem to impinge so particularly upon his own personal fate.

And this was the cause of increasing perturbation and unrest within the heart of Pharazyn: that, strive as he might, he could acquire no certain foreknowledge of that which would soon eventuate, nor even an inkling thereunto. Being a past-master of all magic and divination, and a seer of remote and future things, he made use of his arts in an effort to divine their meaning. But a cloud was upon his eyes through the diurnal hours, and a darkness thwarted his vision when he sought illumination in dreams. His horoscopes were put to naught; his familiars were silent or answered him equivocally; and confusion was amidst all his geomancies and hydromancies and haruspications. And it seemed to Pharazyn that an unknown power worked against him, mocking and rendering impotent in such fashion the sorcery that none had defeated heretofore. And Pharazyn knew, by certain tokens perceptible to wizards, that the power was an evil power, and its boding was of bale to man.

Through the middle summer the fisher-folk who dwelt in wattle huts below the tall towers of Pharazyn went forth daily in their coracles of hide and willow and cast their nets in the accustomed manner of their trade. But all that they gathered from the sea was dead and withered as if in the blast of great coldness such as would emanate from trans-Arctic ice. And they drew forth from their seines living monsters as well, such as their eldest captains had never beheld: things triple-headed and tailed and finned with horror; black, shapeless things that turned to liquid foulness and ran from the net like a vile ichor; or headless shapes like bloated moons with green, frozen rays about them; or things leprous-eyed and bearded with stiffly-oozing slime. It was as if some trans-dimensional and long-blocked channel beneath the known, familiar seas of Earth had opened suddenly into the strange waters of ultra-mundane oceans, teeming with repulsive and malformed life.

In awe and wonder at what had come out of the

sea-horizoned north, the fisher-folk withdrew into their huts, abandoning their wonted pursuits of the season; their boats, which fared no longer to sea, were drawn up on the sands below the tall towers of Pharazyn on the cliff. And Pharazyn himself, descending later, also beheld the rotting and unwholesome monsters drawn dripping from the tainted waters, and pondered much concerning the import of this prodigy. For this ill miracle was, he knew, in sooth a sure prodigy of evil.

Thereafter, for the span of seven days, each time the timid folk would emerge from their huts and sail forth to draw provender from the waves, naught filled their nets but unnatural malignancies. At length, and all aghast, they tarried not but fled swiftly to the uppermost rocks and thence to an inland village which lay hard by, wherein the greater number of them could find haven and refuge from these grisly marvels among their kin. There remained with Pharazyn only his two servants, the boy Ratha and the crone Ahilidis, who had both witnessed many of his conjurations and were thus well inured to sights of magic. And with these two beside him, the prophet felt less alone against whatever the night would bring.

Reascending to his towering abode, he ignited before every portal such suffumigations as are singularly repulsive to the boreal demons; and at each angle of the house where a malign spirit might enter, he posted one of his familiars to guard against all intrusion. Thenceafter, while Ratha and Ahilidis slept, he studied with sedulous care the parchments of Pnom, wherein are collated many strong and potent exorcisms. He bethought him that a dire spell had been laid upon the land of Zabdamar: an ensorcelling such as the wan polar demons might weave, or the chill witches of the moon might devise in their caverns of snow. And he deemed it well to retire for a time, lest the spell should now take effect upon others than the clammy denizens of the oozy-bottomed sea.

But albeit the exorcisms of Pnom were many and mighty, and stood strong against those entities sinister and malign, such as might yearn to work evil upon the life of Pharazyn, he derived little easement of heart from their perusal. For ever and anon, as he read again for his comfort the old rubrics, he remembered ominously the saying of the prophet Lith, which heretofore no man had ever understood: "There is One that inhabits the place of utter cold, and One that respireth where none other may draw breath. In the days to come He shall issue forth among the isles and cities of men, and shall bring with Him as a white doom the wind that slumbereth in his dwelling place."

And he remembered, as well, the grisly and horrific doom which had befallen his sorcerous colleague, the warlock Evagh, in Yikilth the iceisland. There, in the frozen realm of the worm Rlim Shaikorth, Evagh had suffered a metamorphosis so terrible that few savants have dared be specific in their redactions of the tale. But Pharazyn and Evagh had been students of the same master, and following upon the demise or enchantment of the warlock, Pharazyn had been moved to interrogate the wandering spirits of wind and wave until at length he had learned in every dread particular that which had befallen his former comrade. And the portents which had presaged the coming of the white woam and the discarnation of Evagh were not unlike the omens and portents which Pharazyn had observed, and which he knew related to his own doom.

Therefore, he pored long over the exorcisms of Pnom and the prophecies of Lith, and peered as well into the doom-fraught pages of the Pnakotic Manuscripts, wherein there were of old indited much lore both abstruse and recondite, and otherwise forgotten among men.

*

Although a fire of fatty connifer blazed fiercely upon the marble hearth of his tower-top chamber, it seemed that a deathly chill began to pervade the air of the room about the midnight hour. As Pharazyn turned uneasily from the parchments of Pnom, and saw that the hearth was heaped high and the fire burned bright, he heard the sudden turmoil of a great wind full of sea-birds eerily shrieking, and the cries of land-fowl driven on helpless wings, and over all a high laughter of diabolic voices. Madly from the north the wind beat upon his square-based towers; and birds were cast like blown leaves of autumn against the stout-paned windows; and devils seemed to tear and strain at the granite walls. Though the room's door was shut and the windows were tight-closed, an icy gust went round and round, circling the table where Pharazyn sat, snatching the broad parchments of Pnom from beneath his fingers, and plucking at the lamp-flame.

Fruitlessly, with sluggish brain, he strove to remember that counter-charm which is most effective against the spirits of the boreal quarter. Then, strangely, it seemed that the wind fell, leaving a mighty stillness about the house.

Soon he was made aware of a light shining beyond his chamber windows, as if a belated moon had now risen above the rocks. But Pharazyn knew that the moon was at that time a thin crescent, declining with eventide. It seemed that the light shone from the north, pale and frigid as fire of ice; and going to the window he beheld a great beam that traversed all the sea, coming as if from the hidden pole. In that light the rocks were paler than marble, and the sands were whiter than sea-salt, and the huts of the fishermen were as white tombs. The walled garden of Pharazyn was filled with the piercing light, and lo! all of the green had departed from its foliage, and all of the color had been leached from its blossoms until they were like deathly flowers of snow. And the beam fell bleakly upon the lower walls of his house, but left still in shadow the wall of that upper chamber from which he looked.

He thought that the beam poured from a pale cloud that lay athwart the sea-line, or else from a white peak in the direction of the pole, which had never before been visible by day, but seemed to have lifted skyward in the night—of this he was uncertain. Watching, he thought he saw that it rose higher in the heavens, that beam of frigid light, but climb no higher upon the walls of his tower. At length the ice-mountain, wherefrom it seemed that ray of cold light shone, loomed mighty in the boreal heavens, until it was higher even than the dread mountain Achoravomas, which belches rivers of flame and liquid stone that pour unquenched through Tscho Vulpanomi to the austral main; nay steeper still it seemed to him, until it towered above the house of Pharazyn like unto far and fabulous Yarak itself, the mountain of ice that marks the site of the veritable pole.

Scarce could he draw breath in the cold that was on the air; and the light of the mountainous iceberg seared his eyeballs with an exceeding froreness. Yet he perceived an odd thing, that the rays of the glittering light from the pole fell indirectly and to either side of his house; and the lower chambers, where Ratha and Adilidis slept, were bathed in the strange luminance. It would seem that his suffumigations and other precautions had served to preserve at least this chamber of his house from the full fury of the beam of freezing light.

Then the beam swerved from the tall towers of Pharazyn, and passed his house by, questing the night. The chill gust was gone from the room; the lamp and the fire burned steadily; and something of warmth returned slowly into the half-frozen marrow of Pharazyn.

Pondering in vain the significance of the mystery, he then seemed to hear in the air about him a sweet and wizardly voice. And, speaking in a tongue that he knew not, the voice uttered a rune of slumber. And Pharazyn could not resist the rune, and upon him there fell such a numbness of sleep as overcomes the outworn watcher in a place of snow.

*

Waking stiffly at dawn, he rose up from the floor where he had lain, and found himself alive and unharmed by the ordeal: it was as if all which had befallen him during the nocturnal hours had been naught but the phantasmagoria of a dream.

Striding to the window, the prophet threw wide the casement and gazed with fearful trepidation upon the north. But there was nothing which met his eye that he had not beheld a thousand dawns aforetime: the bleak and barren wastes of Mhu Thulan, culminating in a rocky promontory which thrust out into the dark sea; and the white wilderness of northernmost Polarion beyond the snowy bastions of the wall of mountains which stood athwart the horizon. Nowhere in his range of vision could Pharazyn perceive that wanly glittering, that sky-ascending spire, of soaring ice wherefrom had shone the frigid ray.

For all that it was no longer within the scope of his perception, the prophet knew with grim certainty what it had been that he had surely seen. No captain, faring far to sea, had espied its like in the boreal main; no legend had told of it among the dim hyperborean isles; no seer or sage had recorded it from his seething and phantasmal visions: but Pharazyn knew.

Deathly and terrible had been that glittering pinnacle, hung like a djinn-reared tower in the zenith; and he knew with sure and certain knowledge the source of the light he had beheld in the darkness like a far beacon, and that it shone not from any earthly coast, but from remote and trans-telluric gulfs profound.

For the uncanny glitterings of a frost harder than diamonds sheathed the walls of his tower in unmeltable crystal. Yet the walls of the tower were no longer touched by the beam as in the night, for it has passed on many hours since; and upon all his house there was naught but the early sun and the morning shadows.

Again he remembered the saying of Lith; and with much foreboding he descended to the ground story. There, at the northern windows, the boy Ratha and the hag Ahilidis were leaning with faces upturned to the direction wherefrom the icy beacon-light had shone. Stiffly they stood, with wide-open eyes, and a pale terror was in their regard, and upon them was the white death such as has stricken his garden in the night. And, nearing them, the prophet was stayed by a terrible chillness that smote upon him from their bodies, which were pallid as the flesh of leprosy and white as moon-washed marble.

Gazing beyond them through the window, Pharazyn perceived along the sands and rocks of the shore, certain of the fisherfolk as had crept back to their homes were lying or standing upright in stiff, rigid postures, as if they had emerged from their hiding-places to behold the pale beam and had been struck into an enchanted slumber, or else turned to stone by the Gorgon's glare of the polar light. And the whole shore and harbor, and the cliffs, and the garden of Pharazyn, even to the front threshold of his house, was mailed in crystal armor of perdurable frost, as had been the walls of his house.

He would have fled from thence, knowing his magic wholly ineffectual against this thing. But it came to him that death was in the direct falling of the rays from the ice mountain, and, leaving the shelter of the house, he must perforce enter that fatal light when next it shone questing down the darkling skies from the ultimate north. And yet not totally unprotected was he if he remained, for the wards he had erected against supernatural intrusion had in sooth protected him from the doom which had befallen the hapless fisher-folk, and the boy Ratha, and the crone. Or was his inexplicable survival due *only* to the efficacy of his suffumigations and familiars?

Now terror crept into the heart of Pharazyn, for it came to him that he alone, of all who dwelt on that shore, had been *exempted* from the white death. He dared not surmise the reason of his exemption; but he realized the futility of flight, and in the end he deemed it best to remain patiently and without fear, awaiting whatever should befall him with the coming of another night.

Returning to his chamber he busied himself with various conjurations. But his familiars had gone away in the night, forsaking the angles at which he had posted them; and no spirit, human or demoniacal, made reply to his querying. And not in any way known to wizards could he learn aught of the mountain of ice and of its frigid ray, or divine the least inkling of its secret, to confirm the dreadful surmise that had seized upon him.

Deeply immersed in his sorcerous labors, he was unaware of the passage of time and only realized that night was upon him when presently, as he labored with his useless cantrips, he felt upon his face the breathing of a wind that was not air but a subtler and a rarer element cold as the moon's ether. His own breath forsook him with agonies unspeakable, and he fell down on the floor in a sort of waking swoon that was near to death. And again he recalled the hideous metamorphosis that had befallen the unfortunate warlock, Evagh, and his transformation upon Yikilth into a being able to endure the rigors of super-Arctic cold, to whom even the frigid and insubstantial ether was rendered somehow respirable.

In the swoon he was doubtfully aware of voices uttering unfamiliar spells. Invisible fingers touched him with icy pangs; and about him came and went a bleak radiance, like a tide that flows and ebbs and flows again. Intolerable was this luminance to all his senses; but it brightened slowly, with briefer ebbings; and in time his eyes and his flesh were tempered to endure it. Almost fully upon him now shone the mysterious light from the north, blazing through his windows; and it seemed that a great Eye regarded him in the baleful light. He would have risen to confront the Eye, but his swoon held him like a palsy.

After that, he slept again for a certain period. Waking, he found in all his limbs their wonted strength and quickness. The light was still upon his house, its pallid luminance glimmering through his chamber. Then, with inexplicable suddenness, it was gone; but whether it had died at its source or merely turned away to bathe some other place in the freezing regard of its Gorgon-eye, he did not know.

*

Morning lit the east and the second night was ended of this seige. And, peering out, he witnessed a new and more ominous marvel: for, lo! the adamantine frost *had now crept nigh unto the very sill of his casement*. And he was aware of a bleak certainty: that on the third night—should he live to see it—the cold and pallid beam from the icy peak would fully enter into his casement window, and his doom would be upon him everlastingly.

Terror seized upon Pharazyn then, for he saw in all of these phenomena the insidious workings of a wizardry plenipotent and transcendental, and beyond the skill of any terrene sorcerer. All that third day he searched the blood-writ runes of mouldering scrolls of pterodactyl-parchment, and scanned the writings of the elder sages, searching in vain for the means to combat the eerie menace from the pole which close-compassed him and which would, he knew, with the coming of night, drag him down to a doom so profound and unutterable that from its frigid bourn he might never escape.

For it had come to Pharazyn, in the trance-like slumbers of his spell-induced swoon, what secret lurked behind the cryptic sayings of Lith. For he had found amongst the enigmatic utterances of the prophet yet a second passage whose meanings had heretofore eluded the comprehension of the sages: "But even He, who reigns among the lords of death, is made vulnerable by His coming-hence into the world of mortality. Beware, then, the wrath of that Other One which is His Master and far more terrible than He; and Who abideth forever in His cold caverns beneath His mountain, beprisoned there by the Elder Gods. For if that Other seek ye out, Him there is no escaping save in death itself."

Now it seemed to Pharazyn that the One whose coming was foretold by the prophet Lith was the white worm, Rlim Shaikorth; from beyond the limits of the north had he come in his floating citadel, the ice-island, Yikilth, to voyage the mundane oceans and to blast with a chill splendor the puny peoples of humankind. And when Evagh the warlock had been transformed into a being for whom was made respirable the air in which no mortal man may draw breath—even that coldness and the thin ether that go everywhere with Yikilth—he was brought face to face with that being whose advent the prophet Lith had foretold obscurely, and who had vaguely the lineaments of a visage belonging neither to beast of the earth nor ocean-creature.

And unto him Rlim Shaikorth had spake: Wisdom ineffable shalt be thine, and mastery of lore beyond the reach of mortals, if thou wilt but worship me and become my thrall; with me thou shalt voyage amid the kingdoms of the north, and shalt pass among the green southern islands, and we shall smite the fair ports and cities with a blight of trans-Arctic winter: for I am he whose coming even the gods may not oppose.

Thereafter, Pharazyn knew, Evagh had dwelt upon Yikilth, and beneath the instruction of Dooni and Ux Loddhan, captive sorcerers of Thulask, who had as well been tempered to the coldness of Yikilth, together with certain outlandish and uncouth men called Polarians, he performed the sevenfold rite that is scarce suitable for narration here, and sware the threefold vow of unspeakable alienation. Thereafter for many days and nights, he sailed with Rlim Shaikorth adown the coast of Mhu Thulan and the province of Zabdamar, the great iceberg being guided by the sorcery of the worm, prevailing even against the wind and tide. By night and day, like the beams of a deathly beacon, the chill splendor smote afar from Yikilth to freeze flowery Cerngoth and sea-affronting Aguil with boreal stillness. Proud triremes were overtaken as they fled southward, their crews blasted at the oars; and often ships were caught and embedded in the new bastions of ice that formed daily around the base of that ever-growing mountain. But, dwelling upon Yikilth, the sorcerer Evagh and his fellow-wizards were immune to that icy death, even as the worm had promised them. All were united in the worship of the white worm; and all, it seemed, were content in a measure with their lot, and were fain of that unearthly lore and dominion

80

which the worm had promised them.

But Evagh rebelled in secret against his thralldom to Rlim Shaikorth; he beheld with revulsion the doom of cities, and sorrow was in his heart for the fishing-coracles and the biremes of trade and warfare that floated manless after they had met Yikilth. Ever the ice-isle followed its southwardly course, growing vaster and more prodigious by accretion; and ever, at the star-appointed time, which was the forenoon of every third day, the sorcerers convened in the presence of Rlim Shaikorth to do him worship. To the perturbation of all, their numbers unaccountably dwindled, warlock by warlock, first amongst the outlandish men from Polarion. And ever, ominously the worm *greatened* in size; and the increase was visible as a thickening of his whole body from head to tail.

Deeming these circumstances an ill augury, the sorcerers made fearful supplication to the worm in their various tongues, and implored him to enlighten them concerning the fate of their erstwhile fellows. But the reply they received was equivocal at best: sometimes the worm was silent, and sometimes he bespoke them, renewing vaguely the promises he had made. And Ux Loddhan, it seemed, was wholly oblivious to the doom which overtook them slowly, one by one, and was fain to impute an esoteric significance to the ever-growing bulk of the white worm and the vanishing of the wizards. At length Evagh had perceived that his evanished brethren were now merged wholly in the ultraterrestrial being of Rlim Shaikorth, had been devoured by the wan and loathly mouth of the worm, and abode henceforward in the evil blackness of his belly, whereto he himself was doomed to dwell, if he did not foreswear his dreadful vows and strike during those infrequent periods of slumber when even the mighty Rlim Shaikorth was vulnerable. And strike he did, effecting the dissolution both of the white worm and of the ice-isle, Yikilth, itself; while his own spirit was borne shrieking into the boreal solitudes, there to bide forever.

Now it seemed to Pharazyn that the white worm was even that One whereof the prophet Lith had forewarned the world; and that if this was so, then even the terrible Rlim Shaikorth was but the emmisary of another and far more potent and dreadful Being, whose wrath was a peril to all the world, as the prophet Lith had foretold.

In his perusal of the parchments of Pnom, Pharazyn had found certain vague references to an entity of supra-polar cold who had come down from dim Fomalhaut when the world was young, taking as his abode the icy and cavernous bowels of Yarak, the ice-mountain which stands upon the ultimate and boreal pole, bound there forever under the sigil of those eldermost and benign divinities which guard the world and are reputedly disposed to be friendly towards man. All of this seemed to agree with that against which the sayings of Lith had so cryptically warned. And in this the dread name of Aphoom Zhah, concerning whom even the Pnakotic Manuscripts dare only hint, took on a grim and frightful relevance.

For if that which Pharazyn now dared to dream was true, then Rlim Shaikorth was only the minister of that Polar One of whom the legendries of anterior cycles whisper fearful things; and the white spirits of the boreal wastes—the Cold Ones who obey the behests of the worm, and haunt perpetually the frozen wilderness, and shriek upon the nightwind like damned, tormented souls—they were but the minions and servants of Aphoom Zhah, and Rlim Shaikorth their leader. And of this Aphoom Zhah, the Pnakotic Manuscripts alude to him as *a flame of coldness* which shall someday encompass the lands of men, from wintry Polarion in the ultimate north, through all the Hyperborean kingdoms and archipelagoes, even to the southmost isle of Oszhtror. And was it not a very *flame of coldness* which Pharazyn had seen falling adown the nighted skies, from a mountain of ice very like remote and terrible Yarak?

But wherefore was the wrath of the Dweller at the Pole turned against Pharazyn; or, if not from vengeance, for what ulterior purpose did the flame of coldness seek out his high house, night upon night? Here, too, the wisdom of Pnom yielded a clue upon perusal. For had not the sage written thusly: "Neither the Old Ones nor their minions dare to disturb the sigil of the elder gods; the hand of mortal man alone may touch their sign unblasted;" and, in another place, "Power the starborn Ones possess over those hapless mortals in whose natal hour the star of Their origin be ascendant." And well knew Pharazyn that both he and the unhappy Evagh were birthed in the hour when

83

dim Fomalhaut is risen over the edges of the world.

Therein lay the reason whereby had Rlim Shaikorth power to transmute the flesh of Evagh, and to temper it so that the warlock might endure the harsh rigor of Yikilth; therein, too, it might be, was the cause wherefore the light from the pole had sought out the tall towers of Pharazyn, among all the residences of men. *For only his hand could dislodge the sigil the gods had set upon the portals of Yarak: only Pharazyn the prophet could loose the Cold Flame upon the world!*

And thus it came to pass that Pharazyn knew the extremity of horror, and knew himself damned beyond all other dooms eternal: for it is a strange and fearful doom, to know that *by your hand* shall be set upon the flesh of men the seal of that gulf whose rigor paleth one by one the most ardent stars, and putteth rime at the very core of suns — the unutterable coldness of the profound and cosmic deeps!

*

When that the sun rose upon the morning of the third day after the blight of coldness had first touched the coasts of Zabdamar, and the fisher-folk who had fled inland to abide the unseasonable chill in the village of Zuth came to return to their frost-whitened huts, they found the high house of Pharazyn the prophet empty of life.

At first they were timid and trepidatious, and lingered athwart the threshold; later, when naught betide, the younger and bolder men amongst them ventured into the house, but cautiously: for it is never prudent to enter the houses of sorcerers unbidden. In the lower parts of the house the young men found the bodies of the boy Ratha and the crone Ahilidis stark as bone; they gathered their courage and approached the pale corpses, finding them frozen and stony.

In the upper parts of the tower which were untouched by the glittering frost, the fisher-folk discovered the corpse of the prophet himself, seated in his throne-like chair carved of the ivory of mammoths. Upon his thin red lips was a cold smile, and there beneath was another smile, thinner and yet more red; for he had slit his throat from ear to ear, had Pharazyn, heedful of the less cryptic of the two sayings of the prophet Lith, that only by death can a man elude the clutches of Aphoom Zhah the Lord of the Pole.

For generations, each woman of the family had waited to be revenged upon . . .

Someone Named Guibourg

by Hannes Bok

Today, Hannes Bok is best remembered for the many cover paintings and interior illustrations he did for the old *Weird Tales*; what is generally forgotten is that he contributed short stories to the Unique Magazine as well. His first cover painting adorned the issue for December, 1939, and his first story—"Poor Little Tampico"—appeared in the issue for July, 1942, the first of five tales he did for the magazine. After his death on April 11, 1964, I discovered among his papers the manuscripts of five unpublished stories in various stages of rough draft and revision; two of them, however, were finished and neatly typed. "Someone Named Guibourg" is one of these two; it was so obviously intended for *Weird Tales* that I wonder if he ever submitted it. If he ever did, it would seem that the story was rejected. For the life of me, I can't imagine why: it is a model *Weird Tales* yarn, and when you have read it yourself, I believe you will agree with me . . .

Seven-year-old Tim Brent was crawling on his hands and knees over the rug, a popgun in one of his hands. He looked up at his twin-sister on the sofa. "Jeanne, will you pretend to be a tiger? I'm a big game hunter, you see, and I want to shoot a tiger!"

But she seemed not to have heard. He sat back, disgusted. In her right hand was a doll, in her left, a long corsage pin.

"Now you're Guibourg," she told the doll's rapt stare, and then deliberately thrust a pin deep into the poppet's body.

"What're you doing?" Tim asked interestedly, but she was unconscious of his presence, her face twisted by an emotion which he did not recognize. "Jeanne!" But her eyes remained magnetised to the doll.

Puzzled, Tim straightened up, leaving the gun on the rug. "Hey, Jeanne, what kind of a game are you playing? Stop looking that way! You—you scare me!"

She was asleep sitting up. He went hesitantly to her and attempted to take the doll from her. With a jerk, she awoke. Her eyes observed the pin in the body of the little image, and with a gasp of horror, she whipped it out. She kissed the doll's face passionately.

"Oh, darling Edmond, I didn't mean to hurt *you*! I was playing that you were someone *else*!" She hugged the doll as closely as possible, rocking it, and began to cry.

Tim drew back, embarrassed. As he stopped to retrieve his gun, he noticed his mother standing in the doorway. He hurried joyfully to her. "Hello, Mom! I'm glad you're home! What're we goin' to have for dinner tonight?"

His mother's face was far too haggard for a woman of her years. Less gaunt, she would have been very beautiful. Then Tim saw that she was peering beyond him to Jeanne. He turned, worried. "I didn't make her cry, Mom. Honest! She just started in all by herself! She was playing with her doll—"

His mother's hand touched his shoulder lightly. "I saw it all. Never mind. Tim, come here into the bedroom with me."

Her tone troubled him; he raised apprehensive eyes. Her fingers on his back insinuated him out of the living room and into the dark little bedroom which she shared with Jeanne. She pulled off her hat, laid it down, and seated herself on the edge of the bed. She drew the boy to her side, slipped an arm around him.

"Tim, you're mother's little man, aren't you,

now that daddy's gone—away?"

The child stared at her, distrustfully. Her voice was very soft and unhappy. She was not being affectionate, as she was usually when she said this sort of thing.

"Sure, Mom. I'm the head of the house now, like you said."

She averted her face. "Tim, how'd you like to live with your Aunt Esther?"

His eyes widened; he slipped his arms around her. "Oh, but Mom, I don't ever want to live with anybody but you! I got to be around to protect you!" He threw out his chest bravely.

She hugged him tighter. "Yes, I know dear. And I appreciate you so much. Only—if something should happen to Jeanne and me—then you'd like to live with Aunt Esther, wouldn't you?"

"Well, yes. I guess so."

"And you'd always remember that Mom loved you very much!"

"Sure, Mom. But nothing's going to happen, is it? Is it?"

She flinched from his nervous gaze. "No, darling," she answered dully. "Nothing's going to happen."

The boy felt her shaking against him, saw tears in her eyes. "What's the matter, Mom? You've got to tell me! I'm the daddy now!"

She fumbled for a handkerchief, dabbed it on her eyes. "It's no use," she murmured. "I can't keep it up. If Walter were here, he'd help me fight it. But now when I know Jeanne's haunted by it, too—Oh I was a fool to think it wouldn't happen!"

"What wouldn't happen?" Her young son was near tears himself. "Mom, don't act this way! You're looking like—like Jeanne looked a minute ago! Don't, Mom, don't!"

She dropped her arms from around him. "There, dear, don't you be afraid." She pushed him away. "Run out to the other room and send Jeanne in here. Then you go outside for a while into the nice sunshine. Run along now!"

As he started for the door, she arose and went to her dresser, opened one of the bottom drawers. Young Tim hesitated at the threshold, curiously looking back. Tissue paper rattled like feet plodding through dead leaves; Mrs. Brent drew a long knife in a jewelled scabbard from its wrappings. She glimpsed Tim in the mirror, and motioned him to go.

"Hey, Jeanne, Mom wants you!" Tim shouted. His sister came quietly, emptyhanded. "Where?"

Tim said, "Here in the bedroom." Mrs. Brent hastily swathed the knife in paper as her daughter entered, and turned. Her welcoming smile was artificial. "Come to me, Jeanne, sweet. "She enfolded her daughter in her arms. "You go, now, Tim, as I told you. Go out and play."

"No, I want to stay, Mom."

"Run along!" Her voice lifted sharply, a vocal slap. She released Jeanne, and hurried to Tim, pushing him from the room. The door slammed; Tim heard the click of its key. He hesitated, his eyes roving the dim little hall. From the bedroom he heard his mother's voice; he put his ear to the door to listen.

"You recognize this knife?" Mrs. Brent's voice was shaking.

"Yes, Mama," Jeanne said. "It's Guibourg's!"

"Jeanne, where did you hear that name? I never told you—!"

"But Mama, it's the name I hear when I had bad dreams! It's the name you say when you get sick and Mrs. Scarlatti comes in to take care of you!"

"Jeanne, darling—" Mrs. Brent choked, and Tim stiffened anxiously. "You know that Mama loves you very much—"

"Oh, yes, Mama!"

"But Mama can't let this go on any longer. I *won't* have your life wrecked by the torture that's ruined mine!" There was a pause. "Come, Jeanne, darling, kiss me. Now close your eyes and think of something nice. Close them, darling. Come on, be a good girl. Close them. I'll tell you what—make a wish. Try to make it a very good one, and Mama will see if she can give it to you. There, that's better."

Then there was a shrill scream—Jeanne's treble voice, and Mrs. Brent's distraught shriek. "Mama! Mama!" Tim hammered on the door, kicking against it, rattling the knob. "Mom!! Jean! Open the door! Let me in!" But the screams went on and on, their anguish slashing the child's heart like a razor. Then Mrs. Brent's cries thinned away; only Jeanne was screaming. Tim strained against the door, hysterical with terror. "Mom! Jeanne! Open!"

Then Jeanne's cries stopped too. But Tim heard a horrid bubbling sound, as if someone were rhythmically blowing bubbles in very soapy water. . . .

He fled to the apartment's entrance, dragged the door open, and raced down the hall. "Mrs. Scarlatti! Mrs. Scarlatti! Come quick! My Mom's done something to herself and Jeanne!"

The white bandage was still around little Jeanne's throat, and she huddled fearfully against the tall swarthy old lady who was Aunt Esther. Tim stared at the few pathetic flowers on the new grave. "Poor Mom!" he said soberly.

Then he went to his sister, tried to take her hand, but she pulled it from him and put it back around her aunt. "Don't you worry, Jeanne, I'm almost grown-up, now. I'll take care of you."

Jeanne glanced up at her aunt's dark face; the two of them exchanged some kind of silent message that the boy could not comprehend.

"Come, Tim," the aunt said coldly. "It's time we started for home."

Aunt Esther's house was a squat old gingerbread structure which looked as if a giant's dirty hand had tried to smash it flat. It stood alone on the top of the hill, with weeds hanging heavily over the sidewalk leading up to it.

Aunt Esther was very solicitous about the little girl, clinging to the child's fingers; when Tim put up his hand for her to hold, she ignored it. "There's where we're going to live, all by ourselves, away from everybody," she said. "Isn't it nice!"

Jeanne scanned the house. "Aunt Esther?"

"Yes, pet?"

"You didn't forget to bring along the knife?"

Tim stopped, frozen. But Aunt Esther smiled like a witch from a fairy tale. "It's packed in one of the trunks that I had sent up by express." She glanced back, annoyed, at Tim. "Don't stand there! Come along!"

He followed, but slowly.

"Sh!" Jeanne cautioned. "Aunt Esther's sick."

Tim turned from the window overlooking feather-falling snow. "And on her birthday, too — just like Mom always was." He eyed the red scar, like a rope burn, on his sister's throat. "Is she saying — that name?"

Jeanne turned abruptly. "Don't talk about it! Just be quiet! Go upstairs and look at a picture book!"

"Where are you going?"

"Back to help Aunt Esther."

The boy hesitated. "Go on," Jeanne was a miniature adult, a midget copy of her dead mother.

Tim gulped and started away. At the foot of the dark stair he halted. "I wish you'd come along with me."

"No. Aunt Esther needs me."

Tim could not sleep. Shadows hung over his bed like wavering dark draperies. Out in the hall, Aunt Esther was pacing back and forth, the light of the lamp which she carried showing under the crack of the door, dimming, brightening, and fading again. The boy could hear her heavy breathing, as though she were tormented by a very bad cold.

He threw back the bed-clothes, and slipped out of bed to the floor, listened at the door. Then he opened it, peeped out. "Aunt Esther, can I help you?"

She turned sharply. "Get back in your bed and stay there!"

He was downcast. "Yes'm." He closed the door, stood irresolute in the darkness, then went back to bed.

But Aunt Esther still continued her restless shuffling. Worse, she began to murmur something too vague to be intelligible.

Tim tossed unhappily.

In the brilliant sunshine, under tunneling trees, the children were returning from school, bright little beings, the boys swaggering mannishly, the little girls flower-like in pastel-hued dresses. But Jeanne was cornered against a brick wall, her fists rubbing her eyes as she sobbed in despair while a crowd of girls linked hands and danced, surrounding her. *Jeanne is a crazy girl! Jeanne is a crazy girl!*"

Tim happened along with some classmates. He halted, incredulous. Then he rushed forward, tearing an opening among the girls. He stood in front of his sister. "You leave her alone! You get away from us!"

Their chant became even more ecstatic with cruelty. *"Jeanne is a crazy girl, and Tim is just as crazy!"*

In the summer night, the light from the full

moon was strong enough to reveal colors. Dewy grass glinted as though spread with frost. Somewhere a bird piped a few short minor notes.

Tim was older now, a gangling lad of fifteen. The boys with him stopped at the gate.

"Well, here's where we drop you. See you tomorrow, and we'll go boating again. That's if you don't catch john-henry for being out so late."

"Yeah, you said it! Goodnight, fellows."

The boys ambled along, absorbed in horseplay. Tim swung open the gate and started up the path through the orchard.

Something white, speckled by the moonglow shafting through foliage, stirred ahead. It glided to a tree, struck it, felt its way carefully around and continued onward. It was Jeanne, slim in her thin nightgown, walking in her sleep.

Tim hurried to her. As he seized her hands, the knife glinted in one of them. He stepped back. "Jeanne! Wake up! Where do you think you're going?"

She edged around him, her eyes unseeing. "I'm looking for Guibourg. I'm going to kill him." Her voice was listless.

He reached for the dagger, but could not unclench her fingers. He put his hands on her arms and shook her. Awareness returned to her.

"Oh, Tim, my feet are all wet!" she cried, and picked up the skirt of her long robe, tiptoeing with him across the grass toward the crouching house.

"You were walking in your sleep," Tim said sourly.

"I was dreaming." She eyed the knife resentfully.

"Yes, about this Guibourg," Tim answered. "Jeanne, who is he? Why did he wreck Mom's life? What do you know about him? Why won't you ever tell me?"

But she was obdurate, hiding her face from his piercing eyes. They were at the door when Tim continued, "You said a minute ago that you wanted to kill Guibourg. And you have the dagger—the same one Mom used—why, Jeanne, why?" His forehead was wrinkled, his palms stretching toward her.

She inhaled sharply. "Yes, I suppose you do have the right to know, even if you can't do anything about it. But I don't like to tell you, because you'll only be hurt, like daddy was—" She lifted a finger to her mouth. "Sh! Come on upstairs to my room, and I'll tell you. Careful! Don't let Aunt Esther hear!"

Tim sat on the bed. Jeanne enveloped herself in a wrapper. She went to the door, opened it, listened, then closed it again. "I guess she's asleep," she said, and crossed the room to the window-seat.

"I can remember Guibourg as far back as I remember anything," she said. "Aunt Esther remembers him, too—and so did Mama. All the women of our family have remembered him, though he died hundreds of years ago—" She was silent with revery.

Tim shifted impatiently. "What're you talking about? How can you remember someone you've never met?"

She silenced him with a quick gesture. "Grandma Pierce looked him up in our family tree. He really did exist. I've seen the family crest. He was attached to the court of one of the French kings—I think that it was Louis the Fourteenth. The woman he married was our grandmother—a great-great one, of course."

She pressed her fingertips to her temples, shook her head. "It's funny, though, because I'm the woman he married. Yes," she said eagerly, forestalling his attempt at interruption, "I'm Madalene! I can remember it as clearly as if it happened only a few minutes ago. Madalene! That was my name in those days! I was a little older then than now. About eighteen. And beautiful! I remember how I looked in my mirror—my hair was tucked away under an enormous wig; my skin was white with powder, and my eyelids were painted dark. Except for the diamonds which Guibourg had given me, my neck and shoulders were bare. My skirts were a bell of gorgeous silks.

"We all reeked of perfume in those days; we had to. But mine was faint and exquisite, something which had been brought from far Persia.

"And my baby! He was the sweetest thing in the whole wide world!"

Her words blended into a soft curtain of sound, darkening the bedroom, superimposing a different picture.

Madalene rested on a gilded chair whose wooden frame had been carved with sophisticated precision to resemble thin tendrils of smoke. Her baby's long dress was of pearly white satin and creamy old lace. One of his little hands, elfinly small and frail, was curled into a sleepy paw; the other clutched the diamond necklace. Madalene swayed from side to side, smiling, making the jewels sparkle in the glow of the many candles.

The baby gurgled, enchanted, laughing with his toothless mouth all awry, a happy little gnome with blue stars for eyes in a pink heaven of face. Madalene imitated the sounds, blissfully maternal, and shifted his slight weight that one of her hands might wonder at the silk of his short hair.

"You darling! I wish I had a million more like you!" She leaned down, just barely touching the tip of her nose to the pink bud of his. "But it's time for you to go to sleep again." She drifted erect and floated across the polished floor to the small swan-shaped bed under its damask canopy. She settled the infant on the feathery softness, drew cloud-soft coverlets up to his middle. "Let go of mother's necklace, sweet! No, let go!" She gently pried the tiny fingers loose, and the baby laughed again as though at a joke. "Go to sleep, now, darling." She leaned over the small bed, and began to sing. The baby's eyes were enormous with awed admiration, his flower-pink lips pursed as though for a kiss.

When he was slumbering at last, she turned. Guibourg was at the threshold, hardly any taller than she, almost as slight. One hand was effeminately on his hip, the other impatiently toying with the lace cascading down the front of his brocaded coat. After the fashion of that day, he too wore a wig; his face was cold white stone under powder; his brows had been shaved and replaced with perfect thin black painted lines.

He stamped a high heel impatiently. "Come, Madalene. I've something to show you."

She frowned, pressing a forefinger to her mouth to silence him. Her wide skirts whispered as she tiptoed over the floor to him, incredibly graceful, as though every movement were part of a stately dance.

"Yes, my dear?"

"Come. It's upstairs."

Her glance at him was a jerk of pain; her eyes lifted to the high ceiling's gilded plaster ornament and passed through it. "Upstairs?" she asked unwillingly.

He laid fingertips on her back, lightly prodding her out of the baby's room. His heels clattered as they crossed a tiled hall and started up a spiral stairway which looked too frail to bear their weight. Madalene lifted her skirts in front of her.

The second floor was dim, only a few candles burning. Guibourg stretched out a demanding palm to the old servant Pierre, who waited in the doorway, a tired human marionette in gorgeous livery, sagging on loose strings. "A candle, Pierre."

The puppet awoke to life, lifted a crystal candlestick, touched the candle to the flame of a burning one.

"Should I light the way?" he asked, his words the husky scrape of wool rubbed on wool.

"No. Stay where you are." Guibourg took the candle from him. "Come, Madalene."

The polished floor was dark glass under them. The woman glanced nervously from side to side, as though terrors lurked in the shadows, but the man strode ahead confidently and eagerly, as if answering a summons to happiness. The candle's flame flickered, and was echoed by highlights on ponderous gold frames on the walls, on shimmering hangings and in the mirrors panelling the walls. They turned a corner of the hall, halting before large double doors which Guibourg, handing the light to Madalene, unlocked.

He led the way into cavernous darkness. "Come in," he said, taking back the candle, his heels ticking as he sauntered about, lighting other tapers with the flame which he carried.

Madalene ventured within, her eyes following her husband curiously. In the augmenting brightness, she gazed about. There was a large desk littered with ragged big books and piles of manuscript; farther away were chairs and a long table crowded with strangely shaped bowls, long glass tubes and jars filled with scraps of aromatic bark and colored powders. Madalene's eyes winced from the skeleton dangling on a stand; her nostril dilated at an acrid odor rising from a basket, and she stepped away in disgust when she saw that it contained dried lizards, a mouldering snake and shrivelled dead bats.

Guibourg set down the candle and leaned on the edge of the table, smirking.

"You've always wondered what I've done in these rooms, my dear, haven't you? Well—I hadn't any need to tell you. You recognize these things in the basket?"

She nodded dazedly. "The ingredients used in—witchcraft!"

"Tonight I propose to raise the devil for you."

Her hands tightened on her breast in superstitious fear. "But our religion! Witches are damned—"

He snapped his fingers. "Tut, you are only a woman. You know nothing but how to be attractive to men. How do you suppose I learn the things to tell Louis? By communicating with the spirits of the dead!"

She stepped backward, toward the door. He strode to her hastily, his hands gripping her arms. "No, you stay. Here." He kicked a chair; it slid over the floor and thumped against the table. "Sit down!"

She shook her shoulders to loosen his grip, but it did not weaken. "I won't stay!" she said.

Their eyes contended; his will was stronger. His hands forced her down on the chair. She sat round-shouldered, her head drooping. Guibourg stepped smartly around the table and began to dip into the jars, withdrawing pinches of the colored powders, fragments of spice which he dropped into a large basin. He thrust a splinter of wood into the candle's glow, and dropped it, flaming, into the basin. He spread his hands over the bowl, closing his eyes and murmuring gibberish.

A light sprang up in the basin; the mixture within it was burning. There was a sudden uprush of thick yellow smoke which rolled over and over, as though loath to ascend, altering from one fantastic shape to another, whatever the eye chose to see. The flaming matter in the basin bubbled, guggling like an insane echo to the muttered words of

101

Guibourg, whose face was rapt, his head tipped; he appeared to be listening to something. Once his gaze jerked to his wife, beckoning her attention. She waited trembling, her fingers fidgeting. But nothing further happened. The fire died; the smoke gradually lifted to the ceiling and spread over it like misty paint.

Guibourg straightened up. "You saw!" His voice was jubilant. "Now you cannot help but believe!"

Madalene was weak with relief. "I saw only smoke," she said.

"You saw his face in the smoke! You heard his voice in the fire!" The man was panting with excitement, perspiration blistering his mask of powder.

She withdrew from him, her hands reaching out as though to clutch something beside her and steady herself. "I saw only smoke."

His eyes narrowed with suspicion; then his shoulders jerked with a contemptuous snort of laughter. "You can't deceive me! Don't try to hide your fear with lies! You saw him—the devil—the same as I."

"No, Guibourg."

They eyed each other a long silent moment, one of his palms lifting slowly as though he meant to slap her. When he dropped the hand, turned on a heel and went about blowing out all the lamps except the one which he had brought. He took it to her. "You're afraid. You don't want to meet his demands."

She could say nothing.

"You heard what he promised me—influence

over the King. But you don't want to offer the sacrifice he's demanded. Well, I do! I want power and glory! Why should I let our child stand in my way! What's one child's life to all that I can gain? We can always have another."

Her life leaked out of her through the holes that were her eyes. "What do you mean?"

"The devil is hungry; he needs spiritual sustenance. You heard! He wants us to sacrifice a life to him."

She said hopefully, her voice a scratch from her parched throat, "A sheep, perhaps?"

"Of course not, you fool! He wants our baby!"

He leaned toward her intently, the candle at a slant and weeping wax to the floor. She smiled vacuously.

"You're mad, you know," she said. "Utterly mad. Our child! Guibourg, I love my child. I will fight for him until there's not a breath left in my body—"

"I know," he replied. "But don't you love me, too? I tell you, this thing must be, if ever I'm to amount to anything in France."

She shook her head violently, starting away. Guibourg hurried after her, the candle flickering in his hand. He dragged on the lace of her bodice. "If you love me, you'll do this for me."

"No! Never!"

"If you love me," he repeated. How strange he looked in that unsteady light! As if all the expressions in the world were crowding in parade over his features. His hand did not release the lace.

She acted instinctively, moving as swiftly as if lightning coursed her veins. Her hands swept down, lifting her skirts that they might not hinder her steps; she raced for the doors, the lace ripping from her gown, dangling in Guibourg's hold. She threw a shoulder against the doors, pushing one of the massive leaves open. She brushed down the dark hall, past the polite curiosity of the servant Pierre, down the stair's graceful curves, over the gleaming tiles into her baby's room. The child slumbered, a frail little pink-wax doll. She snatched it up from its bed, protectively flinging a fold of her skirts over it. She whirled to the door, and was cut short.

Guibourg blocked her way, the candlestick still in his hand, but the flame extinguished.

Madalene's mouth opened, but there was no breath in her to carry a scream. Guibourg started for her, slowly, on tiptoe, like a stalking beast. She drew back until she bumped against a gilt-patterned wall. He spread his arms. There was no chance of passing him.

His hands closed on the child; Madalene would not relinquish it. She braced herself, wrenching away. Guibourg jerked sidewise, flinging her off balance, but the baby fell with her, shielded from hurt by her arms. Guibourg swooped down, tearing the little body away. As the woman scrambled to her feet, dishevelled, her wig awry, Guibourg ran out with the baby.

Madalene rushed after him, the door slammed in her face. He had not time to lock it; she pushed on it, but he held it shut. Once, hammering her fists, throwing her light weight against it, she almost forced it open. But it was no use. She turned away, aware of her impotence, her eyes seeking help. The portal swung open. Guibourg was running to the stair.

She darted after him, but he was much faster than she. She tripped on her skirt and fell, sliding. She lay stunned, her hands imploring her husband, who clattered heedlessly up the steps. "Guibourg! For the love of God! Guibourg! My baby!"

Then she was on a chair, the servants Pierre and Emile fussing over her. Her wig had been removed. Pierre dabbed a damp kerchief on her temples; Emile kneeled, anxiously chafing her hands! She stiffened erect. "Guibourg! My baby!"

The two lackeys glanced furtively at each other and lowered their gaze. She snatched her hands from Emile, thrust Pierre's moist cloth aside, and tottered to her feet. "Where's my husband? Where's my baby?"

Again the two servants exchanged a fearful scrutiny. Emile gestured toward the stair. Madalene started for the steps; the two men took candles and accompanied her.

The doors of Guibourg's workroom were wide open. Many candles were burning, but as many others had guttered out. The air was diseased with sharp incense. The servants faltered at the door, but Madalene fled within.

Books and papers had been thrown to the floor. The desk had been cleared and draped with crimson velvet. An inverted crucifix stood on the center of the cloth, surrounded by candles.

Before the crucifix, the naked little baby lay, the knife protruding from it, blood blackening the velvet.

Madalene knelt by the swan-shaped bed, the knife in her hands, its ornament of Guibourg's jewelled crest burning her eyes.

"Guibourg, I swear that I'll find you, though I die and am born again through a thousand lives! I'll cut out your heart as surely as you've cut out mine!"

The knife clanked on the floor. She leaned over the still little body. "Oh, my dearest sweet! My baby!"

She laid her cheek on the cold face — and she was Jeanne, in the window-seat, telling a story. She turned to her brother; she was shaking with emotion.

"Aunt Esther says that it was something no woman could ever forget, something so terrible that it left its trace in Aunt Esther's body and was transmitted to all the women who came after her. None of us will ever know peace until we find Guibourg and kill him. That's why Grandma Pierce died in an asylum, not while she was away on a trip, as we were told. And that's why Mama tried to kill me — " She fingered the scar on her throat.

"Jeanne!" Tim cried.

"But it's all true," she insisted.

"Guibourg lived and died centuries ago. You can't hurt a dead man."

"He left other children; there are still Guibourgs in France. Probably some of them have come to America. And if I could find them, I'll kill them all—"

Tim arose, his face wrecked by conflicting thoughts. "I still say it's not true. They've told you so often that you think you remember it yourself. If I'd only have known, long ago, I'd have tried to run off with you somewhere. I don't know what I'd have done, but I wouldn't have let them—"

"One day I'll find him, and kill him," Jeanne repeated.

The bus depot. Aunt Esther had not come along. Tim carried one bag, and Frank Something-or-other carried the other, his free hand around Jeanne's waist, his eyes eager. A couple of girls, leaving the soda fountain, lifted their noses significantly as they passed.

"Wait here, Frank," Tim said, setting down his bag. "Jeanne, please come along with me and help me straighten out this ticket." But when they were out of Frank's earshot, he whispered, "Now there's a good fellow. Why don't you marry him and get out of Aunt Esther's crazy atmosphere?"

She gazed through the crowd to Frank. "Yes, he is nice. But I can't ever marry. Not until I do what's got to be done."

Sick, he turned away. . .

Columbia University. Livingston Hall. Athletic young men were loitering down the hall. Tim stopped to scan the posters on the bulletin board, one of his friends pausing also.

"That's an attractive piece of letterin." Tim pointed to the clever poster, "TYPING—GHOST WRITING. ROOM 417, HARTLEY HALL." The prettily tinted poster depicted a winking spook at a typewriter. Tim pushed his face close to decipher the somewhat overdone signature.

"Oh, Russell Clark made that," Tim's companion said. "That's not anywhere nearly so good as some of his other stuff. He's a real artist. Studied over in France, you know. Say, how'd you like to meet him? I'll take you over to his place."

Russell Clark was rather commonplace: average height, average weight, neither blonde nor dark. But his taste in clothes was dramatic. Just now he wore a basque shirt of wide red-and-blue stripes, a pair of checked trousers whose pattern was visible from a great distance. He simpered over a cup of tea while Tim moved about from picture to picture, for Russell's walls were hidden under large oil paintings.

There were fancifully embellished portraits of weirdly beautiful women in strange flowing gowns, moonlit landscapes peopled by nude dancers, somber interiors depicting unholy rituals. Their colors were sensuously rich; they were executed with exquisite craftsmanship.

"Gosh, I think you're a genius," Tim murmured, awed, and Russell's smirk broadened. Tim stopped. "Say, this one looks almost exactly like my sister! I mean, the way she'd look if she put on a white wig and an old-style dress."

Russell set down his cup and sauntered to Tim. "If your sister really looks like that, I'd like to meet her. This girl's—well, sort of an ideal."

Tim looked him up and down, meditating. "You know, it'd be a good thing if Jeanne met you. You're interesting; you've traveled—it might take her mind off her troubles. We can run up to the old house any time over a week-end. Would you lend me this picture? I'll show it to her. That'll make a good springboard. I'll tell her all about you, and of course she'll ask me to bring you up."

Russell's eyes lighted. "So you really think so?"

"Sure. She'll be tickled pink."

In the dark old house, Jeanne stared at the picture, then secretly glanced at Tim as though afraid he might read her reaction in her face.

"Why, it really does look like me!" she exclaimed. "And look at this crest embroidered on the dress! How beautifully it's been done!" She turned to the tarnished mirror over the mantel and compared her face with the painting. "I wonder if he'll love me," she said thoughtfully, preening.

Tim laughed. "Why, Jeanne! You haven't even seen him yet!"

She laughed too, but nervously, a little embarrassed. "I think we'd better get Aunt Esther's opinion before we ask him up. Do you mind if I take this picture to her room so she can see it?" She started to lift it.

He gallantly brushed her hands aside. "Let me—it's heavy!"

"Nonsense. And anyway, I want her to see it

without your sales talk." She raised the canvas. "Stay here. I'll be back in a few minutes."

When she was gone, he strolled about, peering at the shells in the whatnot, lifting the glass bell over the vase of dried grasses, and setting it down. Then Jeanne came in, radiantly pretty, somehow triumphant. "Aunt Esther says that she doesn't mind," she said, unsuccessful in an effort to restrain her enthusiasm. "When can you bring him?"

He considered. "I don't know. I'll have to ask him when I go back. Then I'll write and let you know."

"Fine," she said, and began to primp again at the mirror.

Russell was unable to sit quietly during the train ride. "What does your sister like to talk about? Tell me everything that she likes. I want to get off on a good start with her. Does she dance? I'm not so good at it. I hope she won't mind."

Tim pushed him back against the plush seat. "Shut up, will you, and relax!"

As they panted up the hill to the old house, Russell said, "It's just the sort of setting I imagined you'd come from." When Tim introduced him to Jeanne, he stared at her sharply. "Excuse my rudeness, but I can't help it. You look just like what I'd hoped—" He flushed. "Gee, I sound like a damn' fool," he told Tim.

"You sound perfectly wonderful," Jeanne soothed, her face radiant. She laid a hand on his arm. "Come along and meet my Aunt. She's simply

110

crazy to get a look at you." She led him away, Tim starting along, but she shook her head at him. "No, Tim, you stay put. We females haven't seen a man for so long that we want to monopolize this one."

Russell was quite dazzled by their contest for his attention at the dinner table. Aunt Esther's eyes hovered on him with almost lovelorn rapture, and Jeanne smiled fascinatingly, placing a hand so close to his that it was an invitation for him to touch it — which he did, then blushed and snatched his fingers away, glancing at the others to see if they had noticed. But Tim was obviously satisfied, and Aunt Esther displayed her ill-matched false teeth in a smile of blessing.

In the bedroom that had been assigned him, Russell paused while untying a shoe.

"Your sister and I were just made for each other," he rhapsodized to Tim. "Just made for each other."

"Not really!"

"Would you try to kind of pump her about me as soon as you see her alone? You know, ask her if I was too forward, or anything. I don't want to make a bad impression." He pulled off the shoe. "Gee, she asked me if she could pose for me sometime. I said yes. That'll give me a lot of time to be alone with her."

"Boy, you've sure got it bad!"

"Yes, haven't I?" But he was not disturbed by it. "I can't help it. I guess we were just fated to meet each other like this."

Tim lounged against the door. "Jeanne was awfully interested in the pattern on the painting's dress. Did you make that up from your imagination, too?"

He flushed as though insulted. "Of course! All my work is purely creative! You don't think I'd copy anything, do you?"

"You artists!" Tim scoffed.

"I paint purely from memory," Russell said firmly. Then he frowned, troubled. "Why was your sister so interested?" he asked. "Did she think it looked—familiar?"

"Familiar—" Tim murmured, and straightened up, alarmed. "Listen, genius—you tumble into bed and get a good night's sleep. I'm going now. Goodnight!"

"Good night. Don't forget to ask her if she likes me."

Tim went straight to Jeanne's room and rapped on the door. "Just a minute!" she called, then opened the portal. She had not prepared for sleep. Her face was strange, her eyes puffy as though from crying. "Yes?"

"I'd just like to come in for a minute and ask you something."

She waved an invitation for him to enter. He dropped on a chair.

"What did you want to know?"

He came to the point at once. "You don't think that Russell is a Guibourg, do you?"

"Russell a Guibourg?" she asked, her eyes wide with what could have been innocence.

"Well, do you?"

She moved to the window and peered out. He turned and gazed, too. Heavy clouds were piling around the moon. There was a flicker of heat-lightning.

"It's probably going to rain," she said.

"Don't evade," Tim said crossly. "Because if you do think he's a Guibourg, don't you see now how perfectly asinine it would be even to think of killing him? He wouldn't be responsible for an act that was committed centuries before he was born."

"If he were a Guibourg," she replied, "and mind, I'm merely saying if, then it's enough that he's of the blood of the man who wronged our grandmother's grandmother. But why should I think he's a Guibourg? His name's Clark, isn't it?"

"Well, I was just wondering," Tim said sulkily, his eyes at the window again. The moon was behind the clouds.

"Oh, you're so foolish!" She approached him, smiling affectionately. "Stop worrying and let me get to bed. I want to get some sleep. I've got to look pretty tomorrow. Russell said he might make a drawing of me."

Tim stood up. "Good night," he said apologetically, on his way to the door.

"Good night," she said.

He went to his room and to bed. He fell asleep to the sound of falling rain.

It was nearly ten in the morning when he awoke. Fingers of rain were patting the windowpane; he looked out on the sodden grey world, then at the clock. "Wow!" he said, and hurried into his clothes; he went downstairs. No one was about. There was no sign of breakfast preparations in the kitchen.

He went back upstairs and knocked on Jeanne's door. "Hey, you in there! Wake up!" She did not reply, and he opened the door, peeped in. Her bed was made; she was not in. Shrugging, he closed the door and went to Russell's room, but Russell was gone, too.

He tried another door. "Aunt Esther! Aunt Esther!" There was nothing but silence.

He scowled. Where were they? He looked through all the rooms, becoming nervous, frightened. He even shouted down the cellar steps.

He opened the back door, peeped out. The door of the unused stable was open. That was odd! As he thudded down the steps into the drizzle, Jeanne emerged from the stable, walking slowly, dazed, as though only half awake. One of her hands seemed partly inserted in a red glove. Then he saw that it was blood.

She did not recognize him as he rushed past her into the stable. She walked somnabulistically up the steps into the house, closing the door without sound.

Laughter gurgled from the stable—the kind of mirth that might come from a parrot's imitative throat. Aunt Esther was on her knees on the floor, her skirt soaked in blood, poring evilly over Russell, who lay very still. They had torn his shirt from him, and his chest was hideous with knife-marks.

Then, from upstairs in the old house, a shot banged.

Columbia University again. Tim sat looking at a book, unable to read it. Someone tapped on his door; he opened it to a slender middle-aged man, whose hand was held out.

"How do you do? You're Tim Brent? One of the students told me that I'd find you here. May I come in?" But he was in already. His eyes lighted on Russell's painting which had resembled Jeanne.

"Ah!" he cried delightedly. "There's what I came to see you about. I'm collecting Russell Clark's paintings. It's a hobby of mine. They said that you have this one. Yes. I have nearly all of them now."

He stood in front of it, enraptured.

"But perfect!" He kissed his fingertips. "A perfect copy! The lengths to which young Clark went! The technique isn't bad at all; the color's amazing! Too bad that he couldn't have been original—"

"What are you saying?" Tim asked.

The visitor turned to him, smiling quizzically. "Don't you know? This Clark boy never had an original idea in his life. Every single one of his paintings was a copy of my work. He studied under me in Paris. Yes—" He was examining the emblem on the painted bodice. "He reproduced even that—every last bit of it. I collect all his things. Imitation, the sincerest form of flattery, you know."

"And your name?" Tim asked.

"Guibourg," he answered. "Raoul de Guibourg."

115

Annals of Arkya . . .

1. The Courier

The darkness trembled with a dream of light,
And flame-tipped shadows whispered in the room:
"Remember." From the lonely sea, a flight
Of eldritch bird-things shrilled of nameless doom.
I fled the cursed house and strode the height
Of cavern-pierced Kondath to resume
My eon-weary search before the night
Expired, and dread day lashed me to the tomb.

From out of the caverns, mewling vashti came
To mock me in my terror, till the same
Fell whisper scattered them and grisly dawn
Destroyed me; yet, before I fell, I heard
The fearful courier's long-awaited word:
"Remember when you were the Eidolon!"

2. The Worshippers

Colossal on the planet's youthful face,
I rose into the azure, cloud-flecked skies,
A thing of frozen midnight's mysteries,
Hewn not by living hands, nor any trace
Of craftsmanship was on me. Emperor
And highest pontiff, soldier, serf, and sage—
None in the golden land would dare engage
In any task without my dark concur.

Great was the land until those latter years,
When from the sea the fearful Vorklai came
To drown in bitter blood and put to flame
The cities, till the very stones shed tears.
Around me did the vile usurpers press
And mouth my name in drooling loathsomeness.

—Robert A. W. Lowndes

116

Bat's Belfry
by August Derleth

It simply would not be an issue of *Weird Tales* without an August Derleth story. He was one of this magazine's discoveries, and his work appeared in almost as many issues as did that of Seabury Quinn. But since his death, no unpublished macabre fiction has been discovered. Fortunately for our purposes, Derleth himself never reprinted his very first story in *Weird Tales* and it seems never to have been anthologized anywhere: so we can present it to you here, a story that will be new to virtually all of our readers.

The following letter was found among the papers of the late Sir Harry Everett Barclay, of Charing Cross, London.

117

June 10, 1925

My Dear Marc:

Having received no answer to my card, I can only surmise that it did not reach you. I am writing from my summer home here on the moor, a very secluded place. I am nursing the hope that you will give me a pleasant surprise by dropping in on me soon (as you hinted you might), for this is just the kind of house that would intrigue you. It is very similar to the Baskerville home which Sir Arthur Conan Doyle describes in his *Hound of the Baskervilles*. Vague rumours have it that the place is the abode of evil spirits, which idea I promptly and emphatically pooh-poohed. You know that in the spiritual world I am but slightly interested, and that it is in wizardry that I delight. The thought that this quiet little building in the heart of England's peaceful moors should be the home of a multitude of evil spirits seems very foolish to me. However, the surroundings are exceedingly healthy and the house itself is partly an antique, which arouses my interest in archaeology. So you see there is enough to divert my attention from these foolish rumors. Leon, my valet, is here with me and so is old Mortimer. You remember Mortimer, who always prepared such excellent bachelor dinners for us?

I have been here just twelve days, and I have explored this old house from cellar to garret. In the latter I brought to light an aged trunk, which I searched, and in which I found nine old books, several of whose title pages were torn away. One of the books, which I took to the small garret window,

I finally distinguished as *Dracula* by Bram Stoker, and this I at once decided was one of the first editions of the book ever printed.

At the cessation of the first three days a typical English fog descended with a vengeance upon the moor. At the first indication of this prank of the elements, which threatened completely to obscure the beautiful weather of the past, I had hauled out all the discoveries I had made in the garret of this building. Bram Stoker's *Dracula* I have aleady mentioned. There is also a book on the Black Art by De Rochas. Three books, by Orfilo, Swedenborg, and Cagliostro, I have laid temporarily aside. Then there are also Strindberg's *The Inferno*, Blavatsky's *Secret Doctrine*, Poe's *Eureka*, and Flammarion's *Atmosphere*. You, my dear friend, may well imagine with what excitement these books filled me, for you know I am inclined toward sorcery. Orfilo, you know, was but a chemist and physiologist; Swedenborg and Strindberg, two who might be called mystics; Poe, whose *Eureka* did not aid me much in the path of witchcraft, nevertheless fascinated me; but the remaining five were as gold to me. Cagliostro, court magician of France; Madame Blavatsky, the priestess of Isis and of the Occult Doctrine; *Dracula*, with all its vampires; Flammarion's *Atmosphere*, with its diagnosis of the Gods of peoples; and De Rochas, of whom all I can say is to quote from August Strindberg's *The Inferno*, the following: 'I do not excuse myself, and only ask the reader to remember this fact, in case he should ever feel inclined to practise magic, especially those forms of it called wizardry, or more

119

properly witchcraft: that its reality has been placed beyond all doubt by De Rochas.'

Truly, my friend, I wondered, for I had good reason to do so, what manner of man had resided here before my coming, who should be so fascinated by Poe, Orfilo, Strindberg, and De Rochas—four different types of authors. Fog or no fog, I determined to find out. There is not another dwelling near here and the nearest source of information is a village some miles away. This is rather odd, for this moor does not seem an undesirable place for a summer home. I stored the books away, and after informing my valet of my intentions to walk some miles to the village, I started out. I had not gone far, when Leon decided to accompany me, leaving Mortimer alone in the fog-surrounded house.

Leon and I established very little in the town. After a conversation with one of the grocers in the village, the only communicative person that we accosted, we found that the man who had last occupied the house was a Baronet Lohrville, It seemed that the people held the late baronet in awe, for they hesitated to speak of him. This grocer related a tale concerning the disappearance of four girls one dark night some years ago. Popular belief had and still has it that the baronet kidnapped them. This idea seems utterly ludicrous to me, for the superstitious villagers cannot substantiate their suspicions. By the way, this merchant also informed us that the Lohrville home is called the 'Bat's Belfry.' Personally I can see no connection between the residence and the ascribed title, as I have not noticed any bats around during my sojourn here.

My meditations on this matter were rudely interrupted by Mortimer, who complained of bats in the cellar—a rather queer coincidence. He said that he continually felt them brushing against his cheeks and that he feared they would become entangled in his hair. Of course, Leon and I went down to look for them, but we could not see any of them. However, Leon stated that one struck him, which I doubt. It is just possible that sudden draughts of air may have been the cause of the delusions.

This incident, Marc, was just the forerunner of the odd things that have been occurring since then. I am about to enumerate the most important of these incidents to you, and I hope you will be able to explain them.

Three days ago activities started in earnest. At that date Mortimer came to me and breathlessly informed me that no light could be kept in the cellar. Leon and I investigated and found that under no circumstances could a lamp or match be kept lit in the cellar, just as Mortimer had said. My only explanation of this is that it is due to the air currents in the cellar, which seemed disturbed. It is true a flashlight could be kept alight, but even that seemed dimmed. I cannot attempt to explain the latter fact.

Yesterday, Leon, who is a devout Catholic, took a few drops from a flask of holy water, which he continually carries with him, and descended into the cellar with the firm intention of driving out, if there were therein ensconced, any evil spirits. On the bottom of the steps I noticed, some time ago, a large stone tablet. As Leon came down the steps a large drop of the blessed fluid fell on this tablet. The drop of water actually sizzled while Leon muttered some incantations, in the midst of which he suddenly stopped and fled precipitantly, mumbling that the cellar was incontestably the very entrance to hell, guarded by the fiend incarnate himself! I confess to you, dear Marc, that I was astounded at this remarkable occurrence.

Last night, while the three of us sat together in the spacious drawing-room of this building, the lamp was blown out. I say 'blown out' because there is no doubt that it was, and by some superhuman agency. There was not a breath of air stirring outside, yet I, who was sitting just across from the lamp, felt a cool draught. No one else noticed this draught. It was just as if someone directly opposite me had blown forcibly at the lamp, or as if the wing of a powerful bird had passed by it.

There can be no doubt there is something radically wrong in this house, and I am determined to find out what it is, regardless of consequences.

(Here the letter terminates abruptly, as if it were to be completed at a later date).

The two doctors bending over the body of Sir Harry Barclay in Lohrville Manor at last ceased their examinations.

'I cannot account for this astounding loss of

blood, Dr. Mordaunt.'

'Neither can I, Dr. Greene. He is so devoid of blood that some supernatural agency must have kept him alive!' He laughed lightly.

'About this loss of blood—I was figuring on internal haemorrhages as the cause, but there are absolutely no signs of anything of the sort. According to the expression of his features, which is too horrible for even me to gaze at—'

'And me.'

'—he died from some terrible fear of something, or else he witnessed some horrifying scene.'

'Most likely the latter.'

'I think we had better pronounce death due to internal haemorrhage and apoplexy.'

'I agree.'

'Then we shall do so.'

The physicians bent over the open book on the table. Suddenly Dr. Greene straightened up and his hand delved into his pocket and came out with a match.

'Here is a match, Dr. Mordaunt. Scratch it and apply the flame to that book and say nothing to anyone.'

'It is for the best.'

Excerpts from the journal of Sir Harry E. Barclay, found besides his body in Lohrville Manor on July 17, 1925.

June 25—Last night I had a curious nightmare. I dreamed that I met a beautiful girl in the wood around my father's castle in Lancaster. Without knowing why, we embraced, our lips meeting and remaining in the position for at least half an hour! Queer dream that! I must have had another nightmare of a different nature, although I cannot recall it; for, upon looking in the mirror this morning, I found my face devoid of all colour—rather drawn.

Later—Leon has told me that he had a similar dream, and as he is a confirmed misogynist, I cannot interpret it. Strange that it should be so parallel to mine in every way.

June 29—Mortimer came to me early this morning and said he would not stay another instant, for he had certainly seen a ghost last night. A handsome old man, he said. He seemed horrified that the old man had kissed him. He must have dreamed it. I persuaded him to stay on these grounds and solemnly told him to say nothing about it. Leon remarked that the dream had returned in every particular to him the preceding night, and that he was not feeling well. I advised him to see a doctor, but he roundly refused to do so. He said, referring to the horrible nightmare (as he termed it), that tonight he would sprinkle a few drops of holy water on himself and that (he stated) would drive away any evil influence, if there were any, connected with his dreams. Strange that he should attribute everything to evil entities!

Later—I made some enquiries today and I find that the description of the Baronet Lohrville fits to every detail the 'ghost' of Mortimer's dream. I also learned that several small children disappeared from the countryside during the life of the last of the Lohrvilles—not that they should be connected, but it seems the ignorant people ascribe their vanishing to the baronet.

June 30—Leon claims he did not have the dream (which, by the way, revisited me last night), because of the potent effect of the holy water.

July 1—Mortimer has left. He says he cannot live in the same house with the devil. It seems he must have actually seen the ghost of old Lohrville, although Leon scoffs at the idea.

July 4—I had the same dream again last night. I felt very ill this morning, but was able to dispel the feeling easily during the day. Leon has used all the holy water, but as tomorrow is Sunday he will get some at the village parish when he attends mass.

July 5—I tried to procure the services of another chef this morning in the village, but I am all at sea. No one in the town will enter the house, not even for one hundred pounds a week, they declare! I shall be forced to get along without one or send to London.

Leon experienced a misfortune today. Riding home after mass, almost all his holy water spilled from the bottle, and later the bottle, containing the remainder of it, fell to the ground and broke. Leon, nonplussed, remarked that he would get another as soon as possible from the parish priest.

July 6—Both of us had the dream again last night. I feel rather weak, and Leon does, too. Leon went to a doctor, who asked him whether he had been cut, or severely injured so as to cause a heavy loss of blood, or if he had suffered from internal haemorrhages. Leon said no, and the doctor prescribed raw onions and some other things for Leon to eat. Leon forgot his holy water.

July 9 — The dream again. Leon had a different nightmare — about an old man, who, he said, bit him. I asked him to show me where the man had bitten him in his dream, and when he loosened his collar to show me, sure enough, there were two tiny punctures on his throat. He and I are both feeling miserably weak.

July 15 — Leon left me today. I am firmly convinced that he went suddenly mad, for this morning he evinced an intense desire to invade the cellar again. He said that something seemed to draw him. I did not stop him, and some time later, as I was engrossed in a volume of Wells, he came shrieking up the cellar steps and dashed madly through the room in which I sat. I ran after him and, cornering him in his room, forcibly detained him. I asked for an explanation and all he could do was moan over and over.

'*Mon Dieu, Monsieur*, leave this accursed place at once. Leave it, *Monsieur*, I beg of you. *Le diable — le diable!*' At length he dashed away from me and ran at top speed from the house, I after him. In the road I shouted after him, and all I could catch of the words wafted back to me by the wind, were: '*Lamais — le diable — Mon-Dieu — tablet — Book of Thoth.*' All very significant words, '*Le Diable*' and '*Mon Dieu*' — 'the devil' and 'my God' — I paid little attention to. But Lamais was a species of female vampire known intimately to a few select sorcerers only, and the *Book of Thoth* was the Egyptian book of magic. For a few

126

minutes I entertained the rather wild fancy that the *Book of Thoth* was ensconced somewhere in this building, and as I racked my brains for a suitable connection between 'tablet' and *Book of Thoth* I at last became convinced that the book lay beneath the tablet at the foot of the cellar steps. I am going down to investigate.

July 16—I have it! The *Book of Thoth*! It was below the stone tablet as I thought. The spirits guarding it evidently did not wish me to disturb its resting place, for they roused the air currents to a semblance of a gale while I worked to get the stone away. The book is secured by a heavy lock of antique pattern.

I had the dream again last night, but in addition I could almost swear that I saw the ghosts of old Lohrville and four beautiful girls. What a coincidence! I am very weak today, hardly able to walk around. There is no doubt that this house is infested, not by bats, but by vampires! Lamais! If I could only find their corpses I would drive sharp stakes through them.

Later—I made a new and shocking discovery today. I went down to the place where the tablet lay, and another rock below the cavity wherein the *Book of Thoth* had lain gave way below me and I found myself in a vault with about a score of skeletons—all of little children! If this house *is* inhabited by vampires, it is only too obvious that these skeletons are those of their unfortunate victims. However, I firmly believe that there is another cavern somewhere below, wherein bodies of the vampires are hidden.

Later — I have been looking over the book by De Rochas and I have hit upon an excellent plan to discover the bodies of the vampires! I shall use the *Book of Thoth* to summon the vampires before me and force them to reveal the hiding place of their voluptuous bodies! De Rochas says that it can be done.

Nine o'clock — As the conditions are excellent at this time I am going to start to summon the vampires. Someone is passing and I hope he or she does not interrupt me in my work or tell anyone in the town to look in here. The book, as I mentioned before, is secured by a heavy seal, and I had trouble to loosen it. At last I succeeded in breaking it and I opened the book to find the place I need in my work of conjuring up the vampires. I found it and I am beginning my incantations. The atmosphere in the room is changing slowly and it is becoming intolerably dark. The air currents in the room are swirling angrily, and the lamp has gone out . . . I am confident that the vampires will appear soon.

I am correct. There are some shades materialising in the room. They are becoming more distinct . . . there are five of them, four females and one male. Their features are very distinct . . . They are casting covert glances in my direction . . . Now they are glaring malevolently at me.

Good God! I have forgotten to place myself in a magic circle and I greatly fear the vampires will attack me! I am only too correct. They are moving in my direction. My God! . . . But stay! They are halting! The old baronet is gazing at me with his glittering eyes fiery with hate. The four female vampires smile voluptuously upon me.

Now, if ever, is my chance to break their evil spell. *Prayer*! But I cannot pray! I am forever banished from the sight of God for calling upon Satan to aid me. But even for that I cannot pray . . . I am hypnotised by the malefic leer disfiguring the countenance of the baronet. There is a sinister gleam in the eyes of the four beautiful ghouls. They glide towards me, arms outstretched. Their sinuous, obnoxious forms are before me; their crimson lips curved in a diabolically triumphant smile. I cannot bear to see the soft caress of their tongues on their red lips. I am resisting with all the power of my will, but what is one mere will against an infernal horde of ghouls?

God! Their foul presence taints my very soul! The baronet is moving forward. His mordacious propinquity casts a reviling sensation of obsenity about me. If I cannot appeal to God I must implore Satan to grant me time to construct the magic circle.

I cannot tolerate their virulence . . . I endeavoured to rise but I could not do so . . . I am no longer master of my own will. The vampires are leering demonically at me . . . I am doomed to die . . . and yet to live forever in the ranks of the Undead.

Their faces are approaching closer to mine and soon I shall sink into oblivion . . . but anything is better than this . . . to see the malignant Undead around me . . . A sharp stinging senstion in my throat . . . My God! . . . it is . . . .

Some things are better left undisturbed . . .

The Pit
by Carl Jacobi

The country of Sleep has no borders, but many roads and the Dream Traveler needs no visa.

IMAGES AND FANCIES
Giles Balinton

Chadwick walked slowly up the lane and gazed with satisfaction at his property. The more he saw of it, the more he considered it a stroke of luck. It wasn't often that one could buy ten acres of land and a house of his particular needs for the small amount he had paid. He had wanted a house, modern, yet with an architecture of the past, in an isolated location where he could continue the recluse-like existence he had led in the city.

Owego House answered all those wants. Owego. It was an Indian name, he had been told.

Seen through a copse of cedars, the house looked friendly and inviting, with a wide veranda, over-sized burgundy shutters and a new substantial roof tile. Then Chadwick's gaze turned fifty yards east. If Owego was an odd name for a house, Dead Man's Pit was an appropriate name for the great sink hole that marked the end of his property.

Here were rank weeds, thorn bushes and ragged outcroppings. In the center of this wasteland was a deep depression filled with water so black it didn't even reflect the sky. The borders were strewn with rocks.

Sight of the place depressed Chadwick, and he turned back down the lane toward his house. In the driveway his parked station wagon reminded him that his weekly trip to town for supplies was overdue. He got into the car and headed toward blacktop 3.

In Chaska he parked and went to several shops, where he talked very little to the tradespeople. In the hardware store, however, he found conversation pressed upon him.

"How do yo like your new place?" the hardware man said as he packaged the nails Chadwick had purchased.

"I like it all right," Chadwick said.

"It's a nice house," the man said, "considering that it's been there close to a hundred years."

"I thought a hundred years ago this was all Indian country."

The man rang up the register. "Farther north, mebbe. Not here. But that Pit on your place was once an old Indian burial mound. The first two owners dug it all up, looking for treasure or somethin'."

"Did they find any?" Chadwick asked.

"I don't think so. The first was before my time, but he's supposed to have shot himself. Accidentally. The second just went away and never came back. Nobody ever saw or heard of him."

Chadwick turned to go. "Well, it's an eyesore," he said. "I suppose I'll have it filled up one of these days."

The man's face darkened perceptibly. "I don't think I'd do that," he said. "If I were you, I'd just leave it alone."

Chadwick went out to his car, musing over the merchant's words. He tossed his packages into the rear seat. The August street was hot and sultry, and by contrast the library on the opposite corner a block away, shaded by a couple of elms, looked cool and inviting. On impulse, he crossed the street, walked the block and climbed the steps. Inside, to the girl behind the desk, he said,

"I'd like some information on the building of a summer house. Plans . . . pictures . . . anything you have."

She was gone almost ten minutes. When she returned, she looked at Chadwick with interest.

"You rarely hear of such things anymore. Are you planning to build one yourself?"

132

She was attractive in a fragile way, with long dark hair and lustrous eyes. It had been a long time since Chadwick had been attracted to a girl, but now he felt himself talking without restraint. She was a ready listener. Before leaving, he learned her name, Emily Hunter. With a lighter step than he had known in years, he went out again into the blazing street.

Chaska was an old town, built along the Minnesota River. A German settlement with the characteristic neatness evident on all sides, its streets were redolent with the summer musk from the bottomlands. The county seat courthouse faced the center park, and as Chadwick strode past, a heavy set, redfaced man with a wide brimmed hat came out and hailed him. It was the sheriff, Tom Blunt.

"Just wondered how you were gettin' along," Blunt said, lighting a cigar with a kitchen match.

"I'm okay," Chadwick said.

"You figgerin' on stayin' in your new place alone?"

"I don't suppose there's any law that says a man has to have a regiment around him," Chadwick replied testily.

Blunt grinned. "No law. Only your place is pretty far out."

"I'm used to being alone."

"What are you figgerin' on doin' with the Pit?"

"What do you mean, what am I going to do with it?"

"Well, it's a dangerous place. The Caston boy drowned there a year ago. He'd been studyin' anthropology and he was lookin' for relics."

All this talk about what he considered the one disagreeable feature of his property irritated Chadwick. "I suppose I'll have it filled up," he said.

It was the second time that day he had made that statement, and for the second time it prompted an odd reply.

"I don't think it's necessary to do that," Blunt said quickly. "Why don't you just fence it off and put up a few warning signs?"

Chadwick said that he would consider the matter and as soon as he decently could, he broke away, returned to his car and headed back for home.

For several weeks after that he busied himself repairing the veranda railing, some of the rungs had rotted out — tidying up the grounds and poring over the construction books that Emily had selected for him. It was true that he had wanted a summer house for a long time. Such a building had lingered in his memories since childhood, and it was the desire for one that had been a major reason behind his move from the city.

He decided to build a conventional struture with a stonework lower portion and a screened upper part open to the air. Most of the material he could obtain in Chaska. The stones for the lower portion were available close at hand — in the Pit.

He went to the sink hole, selected the stones with care and trundled them in a barrow to the house grounds. The work was hard and he was disconcerted to find himself so completely exhausted. Not only did he have tired muscles, but the task, particularly while he was in the Pit, for some reason affected his eyes. Once he fancied he saw a head-shaped rock in the center come to life and move toward him, and once, when he peered down into the black water, he thought he saw an elongated shadow like a sea serpent writh and twist just below the surface.

But all his troubles vanished several weeks later when the summer house, with the aid of two Chaska youths, was finally completed. Quickly the building molded itself into his life. He began to spend the long summer afternoons there. A strange quality of contentment fell over him as he sat at the little iron table in the circular room, drinking juleps from a frosty glass. He installed a couch and passed the sultry nights stretched out upon it. To his surprise he found that sleep, which had always been a problem with him now came with ease.

His sleep, however, was marred by dreams.

Like all men, Chadwick had had his share of dreams since childhood. And as with most persons, these dreams were usually disconnected, distorted and marked by complete lack of logic. Now, however, they were different.

Though he could remember no details, he now retained three impressions upon awakening: search, flight, and pursuit by persons or things unknown. What he was searching for was not clear. Sometimes it was for a jungle beast, sometimes a composite, always female. The "flight" followed immediately, whether the search was successful or not. He fled panic-stricken with leaden feet, unable to run or hurry. The "pursuit" was a relentless thing that followed him, and constituted a horror from which he knew there was no escape. These dreams formed a cohesive unit too. That is, the action continued chronologically from one night to another.

But the aspect that was incredible, which he could not at first make himself believe, was the fact that these dreams came only when he slept in the summer house. On those occasions when he spent the night in the house bedroom, the sequence was broken, and he either did not dream at all or his sleeping fantasies were the usual bland meaningless affairs of before.

Sometimes he awoke in the middle of the night, bathed in perspiration, shaking with fear, to discover odd things: the door unlocked or his clothes piled in a disorderly heap in the middle of the floor. Yet the very anticipation of those dreams affected him like an opiate and he could not force himself to stay away from the summer house.

On a morning following several nights when the dreams had been particularly enervating, Chadwick was on his veranda when Sheriff Blunt drove up.

"In the neighborhood," Blunt said, "so I thought I'd stop by. Seen any strangers around?"

"I haven't seen anybody," Chadwick said.

"Then you haven't heard what's happened the last few days?"

Chadwick shook his head. "I haven't been to town in more than a week."

"We've had a murder," Blunt said. "And a disappearance which might well be a second."

Chadwick stared.

"We found Jim Evans' wife—he's the Chaska jeweler—strangled in a ditch along 41. And Irene Trask hasn't been seen since Wednesday night."

"I've got two deputies working around the clock," Blunt continued, "but so far we haven't come up with anything. You'd better keep an eye out, living all alone out here."

Chadwick got up and walked to the end of the veranda. He came back slowly and sat down again. A distant look entered his eyes.

"A long time ago," he said haltingly, "it must have been around '55, I did a hitch on the Chicago police force. That's ancient history, of course, but I'd be glad to help in any way I can."

Blunt nodded. "I may take you up on that," he said. "Did you know a detective sergeant named Fallon? I think he was in Chicago about that time."

"I don't recall the name."

In spite of the police background that he had mentioned, Chadwick was disturbed by the sheriff's warning. After Blunt had gone, he began a search of his grounds, although he had no idea what he was looking for. The doom which had seemed to lie in wait for him in his dreams now became almost a reality. He was chagrined to find himself glancing over his shoulder at every wind-tossed clump of foliage.

In the back of the house, facing the direction of the Pit, he found one of the lower windows open. But there were no footprints near, so he attributed it to his own negligence. There were, however, footprints leading to the driveway where he parked his car. Not far away was a little pile of cigarette stubs, as if someone had stood there a long time. Then he saw that they were his brand and realized that he must have forgotten being there. His car gave him more concern. Though he couldn't be sure, the gas supply seemed less and the odometer reading more than when he had last driven. But it would have been impossible for anyone to have taken the car without awakening him, even though the driveway was some distance from the house. He had a vague impression of night driving and of walking in the darkness. But this, he knew, was only a residue of his summer house dreams. For years he had never gone anyplace after sundown. The loneliness of his property began to weigh on him. He had the unpleasant feeling of being watched by unseen eyes.

On Friday he drove to Chaska. The town was in a state of excitement. The body of the missing girl, Irene Trask, had been found strangled and there was another disappearance. Sheriff Blunt stood on the courthouse steps talking to his deputies and a state police officer.

Chadwick went into the library to return the construction books. He found Emily Hunter almost in a state of hysteria. She told him the missing girl, Mary Philbin, was one of her closest friends.

"I can't understand why anyone would want to harm her," she said. "She was liked by everybody."

"A tall, thin girl with reddish hair?"

"Yes. Do you know her?"

He shook his head. "I've probably seen her around town." In an effort to calm her, he changed the subject and talked of casual things.

She quieted and smiled a little.

"Anyone would know you're a bachelor," she said. "You're wearing one black sock and one brown. And you really should stay out of the mud, Mr. Chadwick. Tell me, did you finish your summer house?"

Chadwick nodded. "Yes, but I'm afraid the job was a little too much for me. I had help on all except the stonework."

"Where did you get the stones?"

"In the Pit. That's a sort of sink hole on my property."

Her face clouded. "Yes, I know the Pit. You shouldn't have taken the stones from there, Mr. Chadwick."

"Why not?"

She fingered her pendant. "Let's just say it isn't a healthy place. It . . . has an evil reputation."

"Yes, I know," Chadwick said. "The Caston boy drowned there a year ago, but he was . . . ."

"Billy Caston was one of the finest swimmers in Carver County."

Back home Chadwick tried to think more of his days as a police officer. He had told Blunt that he was on the Chicago force in '55. But he could recall little of that work save a few trips in a prowl car, and even these were hazy, like the recollection of an old gangster movie.

It now occurred to him that there were still some parts of his house that he had not fully examined. It seemed to him as good a time as any to do a little exploring. He took a flashlight and descended to the cellar. There were actually two cellars, one opening off the other, but there was nothing in either except a plenitude of cobwebs and some empty boxes. He went up to the second floor and prowled down the corridor. Toward the rear he came upon a room he had not entered before. Here a wan shaft of sunlight filtered through a dirty pane to reveal a few pieces of discarded furniture and a carpet grey with dust. About to leave, he saw a large cabinet, almost hidden by a pile of drapery. It was filled with books.

Chadwick stepped closer and ran his eyes over the titles. They were a curious assortment. Many were cheap novels of a generation ago, but there were also a few authoritative volumes on psychology, psychic research, strange myths and primitive beliefs. One of the last bore the title, THE PREHISTORIC HOPEWELL CULTURE.

Chadwick riffled through the pages. He stopped at a passage marked with a pencil check:

"*An utterly strange culture preceded the North American Indian by several thousand years. It was unique for its complex burial mounds and its so-called 'Cult of the Dead'.*

"*It is the warnings of this Cult of the Dead which have come down to us through the mists of the past. Defilers of the burial mounds were promised all the avenging horrors of the culture's diabology.*"

Chadwick closed the book thoughtfully. He selected several psychology volumes which, at the moment, were of more interest to him and carried them downstairs. He had become increasingly concerned with dreams the last few days, and each of the books had one or more chapters on this subject. For his nightmares in the summer house had grown more and more disturbing. Although he still could remember no specific details upon awakening, the three impressions—search, flight and pursuit, continued. Now the "search" was intensified, a powerful urge to seek out something. The "flight" too was more frantic. And the "pursuit" was a nameless terror that followed him relentlessly.

These dreams were debilitating too. They left Chadwick exhausted, almost as if he had not slept at all. Yet though he knew that he had only to move from the summr house to end them, somehow he couldn't do that. It was as if he were taking a stimulant, sweet, bitter, unpleasant, habit-forming.

Late on a cheerless morning, three days after his trip to Chaska, he was awakened by a distant pistol shot. Ten minutes later Sheriff Blunt appeared at the edge of his grounds, followed by one of his deputies.

"Thought we saw him," Blunt said disgustedly. "But it was only this jacket hanging on a bush."

"We traced him across Barlow's Swamp," Blunt continued. "He seemed to be heading for the Pit. Then Jake here saw the jacket and took a shot. But the trail was cold. Have you seen anyone?"

"Not a soul," Chadwick said. "Have there been any more killings?"

Blunt looked at his deputy and frowned. "No," he said, "no more murders. But another disappearance. I believe you know her. The Hunter girl."

Chadwick's jaw went slack. "Not Emily!" he cried. "The girl who works in the library?" He made fists of his hands. "Blunt," he said after a long moment of silence, "you've got to deputize me. If you don't I'll go on my own."

The sheriff nodded sympathetically. "All right," he said. "I understand."

After Blunt had gone, Chadwick went into his house and looked for his revolver. He found a gun; it wasn't a police special but an old Webley Scott automatic. Outside, he got into his station wagon and drove fast to Blacktop 3. There were a thousand places he could search. Emily Hunter lived close to Chaska on 41, but almost automatically he headed in the opposite direction toward the Victoria cutoff. He didn't know why he did this. He had never driven the cutoff, yet a recollection of this road seemed to come to him. His mind seethed. If only it had been someone else. The thought struck him that his actions now were repetitive, like scenes from a movie run many times. And then abruptly the spell was broken. He looked upon his surroundings with complete unfamiliarity. Puzzled, he turned the car and headed for home.

In the central room he buried his head in his hands. He must do something . . . He must think . . .

From the table he took up one of the psychology books he had brought down from the little room upstairs. As if it had been read many times at that place, the book fell open to the chapter on dreams. Half unconsciously, Chadwick began to read:

"The dream is the least understood part of the human psyche. The distortion, irrationality and lack of logical coherance which characterize many of them is no doubt the result of a multitude of subliminal perceptions and is almost impossible to explain."

He turned a page:

"No interpretation of the dream can be made without liberal references to mythology, folklore and primitive beliefs such as witchcraft, lycanthropy, etc. It is a curious fact that the dreamer need have no prior knowledge of these cabala. They are universal in their distribution."

Chadwick discarded the book and took up another. It too opened of its own accord to the dream chapter:

"In 1945 the Belgian, Anatole Arman, quoted the case of a man who, while asleep, not only noctambulated a considerable distance but also lived a life completely divorced from his waking hours. Yet he had no knowledge of that life. To offset this, he created for himself a fantasy past. Such cases are extremely rare, and it is thought that only some malignant influence could induce such a condition."

Chadwick's eyes drifted from the page to the table. There, where he had emptied his pockets upon coming in from outside, were a couple of objects he didn't remember seeing before: a length of window sash cord with each end carefully bound with tape to prevent fraying, and a short piece of rounded wood with a wide, deep notch cut about six inches from one end. He looked at them, puzzled, for the moment unable to explain their presence.

It was now several hours since Sheriff Blunt had told him about Emily Hunter, and he suddenly realized he had done absolutely nothing. A confused picture flashed before his inner eye of her, standing at his side, now running before him. He gathered up his things from the table, went back out to his car and headed for Chaska. He seemed to be viewing his surroundings through a prism, with everything strange and out of proportion. At the town outskirts a car suddenly pulled diagonally across the road in front of his, blocking the way.

The sheriff emerged and approached. "Oh, it's you. We're stoppin' all cars. Where you headin', Chadwick?"

Chadwick spread his hands on the wheel.

"Well, there's no sense to our drivin' two cars," Blunt said. "I'll go along with you."

He walked back, drove his car onto the side of the road, and a moment later climbed in beside Chadwick.

Uncertainly, Chadwick shifted gears. For some time he drove in silence. Then he burst into speech.

"We can't just go blind! You must have some idea. . . ."

144

"No, I haven't." The sheriff's face was immobile. "We don't know if Emily Hunter is alive or dead. We do know that with the other two victims there was an interlude of about forty hours between the time of their disappearance and their death. We know that both were kept alive in one place and then taken somewhere else to be murdered. I'm hoping the killer will keep to the same schedule. If he does, we may have a small margin of time left."

"Why would he do that?" Chadwick heard himself ask.

The sheriff shrugged. "There's no explaining a psychotic killer. I figure he can go just so far in his lust for blood, then he cools. When the urge comes upon him again, he goes back and finishes the job."

"But why forty hours?"

"After a day and a night. I suppose he's got to sleep."

Blunt was a fool, Chadwick thought. A busybody and a fool. Not even a good sheriff. The car swung past Houseman's Woods. When another fork appeared, he swung into it.

"Now you're going in a circle."

"I know." Chadwick did not say that a strange compulsion was guiding his movements.

"When you were in Chicago, did you ever run into a case of this kind?" The sheriff seemed to be talking only to pass the time.

"No."

"Know anything about fingerprints?"

"I know Bertillion discovered them."

"How about ballistics?"

Chadwick shook his head.

"Most premeditary criminals don't use guns anymore. They use too much noise and bullets can be traced. They prefer a knife."

"Knives can be traced too," Chadwick said.

"I suppose so," Blunt said. "But that pretty well exhausts the field."

"There's the garotte." Chadwick's words were automatic.

"Oh, yes. The garotte. But I'd hardly call that a weapon, would you?"

"Yes, I would," Chadwick said. "It goes back to the fifteenth century. In Spain it was a method of injuring the spinal cord at the base of the brain."

"I didn't know that. Have you done much reading along those lines?"

"It used to be my hobby," Chadwick said.

Blunt expelled a mouthful of smoke. "Where are we? Oh, yes, the old Lake Virginia road."

"It comes to the Pit from the other side," Chadwick said. "Nobody uses it anymore."

"The road was deep rutted and the willows along the narrow shoulders pressed close. Presently the forlorn wasteland that was the Pit opened before them.

It was a different view than Blunt was accustomed to seeing. From this angle, the loneliness of the place was more pronounced. The piles of rock were larger and the black water left only a thin corridor for the car to pass. Then this too ended and Blunt understood why the road was no longer used. It should be posted "Dead-End", he thought.

Chadwick stopped the car. He got out and like

an automaton, body stiff, muscles unflexed, began to pace slowly along the water's edge. His gait was shambling, uneven. He stared straight ahead with all the fixed intensity of a sleepwalker.

Quietly Blunt began to follow a few steps behind.

And now, what seemed like Chadwick's destination looked up, an ugly cairn of black boulders fashioned by nature into a grotto-like structure with a jagged opening on one side and a roof formed by an uptilted rock slab.

Suddenly with a hoarse cry, Chadwick stopped and turned. "Over there!" he cried. "Behind you! Back of that rock!"

Even as Blunt spun around in obayance to the command, he realized his mistake. But before he could move, a rope encircled his throat, twisted tight with lightning rapidity and choked off his windpipe. The garotte!

He jerked both hands upward in vain effort to tear it away. His throat constricted as his breath was shut off. With the wooden fulcrum turning, exerting double strength, he felt his senses begin to leave him, blackness rise up to shroud his vision. His legs buckled.

But with a final lunge born of desperation, his right hand reached down and grasped his holstered revolver. He clawed the weapon free, twisted his body sideways, spun the gun barrel down and back, and fired.

The shot echoed across the Pit. Behind him, Chadwick uttered a low cry and released his grip. The garotte fell free. Blunt swiveled, brought back his left arm and delivered a final blow. Chadwick fell, almost at the opening of the cairn.

In that opening a third figure now became visible, a girl bound hand and foot, her mouth gagged with a wad of cloth. The sheriff gave a sigh of relief as he saw that she was still alive. And minutes later he assured himself that Emily Hunter was unharmed. He carried her across to the car and lifted her gently into the seat.

"Take it easy, Miss," he said. "I'll have you out of here in a moment."

With Chadwick he was not so gentle. He saw that his bullet had struck the other man's thigh and although not serious, was completely incapacitating. Nevertheless he snapped on handcuffs and half dragged him to the car. He turned the car around and headed up the Virginia road. At the fork he swung left toward Chaska.

"You've been a busy man," he said to Chadwick. "And you'll pay, one way or another, even though you didn't know what you were doing."

* * * * *

Vengeance rises from the grave

When The Clock Strikes
by Tanith Lee

Yes, the grand ballroom is filled only with dust
now. The slender columns of white marble and the
slender columns of rose-red marble are woven
together by cobwebs. The vivid frescoes, on which
the Duke's treasury spent so much, are dimmed by
the dust; the faces of the painted goddesses look
grey. And the velvet curtains — touch them, they
will crumble. Two hundred years now, since
anyone danced in this place on the sea-green floor
in the candle-gleam. Two hundred years since the
wonderful clock struck for the very last time.

I thought you might care to examine the clock.
It was considered exceptional in its day. The
pedestal is ebony and the face fine porcelain. And
these figures, which are of silver, would pass slowly

149

about the circlet of the face. Each figure represents, you understand, an hour. And as the appropriate hours came level with this golden bell, they would strike it the correct number of times. All the figures are unique, as you see. Beginning at the first hour, they are, in this order, a girl-child, a dwarf, a maiden, a youth, a lady and a knight. And here, notice, the figures grow older as the day declines: a queen and king for the seventh and eighth hours, and after these, an abbess and a magician, and next to last, a hag. But the very last is the strangest of all. The twelfth figure; do you recognize him? It is Death. Yes, a most curious clock. It was reckoned a marvellous thing then. But it has not struck for two hundred years. Possibly you have been told the story? No? Oh, but I am certain that you have heard it, in another form, perhaps.

However, as you have some while to wait for your carriage, I will recount the tale, if you wish.

I will start with what was said of the clock. In those years, this city was prosperous, a stronghold—not as you see it today. Much was made in the city that was ornamental and unusual. But the clock, on which the twelfth hour was Death, caused something of a stir. It was thought unlucky, foolhardy, to have such a clock. It began to be murmured, jokingly by some, by others in earnest, that one night when the clock struck the twelfth hour, Death would truly strike with it.

Now life has always been a chancy business, and more so then. The Great Plague had come but twenty years before and was not yet forgotten.

Besides, in the Duke's court there was much intrigue, while enemies might be supposed to plot
beyond the city walls, as happens even in our present age. But there was another thing.

It was rumoured that the Duke had obtained
both his title and the city treacherously. Rumour
declared that he had systematically destroyed those
who had stood in line before him, the members of
the princely house that formerly ruled here. He
had accomplished the task slyly, hiring assassins
talented with poisons and daggers. But rumour
also declared that the Duke had not been suffi-
ciently thorough. For though he had meant to rid
himself of all that rival house, a single descendant
remained, so obscure he had not traced her—for it
was a woman.

Of course, such matters were not spoken of
openly. Like the prophecy of the clock, it was a
subject for the dark.

Nevertheless, I will tell you at once, there was
such a descendant he had missed in his bloody
work. And she was a woman. Royal and proud she
was, and seething with bitter spite and hunger for
vengeance, and as bloody as the Duke, had he
known it, in her own way.

For her safety and disguise, she had long ago
wed a wealthy merchant in the city, and presently
bore the man a daughter. The merchant, a dealer
in silks, was respected, a good fellow but not wise.
He rejoiced in his handsome and aristocratic wife.
He never dreamed what she might be about when
he was not with her. In fact, she had sworn
allegiance to Satanas. In the dead of night she

would go up into an old tower adjoining the merchant's house, and there she would say portions of the Black Mass, offer sacrifice, and thereafter practice witchcraft against the Duke. This witchery took a common form, the creation of a wax image and the maiming of the image that, by sympathy, the injuries inflicted on the wax be passed on to the living body of the victim. The woman was capable in what she did. The Duke fell sick. He lost the use of his limbs and was racked by excruciating pains from which he could get no relief. Thinking himself on the brink of death, the Duke named his sixteen year old son his heir. This son was dear to the Duke, as everyone knew, and be sure the woman knew it too. She intended sorcerously to murder the young man in his turn, preferably in his father's sight. Thus, she let the Duke linger in his agony, and commenced planning the fate of the prince.

Now all this while she had not been toiling alone. She had one helper. It was her own daughter, a maid of fourteen, that she had recruited to her service nearly as soon as the infant could walk. At six or seven, the child had been lisping the satanic rite along with her mother. At fourteen, you may imagine, the girl was well versed in the Black Arts, though she did not have her mother's natural genius for them.

Perhaps you would like me to describe the daughter at this point. It has a bearing on the story, for the girl was astonishingly beautiful. Her hair was the rich dark red of antique burnished copper, her eyes were the hue of the reddish-golden amber that traders bring from the East. When she walked, you would say she was dancing. But when she danced, a gate seemed to open in the world, and bright fire spangled inside it, but she was the fire.

The girl and her mother were close as gloves in a box. Their games in the old tower bound them closer. No doubt the woman believed herself clever to have got such a helpmate, but it proved her undoing.

It was in this manner. The silk merchant, who had never suspected his wife for an instant of anything, began to mistrust the daughter. She was not like other girls. Despite her great beauty, she professed no interest in marriage, and none in clothes or jewels. She preferred to read in the garden at the foot of the tower. Her mother had taught the girl her letters, though the merchant himself could read but poorly. And often the father peered at the books his daughter read, unable to make head or tail of them, yet somehow not liking them. One night very late, the silk merchant came home from a guild dinner in the city, and he saw a slim pale shadow gliding up the steps of the old tower, and he knew it for his child. On impulse, he followed her, but quietly. He had not considered any evil so far, and did not want to alarm her. At an angle of the stair, the lighted room above, he paused to spy and listen. He had something of a shock when he heard his wife's voice rise up in glad welcome. But what came next drained the blood from his heart. He crept away and went to his cellar for wine to stay himself.

After the third glass he ran for neighbors and for the watch.

The woman and her daughter heard the shouts below and saw the torches in the garden. It was no use dissembling. The tower was littered with evidence of vile deeds, besides what the woman kept in a chest beneath her unknowing husband's bed. She understood it was all up with her, and she understood too how witchcraft was punished hereabouts. She snatched a knife from the altar.

The girl shrieked when she realized what her mother was at. The woman caught the girl by her red hair and shook her.

"Listen to me, my daughter," she cried, "and listen carefully, for the minutes are short. If you do as I tell you, you can escape their wrath and only I need die. And if you live I am satisfied, for you can carry on my labour after me. My vengeance I shall leave you, and my witchcraft to exact it by. Indeed, I promise you stronger powers than mine. I will beg my lord Satanas for it and he will not deny me, for he is just, in his fashion, and I have served him well. Now, will you attend?"

"I will," said the girl.

So the woman advised her, and swore her to the fellowship of hell. And then the woman forced the knife into her own heart and dropped dead on the floor of the tower.

When the men burst in with their swords and staves and their torches and their madness, the girl was ready for them.

She stood blank-faced, blank-eyed, with her arms hanging at her sides. When one touched her, she dropped down at his feet.

"Surely she is innocent," this man said. She was lovely enough that it was hard to accuse her. Then her father went to her and took her hand and lifted her. At that the girl opened her eyes and she said, as if terrified: "How did I come here? I was in my chamber sleeping—"

"The woman has bewitched her," the father said.

He desired very much that this be so. And when the girl clung to his hand and wept, he was certain of it. They showed her the body with the knife in it. The girl screamed and seemed to lose her senses totally.

She was put to bed. In the morning, a priest came and questioned her. She answered steadfastly. She remembered nothing, not even of the great books she had been observed reading. When they told her what was in them, she screamed again and apparently would have thrown herself from the narrow window, only the priest stopped her.

Finally, they brought her the holy cross in order that she might kiss it and prove herself blameless.

Then she knelt, and whispered softly, that nobody should hear but one—"Lord Satanas, protect thy handmaid." And either that gentleman has more power than he is credited with, or else the symbols of God are only as holy as the men who deal in them, for she embraced the cross and it left her unscathed.

At that, the whole household thanked God. The whole household saving, of course, the woman's daughter. She had another to thank.

The woman's body was burnt, and the ashes put into unconsecrated ground beyond the city gates. Though they had discovered her to be a witch, they had not discovered the direction her witchcraft had selected. Nor did they find the wax image with its limbs all twisted and stuck through with needles. The girl had taken that up and concealed it. The Duke continued in his distress, but he did not die. Sometimes, in the dead of night, the girl would unearth the image from under a loose brick by the hearth, and gloat over it, but she did nothing else. Not yet. She was fourteen and the cloud of her mother's acts still hovered over her. She knew what she must do next.

The period of mourning ended.

"Daughter," said the silk merchant to her, "why do you not remove your black? The woman was malign and led you into wickedness. How long will you mourn her, who deserves no mourning?"

"Oh my father," she said, "never think I regret my wretched mother. It is my own unwitting sin I mourn." And she grasped his hand and spilled her tears on it. "I would rather live in a convent," said she, "than mingle with proper folk. And I would seek a convent too, if it were not that I cannot bear to be parted from you."

Do you suppose she smiled secretly as she said this? One might suppose it. Presently she donned a robe of sackcloth and poured ashes over her red-copper hair. "It is my penance," she said, "I am glad to atone for my sins."

People forgot her beauty. She was at pains to obscure it. She slunk about like an aged woman, a rag pulled over her head, dirt smeared on her cheeks and brow. She elected to sleep in a cold cramped attic and sat all day by a smoky hearth in the kitchens. When someone came to her and begged her to wash her face and put on suitable clothes and sit in the rooms of the house, she smiled modestly, drawing the rag or a piece of hair over her face. "I swear," she said. "I am glad to be humble before God and men."

They reckoned her pious and they reckoned her simple. Two years passed. They mislaid her beauty altogether, and reckoned her ugly. They found it hard to call to mind who she was exactly, as she sat in the ashes or shuffled unattended about the streets like a crone.

At the end of the second year, the silk merchant married again. It was inevitable, for he was not a man who liked to live alone.

On this occasion, his choice was a harmless widow. She already had two daughters, pretty in an unremarkable style. Perhaps the merchant hoped they would comfort him for what had gone before, this normal cheery wife and the two sweet, rather silly daughters, whose chief interests were clothes and weddings. Perhaps he hoped also that his deranged child might be drawn out by company. But that hope foundered. Not that the new mother did not try to be pleasant to the girl. And the new sisters, their hearts grieved by her condition, went to great lengths to enlist her friendship. They begged her to come from the kitchens or the attic. Failing in that, they sometimes ventured to join her, their fine silk dresses trailing on the greasy floor. They combed her hair, exclaiming, when some of the ash and dirt were removed, on its colour. But no sooner had they turned away, than the girl gathered up handfuls of soot and ash and rubbed them into her hair again. Now and then, the sisters attempted to interest their bizarre relative in a bracelet or a gown or a current song. They spoke to her of the young men they had seen at the suppers or the balls which were then given regularly by the rich families of the city. The girl ignored it all. If she ever said anything it was to do with penance and humility. At last, as must happen, the sisters wearied of her, and left her alone. They had no cares and did not want to share in hers. They came to resent her moping greyness, as indeed the merchant's second wife had already done.

"Can you do nothing with the girl?" she demanded of her husband. "People will say that I and my daughters are responsible for her condition, and that I ill-treat the maid from jealousy of her dead mother."

"Now how could anyone say that?" protested the merchant, "when you are famous as the epitome of generosity and kindness."

Another year passed, and saw no huge difference in the household.

A difference there was, but not visible.

The girl who slouched in the corner of the hearth was seventeen. Under the filth and grime she was, impossibly, more beautiful, although no one could see it.

And there was one other invisible item — her

powers, (which all this time she had nurtured, saying her prayers to Satanas in the black of midnight), her powers were rising like a dark moon in her soul.

Three days after her seventeenth birthday, the girl straggled about the streets as she frequently did. A few noted her and muttered it was the merchant's ugly simple daughter and paid no more attention. Most did not know her at all. She had made herself appear one with the scores of impoverished flotsam which constantly roamed the city, beggars and starvelings. Just outside the city gates, these persons congregated in large numbers, slumped around fires of burning refuse or else wandering to and fro in search of edible weeds, scraps, the miracle of a dropped coin. Here the girl now came, and began to wander about as they did. Dusk gathered and the shadows thickened. The girl sank to her knees in a patch of earth as if she had found something. Two or three of the beggars sneaked over to see if it were worth snatching from her—but the girl was only scrabbling in the empty soil. The beggars, making signs to each other that she was touched by God—mad—left her alone. But, very far from mad, the girl presently dug up a stoppered clay urn. In this urn were the ashes and charred bones of her mother. She had got a clue as to the location of the urn by devious questionings here and there. Her occult power had helped her to be sure of it.

In the twilight, padding along through the narrow streets and alleys of the city, the girl brought the urn homewards. In the garden at the foot of the old tower, gloom-wrapped, unwitnessed, she unstoppered the urn and buried the ashes freshly. She muttered certain unholy magics over the grave. Then she snapped off the sprig of a young hazel tree, and planted it in the newly-turned ground.

* * * * *

I hazard you have begun to recognize the story by now. I know you suppose I tell it wrongly. Believe me, this is the truth of the matter. But if you would rather I left off the tale . . . No doubt your carriage will soon be here—No? Very well. I shall continue.

I think I should speak of the Duke's son at this juncture. The prince was nineteen, able, intelligent and of noble bearing. He was of that rather swarthy type of looks one finds here in the north, but tall and slim and clear-eyed. There is an ancient square where you may see a statue of him, but much eroded by two centuries, and the elements. After the city was sacked, no care was lavished on it.

The Duke treasured his son. He had constant delight in the sight of the young man and what he said and did. It was the only happiness the invalid had.

Then, one night, the Duke screamed out in his bed. Servants came running with candles. The Duke moaned that a sword was transfixing his heart, an inch at a time. The prince hurried into the chamber, but in that instant the Duke spasmed horribly and died. No mark was on his body.

There had never been a mark to show what ailed him.

The prince wept. They were genuine tears. He had nothing to reproach his father with, everything to thank him for. Nevertheless, they brought the young man the seal-ring of the city, and he put it on.

It was winter, a cold, blue-white weather with snow in the streets and countryside and a hard wizened sun that drove thin sharp blades of light through the sky, but gave no warmth. The Duke's funeral cortege passed slowly across the snow, the broad open chariots draped with black and silver, the black-plumed horses, the chanting priests with their glittering robes, their jewelled crucifixes and golden censers. Crowds lined the roadways to watch the spectacle. Among the begger women stood a girl. No one noticed her. They did not glimpse the expression she veiled in her ragged scarf. She gazed at the bier pitilessly. As the young prince rode by in his sables, the seal-ring on his hand, the eyes of the girl burned through her ashy hair, like a red fox through grasses.

The Duke was buried in the mausoleum you can visit to this day, on the east side of the city. Several months elapsed. The prince put his grief from him, and took up the business of the city competently. Wise and courteous he was, but he rarely smiled. At nineteen his spirit was worn. You might think he guessed the destiny that hung over him.

The winter was a hard one, too. The snow had come, and having come was loath to withdraw. When at last the spring returned, flushing the hills with colour, it was no longer sensible to be sad.

The prince's name day fell about this time. A great banquet was planned, a ball. There had been neither in the palace for nigh on three years, not since the Duke's fatal illness first claimed him. Now the royal doors were to be thrown open to all men of influence and their families. The prince was liberal, charming and clever even in this. Aristocrat and rich trader were to mingle in the beautiful dining room, and in this very chamber, among the frescoes, the marbles and the candelabra. Even a merchant's daughter, if the merchant were notable in the city, would get to dance on the sea-green floor, under the white eye of the fearful clock.

The clock. There was some renewed controversy about the clock. They did not dare speak to the young prince. He was a sceptic, as his father had been. But had not a death already occurred? Was the clock not a flying in the jaws of fate? For those disturbed by it, there was a dim writing in their minds, in the dust of the street or the pattern of blossoms. *When the clock strikes*—But people did not positively heed these warnings. Man is afraid of his fears. He ignores the shadow of the wolf thrown on the paving before him, saying: "It is only a shadow."

The silk merchant received his invitation to the palace, and to be sure, thought nothing of the clock. His house had been thrown into uproar. The most luscious silks of his workshops were carried into the house and laid before the wife and her two daughters who chirruped and squealed with excitement. The merchant stood smugly by, above it all yet pleased at being appreciated. "Oh, father!" cried the two sisters, "may I have this one with the gold piping?" "Oh, father, this one with the design of pineapples?" Later, a jeweller arrived and set out his trays. The merchant was generous. He wanted his women to look their best. It might be the night of their lives. Yet all the while, at the back of his mind, a little dark spot, itching, aching. He tried to ignore the spot, not scratch at it. His true daughter, the mad one. Nobody had bothered to tell her about the invitation to the palace. They knew how she would react, mumbling in her hair about her sin and her penance, paddling her hands in the greasy ash to smear her face. Even the servants avoided her as if she were just the cat seated by the fire. Less than the cat, for the cat saw to the mice—Just a block of stone. And yet, how fair she might have looked, decked in the pick of the merchant's wares, jewels at her throat. The prince himself could not have been unaware of her. And though marriage was impossible, other less holy, though equally honourable contracts might have been arranged to the benefit of all concerned. The merchant sighed. He had scratched the darkness after all. He attempted to comfort himself by watching the two sisters exult over their apparel. He refused to admit that the finery would somehow make them seem but more ordinary than they were by contrast.

The evening of the banquet arrived. The family set off. Most of the servants sidled after. The prince had distributed largesse in the city; oxen roasted in the squares and the wine was free by royal order.

The house grew sombre. In the deserted kitchen the fire went out.

By the hearth, a segment of the gloom rose up.

The girl glanced around her, and she laughed softly and shook out her filthy hair. Of course, she knew as much as any one, and more than most. This was to be her night, too.

A few minutes later she was in the garden beneath the old tower, standing over the young hazel tree which thrust up from the earth. It had become strong, the tree, despite the harsh winter. Now the girl nodded to it. She chanted under her breath. At length a pale light began to glow, far down near where the roots of the tree held to the ground. Out of the pale glow flew a thin black bird, which perched on the girl's shoulder. Together, the girl and the bird passed into the old tower. High up, a fire blazed that no one had lit. A tub steamed with scented water that no one had drawn. Shapes that were not real and barely seen flitted about. Rare perfumes, the rustle of garments, the glint of gems as yet invisible filled and did not fill the restless air.

Need I describe further? No. You will have seen paintings which depict the attendance upon a witch of her familiar demons. How one bathes her, another anoints her, another brings clothes and ornaments. Perhaps you do not credit such things in any case. Never mind that. I will tell you what happened in the courtyard before the palace.

Many carriages and chariots had driven through

the square, avoiding the roasting oxen, the barrels of wine, the cheering drunken citizens, and so through the gates into the courtyard. Just before ten o'clock (the hour, if you recall the clock, of the magician) a solitary carriage drove through the square and into the court. The people in the square gawped at the carriage and pressed forward to see who would step out of it, this latecomer. It was a remarkable vehicle that looked to be fashioned of solid gold, all but the domed roof that was transparant flashing crystal. Six black horses drew it. The coachman and postilion were clad in crimson, and strangely masked as curious beasts and reptiles. One of these beast-men now hopped down and opened the door of the carriage. Out came a woman's figure in a cloak of white fur, and glided up the palace stair and in at the doors.

There was dancing in the ballroom. The whole chamber was bright and clamorous with music and the voices of men and women. There, between these two pillars, the prince sat in his chair, dark, courteous, seldom smiling. Here the musicians played, the deep-throated viol, the lively mandolin. And there the dancers moved up and down on the sea-green floor. But the music and the dancers had just paused. The figures on the clock were themselves in motion. The hour of the magician was about to strike.

As it struck, through the doorway came the figure in the fur cloak. And, as if they must, every eye turned to her.

For an instant she stood there, all white, as though she had brought the winter snow back with her. And then she loosed the cloak from her shoulders, it slipped away, and she was all fire.

She wore a gown of apricot brocade embroidered thickly with gold. Her sleeves and the bodice of her gown were slashed over ivory satin sewn with large rosy pearls. Pearls, too, were wound in her hair that was the shade of antique burnished copper. She was so beautiful that when the clock was still, nobody spoke. She was so beautiful it was hard to look at her for very long.

The prince had got up from his chair. He did not know he had. Now he started out across the floor, between the dancers, who parted silently to let him through. He went towards the girl in the doorway as if she drew him by a chain.

The prince had hardly ever acted without considering first what he did. Now he did not consider. He bowed to the girl.

"Madam," he said, "you are welcome. Madam," he said, "tell me who you are."

She smiled.

"My rank," she said. "Would you know that, my lord? It is similar to yours, or would be were I now mistress in my dead mother's palace. But unfortunately, an unscrupulous man caused the downfall of our house."

"Misfortune indeed," said the prince. "Tell me your name. Let me right the wrong done you."

"You shall," said the girl. "Trust me, you shall. For my name, I would rather keep it secret for the present. But you may call me, if you will, a pet name I have given myself—Ashella."

"Ashella . . . But I see no ash about you," said

166

the prince, dazzled by her gleam, laughing a little, stiffly, for laughter was not his habit.

"Ash and cinders from a cold and bitter hearth," said she. But she smiled again. "Now everyone is staring at us, my lord, and the musicians are impatient to begin again. Out of all these ladies, can it be you will lead me in the dance?"

"As long as you will dance," he said, "you shall dance with me."

And that is how it was.

There were many dances, slow and fast, whirling measures and gentle ones. And here and there, the prince and the maiden were parted. Always then he looked eagerly after her, sparing no regard for the other girls whose hands lay in his. It was not like him, he was usually so careful. But the other young men who danced on that floor, who clasped her fingers or her narrow waist in the dance, also gazed after her when she was gone. She danced, as she appeared, like fire. Though if you had asked those young men whether they would rather tie her to themselves, as the prince did, they would have been at a loss. For it is not easy to keep pace with fire.

The hour of the hag struck on the clock.

The prince grew weary of dancing with the girl and losing her in the dance to others and refinding her and losing her again.

Behind the curtains there is a tall window in the east wall that opens on the terrace above the garden. He drew her out there, into the spring night. He gave an order, and small tables were brought with delicacies and sweets and wine. He sat by her, watching every gesture she made, as if he would paint her portrait afterwards.

In the ballroom, here, under the clock, the people murmured. But it was not quite the murmur you would expect, the scandalous murmur about a woman come from nowhere that the prince had made so much of. At the periphery of the ballroom, the silk merchant sat, pale as a ghost, thinking of a ghost, the living ghost of his true daughter. No one else recognized her. Only he. Some trick of the heart had enabled him to know her. He said nothing of it. As the step-sisters and wife gossiped with other wives and sisters, an awful foreboding weighed him down, sent him cold and dumb.

And now it is almost midnight, the moment when the page of the night turns over into day. Almost midnight, the hour when the figure of Death strikes the golden bell of the clock. And what will happen when the clock strikes? Your face announces that you know. Be patient; let us see if you do.

"I am being foolish," said the prince to Ashella on the terrace. "But perhaps I am entitled to be foolish, just once in my life. What are you saying?" For the girl was speaking low beside him, and he could not catch her words.

"I am saying a spell to bind you to me," she said.

"But I am already bound."

"Be bound then. Never go free."

"I do not wish it," he said. He kissed her hands and he said, "I do not know you, but I will wed you. Is that proof your spell has worked? I will wed you, and get back for you the rights you have lost."

"If it were only so simple," said Ashella, smiling, smiling, "but the debt is too cruel. Justice requires a harsher payment."

And then in the ballroom, Death struck the first note on the golden bell.

The girl smiled and she said, "I curse you in my mother's name."

The second stroke.

"I curse you in my own name."

The third stroke.

"And in the name of those that your father slew."

The fourth stroke.

"And in the name of my Master, who rules the world."

As the fifth, the sixth, the seventh strokes pealed out, the prince stood nonplussed. At the eighth and the ninth strokes, the strength of the malediction seemed to curdle his blood. He shivered and his brain writhed. At the tenth stroke, he saw a change in the loveliness before him. She grew thinner, taller. At the eleventh stroke, he beheld a thing in a ragged black cowl and robe. It grinned at him. It was all grin below a triangle of sockets of nose and eyes. At the twelfth stroke, the prince saw Death and knew him.

In the ballroom, a hideous grinding noise, as the gears of the clock failed. Followed by a hollow booming, as the mechanism stopped entirely.

The conjuration of Death vanished from the terrace.

Only one thing was left behind. A woman's shoe.

A shoe no woman could ever have danced in. It
was made of glass.

*   *   *   *   *

Did you intend to protest about the shoe? Shall I
finish the story, or would you rather I did not? It is
not the ending you are familiar with. Yes, I
perceive you understand that, now.

I will go quickly, then, for your carriage must
soon be here. And there is not a great deal more to
relate.

The prince lost his mind. Partly from what he
had seen, partly from the spells the young witch
had netted him in. He could think of nothing but
the girl who had named herself Ashella. He raved
that Death had borne her away but he would
recover her from Death. She had left the glass shoe
as token of her love. He must discover her with the
aid of the shoe. Whomsoever the shoe fitted would
be Ashella. For there was this added complication,
that Death might hide her actual appearance.
None had seen the girl before. She had disappeared like smoke. The one infallible test was the
shoe. That was why she had left it for him.

His ministers would have reasoned with the
prince, but he was past reason. His intellect had
collapsed as totally as only a profound intellect
can. A lunatic, he rode about the city. He struck
out at those who argued with him. On a particular
occasion, drawing a dagger, he killed not
apparently noticing what he did. His demand

170

was explicit. Every woman, young or old, maid or married, must come forth from her home, must put her foot into the shoe of glass. They came. They had no choice. Some approached in terror, some weeping. Even the aged beggar women obliged, and they cackled, enjoying the sight of royalty gone mad. One alone did not come.

Now it is not illogical that out of the hundreds of women who's feet were put into the shoe, a single woman might have been found that the shoe fitted. But this did not happen. Nor did the situation alter, despite a lurid fable that some, tickled by the idea of wedding the prince, cut off their toes that the shoe might fit them. And if they did, it was to no avail, for still the shoe did not.

Is it really surprising? The shoe was sorcerous. It constantly changed itself, its shape, its size, in order that no foot, save one, could ever be got into it.

Summer spread across the land. The city took on its golden summer glaze, its fetid summer smell.

What had been a whisper of intrigue, swelled into a steady distant thunder. Plots were being hatched.

One day, the silk merchant was brought, trembling, and grey of face, to the prince. The merchant's dumbness had broken. He had unburdened himself of his fear at confession, but the priest had not proved honest. In the dawn, men had knocked on the door of the merchant's house. Now he stumbled to the chair of the prince.

Both looked twice their years, but, if anything, the prince looked the elder. He did not lift his eyes.

Over and over in his hands he turned the glass shoe.

The merchant, stumbling too in his speech, told the tale of his first wife and his daughter. He told everything, leaving out no detail. He did not even omit the end: that since the night of the banquet the girl had been absent from his house, taking nothing with her—save a young hazel from the garden beneath the tower.

The prince leapt from his chair.

His clothes were filthy and unkempt. His face was smeared with sweat and dust . . . it resembled, momentarily, another face.

Without guard or attendant, the prince ran through the city towards the merchant's house, and on the road, the intriguers waylaid and slew him. As he fell, the glass shoe dropped from his hands, and shattered in a thousand fragments.

There is little else worth mentioning.

Those who usurped the city were villians and not merely that, but fools. Within a year, external enemies were at the gates. A year more, and the city had been sacked, half burned out, ruined. The manner in which you find it now, it is somewhat better than it was then. And it is not now anything for a man to be proud of. As you were quick to note, many here earn a miserable existence by conducting visitors about the streets, the palace, showing them the dregs of the city's past.

Which was not a request, in fact, for you to give me money. Throw some from your carriage window if your conscience bothers you. My own wants are few.

No, I have no further news of the girl, Ashella, the witch. A devotee of Satanas, she has doubtless worked plentiful woe in the world. And a witch is long-lived. Even so, she will die eventually. None escape Death. Then you may pity her, if you like. Those who serve the gentleman below—who can guess what their final lot will be? But I am very sorry the story did not please you. It is not, maybe, a happy choice before a journey.

And there is your carriage at last.

What? Ah, no, I shall stay here in the ballroom where you came on me. I have often paused here through the years. It is the clock. It has a certain—what shall I call it—power, to draw me back.

I am not trying to unnerve you. Why should you suppose that? Because of my knowledge of the city, of the story? You think that I am implying that I myself am Death? Now you laugh. Yes, it is absurd. Observe the twelfth figure on the clock. Is he not as you have always heard Death described? And am I in the least like that twelfth figure?

Although, of course, the story was not as you had heard it, either.

RED THUNDER

Thunder in the black skies, beating down the rain,
Thunder in the black cliffs looming o'er the main,
Thunder on the black sea and thunder in my brain.

God's on the night wind, Satan's on his throne
By the red lake lurid and the great grim stone—
Still through the roofs of hell, the brooking thunders
drone.

Trident for a rapier, Satan thrusts and foigns,
Crouching on his throne with his great goat loins—
Souls are his footstools and heads are his coins.

Slave of all the ages, though lord of the air;
Solomon o'er came him, set him roaring there,
Crouching on the coals where the great flames flare.

Thunder from the grim gulfs, out of the cosmic deep,
Where the red eyes glimmer and the black wings sweep,
Thunder down to Satan, wake him from his sleep!

Thunder on the shores of hell, scattering the coals,
Riding down the mountain on the moon mare's foals,
Blasting out the caves of the gnomes and the trolls.

Satan, brother Satan, rise and break your chain!
Solomon is dust and his spells grown vain;
Rise through the world in the thunder and the rain.

Rush upon the cities, roaring in your might,
Break down the towers by the moon's pale light—
Oh, the red thunder-dreams in my brain this night!

—Robert E. Howard

Some Day I'll Kill You
by Seabury Quinn

Some promises take more than a lifetime to keep . . .

The seventh issue of *Weird Tales* contained a first story and also an article by a new writer, one Seabury Quinn. The story was titled "The Phantom Farmhouse," and it has often been reprinted. As a newcomer, Quinn was not to remain a stranger for very long, as things worked out: in fact, he became in due time the most faithful and devoted of all the many contributors to the Unique Magazine. In all, his work appeared in some one hundred sixty-four issues of *Weird Tales*, which makes him its most frequent contributor of them all. While his most famous creation was, of course, the immortal Jules de Grandin, from the very beginning Seabury Quinn interspersed tales in the de Grandin sequence with stories of supernatural menace laid all over the world, in every land and age. The most interesting thing about Quinn is, perhaps, his immense and enduring popularity with the readers: over many years, and even in the great days when Howard, Smith and Lovecraft were appearing in almost every issue, Quinn's stories still averaged first place in the reader's poll.

No other name is more closely and intimately associated with the long history of *Weird Tales* than is that of Seabury Quinn. And it seemed inconceivable to publish this first issue in the new sequence without a story by Seabury Quinn in it. The story which follows appeared in a rival pulp back in 1939 and has never been reprinted or anthologized. For that reason it will surely be "new" to most of our readers . . .

William Seffington Jeffers, Jr., and Marilyn Hosmer, were born within twenty-four hours and twenty-five feet of each othere, for their mothers occupied adjoining rooms at the Lamson Peel Memorial Hospital. When the nurse wheeled William from the baby-room for periodic feedings, Marilyn lay in the next basket in the carriage and seconded his lusty cries for nourishment with her shrill piping treble. When the time came for them to go home they rode in the same car, but William got out first, for he was going to live at 1632 Bay Avenue, while Marilyn's family lived next door at 1634.

The elder Jeffers was in the insurance business, Mr. Hosmer was a realtor. Both were active in Kiwanis, held memberships in the Shore Acres Country Club, subscribed to the same newspaper and voted the same ticket on election day.

When Bill—they had begun to call him that already—and Marilyn were four, their mothers entered them at Mrs. Brink's Select Kindergarten. When they were six they entered public school together. Thereafter Bill was waiting at the front gate every morning and walked home with her each afternoon. When they graduated to the upper classes and homework was required of them, Bill strapped their books into a common bundle and bore the burden as a matter of course. On Saturdays they played croquet in her back yard, or, in Indian suit and armed with tomahawk and wooden scalping-knife, Bill rescued Marilyn from hostile Redskins, or sometimes, by way of diversion, scalped Mary Jane, her favorite doll, while she emitted piercing shrieks and begged mercy for her child.

When they were twelve the Jeffers family took a cottage in the Poconos and the Hosmers rented one next to it. That was a wonderful summer. Bill had a new book, "King Arthur and his Knights of the Round Table," and within a week the children knew it by heart.

There was an added zest of adventure when you went for apples if you could tell yourself that they weren't really apples, byt a hoard of precious "jools" to be recaptured from a wicked knight, and that the old gnarled tree wasn't just a tree, but a darksome castle, moated and battlemented, which had to be attacked by storm. The war-cry of King Arthur's doughty knights rang through the orchard while Bill swarmed up the tree and shook the apples down for Marilyn to gather in her pinafore, and "Well done, Sir Gawain!" or "Strike bravely, Lancelot!" Marilyn encouraged while she retrieved the booty from the orchard grass.

High summer passed and on the hilltops fox-grapes ripened. On the tangle-wooded slopes the purple fruit hid under notched leases, pungent with the tang of wild growth and cool from its shadowed secret places. Both Mrs. Jeffers and Mrs. Hosmer were enthusiastic at the prospect of wild grape jelly, and a bounty of a quarter a basket was proclaimed.

"Why Marilyn, we'll make our fortunes!" Bill declared. "We ought to get at least a dozen baskets. That'll be three dollars, an' we can have a choc'late soda every afternoon 'til a'most Thanksgiving!"

It was September, but the sun was hot. The world was fairly drenched with warmth, late locusts whirred their strident cries in the heat, the golden light made latticed patterns on tree-shaded paths, the woods smelt sweet and moist. Bill walked a pace or two ahead, a basket of the precious grapes in each hand, Marilyn brought up the rear with a hamper dripping purple fruit. They were barefoot, a little travel-stained, more than a little dirty. Bill was jubilant.

"Seventy-five cents!" he gloated. "We've made a'most a whole dollar, just this afternoon—hey!"

He broke his computation of their riches on a sharp note of protest, for she pushed against him roughly, forcing him into the pathside bushes.

"Look what you're doin'," he admonished as he scrambled through the briars, for she had dropped her basket in the path and grapes were spilling on the stones like rice from a burst bag.

"Stay back, Bill; keep away!" she panted, reaching for a stick that lay across the trail.

Then he saw. The "stick" she seized with her bare hands was a two-foot copperhead which had been lying stretched full length in a warm patch of sunlight. Another step and he'd have put his unprotected foot upon it.

The reptile had the sinuous strength of its kind, but desperation gave her greater strength. Before it could writhe from her grasp or slip its head far enough forward to sink its fangs into her wrist she had thrown it twenty feet away into the bushes, and she and Bill were racing down the path in panic flight.

"Gosh, but you're brave!" he complimented when they finally paused for breath. "Weren't you scared a'tall?"

"More than I've ever been in my life," she panted, "but I was more scared that the snake would bite you than of what it might do to me, Bill dear." Then she began to cry.

Bill suffered oddly mixed emotions. No female, other than his mother, aunts and cousins, had ever called him "dear" before. Certainly none had used the term in that tone. It gave him a queer and rather puffed-up feeling. Then, too, Marilyn was crying. In their twelve years of companionship he'd seen her cry perhaps a thousand times, but somehow this seemed different. What would Galahad, or Gawain, or Lancelot du Lac have done in such conditions? He had the answer instantly—a grand and noble, knightly gesture.

Down on one knee he went before her, took the hem of her dress in his hand.

"When anybody saves another person's life, that life belongs to him or her," he announced solemnly, and raised the hem of her brief gingham pinafore to his lips.

She laid her hand on his hair, and it was like an accolade.

"I am your liege lady, and you are my true knight," she answered. "You will bear me true and faithful service, and when we're grown I'll marry you and you must love me always—oh, Bill, please do!" she ended in entreaty. "I'll just die if you don't."

"Course, I will," he replied stoutly. "Didn't I *swear* it?"

So, armed with stick and treading warily, they went back for the grape baskets, and in due time received their reward. But neither of them told of the adventure. Parents had a queer way of misunderstanding, and there were too many pleasant walks in the woods to be taken in the two remaining weeks of vacation.

They went to their first formal dance together, and it was there that Marilyn began to have misgivings. For two years she had known, with all the certainty that she knew sunrise follows darkness, that they would be married. Secure in this knowledge, she planned their life together serenely, longing with impatience hardly bearable for the time when they'd be old enough to marry and settle down.

But Bill had grown into a handsome boy, tall, slim, attractive, laughing readily, wearing his clothes with an air of smart distinction. And she was not a pretty girl. Her little, heart-shaped, sharp-chinned face was too small for her large, brown trustful eyes, and though her mouth was sweet and tender it seemed almost childish in its smallness. The slenderness which might have seemed alluring in another girl seemed adolescent immaturity in her. Her clothes were well made and expensive, but they hung on her like smart gowns shown on window-mannikins—well displayed but definitely no part of her personality.

Only her hair was remarkable. She had never had it cut. In childhood she had worn it rippling down her back, or in two long braids. Now, unbound, it reached well past her knees. Braided and wrapped about her head in a coronal, it was like a Grecian head-dress and made wearing almost any hat with *chic* impossible.

When she was in Bill's arms as they danced she was ecstatic. She never noticed that he did not talk, she did not know if he smiled at her or not. Her eyes were always closed. But when another partner claimed her, she was like a bird in a strange nest, and her eyes were opened and alert. Watching Bill and the girl he danced with, seeing how he smiled at her, noting how he kept up a continual flow of small talk.

Bill was too used to her, too certain, accepting her as he might take a match or lighter proffered when he lit a cigarette. She must make him jealous—coquette with other boys. . . . Pshaw, this was childishness! He might flirt with other girls; he belonged to her. He'd sworn it. . . . "My life belongs to you. . . ." Soon they'd be out of school, Bill would go in business with his father, then. . . .

They were in their senior year at college when the Serpent entered her Eden. A very lovely Serpent, all the more disquieting for that reason.

Ernestine McMurtie was the essence of everything Marilyn was not. Tall, willowy, smooth-skinned, with a red mouth chiseled in long curves, raven black hair piled in Vigée Lebrun curls upon her sleek head, she made every move in the way of a lithe silky cat. There were flecks of yellow in her amber eyes, giving them the effect of hot green. She knew her beauty. All her life the applause of men's eyes had told her she was different from other girls, more alluring, more desirable. Her father had some sort of vague connection with the theater, and she brought all the glamor of the mummer's art with her when she enrolled at State College. The sophomores were wild about her, juniors fought to dance with her, the senior class were her slaves to a man.

Sangreal, the quest of Galahad for the Holy Cup of Antioch, was the class play. Bill played Sir Galahad; Marilyn and Ernestine both tried for the part of Sir Percival's sister. Perhaps the acting honors went to Ernestine, but when Marilyn let down her hair so that it almost swept the floor and recited:

The girdle, lords, I'll weave of mine own hair
Which while I yet was in the world I loved full
well . . .

the rôle was given her.

But triumph could be as bitter as defeat. At the dance held after the play, Bill waltzed the first number with her, and was her partner in the rhumba just before the intermission. Every other dance he had with Ernestine, and when the other men cut in he stood against the wall, hands almost elbow-deep in trouser pockets, and glowered jealously.

The two girls joined issue in the powder room. Ernestine pre-empted the best mirror, posing and preening before it as she renewed her make-up. She spoke, and at once it was evident that the loss of the part was still on her mind.

"Some day," she threw the threat across her shoulder, looking from her reflection for a moment, "I'm going to crop that mane of yours, my dear, and you'll not raise a hand to stop me."

Smoldering anger and resentment rose and washed a flush across Marilyn's cheeks.

"You *are* a pirate, aren't you?" she replied.

"Oh? Touched on the raw?" Ernestine laughed brittlely. "Don't worry about your boy friend, dear. You can have him—now. I can take him any time I want, you know."

Hatred came into Marilyn's heart then, and she

answered almost automatically.

"Some day," she promised in a passionless, cold little voice, "I'm going to kill you, Ernestine."

That autumn Ernestine secured a little part in a road company of *Salute the Gentlemen*, and Marilyn and Bill were married.

To Marilyn, marriage proved an exception to the rule that realization fails to match anticipation. When the clergyman proclaimed, "Whom therefore God hath joined together let no man put asunder," and Bill put back her veil and kissed her, she responded with the last small cell of her being. It seemed to her that she had everything that she had ever dreamed of wanting.

Life flowed evenly and peacefully, almost monotonously for them. Bill joined his father in the office, joined the Shore Acres Country Club, addressed the Kiwanis at luncheon conferences, became a member of the Board of Trade.

Marilyn played bridge and attended meetings of the Ladies' Thursday Garden Club. When Bill junior and little Marilyn were old enough for school, she joined the P.T.A. and finally became its president. Everything went on and on, the groove of life deepened, but its course and pattern never changed. She loved it.

One afternoon, as she was coming home from a club meeting, she felt a sudden twinge of searing pain in her right side. For several months she'd suffered from recurrent aches like neuralgia in her stomach and had dosed herself with bismuth, peppermint and all the simple, harmless nostrums from the bathroom shelf, but this was withering in its suddenness. Hardly able to endure it, but fighting with the desperate ability women have to outface pain, she drove to Dr. Trowbridge's. By the time she reached his office the shrill torment had subsided, but her brow was beaded with small gouts of perspiration. She found it difficult to breathe, and where the pain had been there was an all-pervading, spreading numbness.

"Is—is it appendicitis, Doctor? she asked as he completed his examination.

"No," Dr. Trowbridge answered slowly. "It's certainly not that, but I'd like to have you call on Dr. Van Raalte. He's a specialist, you know; more competent to put his finger on obscure ailments."

"Then you think it's something serious?"

The doctor pursed his bearded lips. "One never knows, my dear, and it's best to take Time by the forelock when we're not quite sure."

As the door of the consulting room closed behind her, Dr. Trowbridge reached for the cigar that he'd been wanting for the last half hour.

"I'm not the hanging judge," he murmured as he snapped his lighter. "Let Van Raalte pronounce sentence."

Bill was going out of town that evening. There was a meeting of insurance men at Watertown and he was scheduled to address it.

"But Bill, dear, you don't have to speak till Saturday and this is only Thursday," she protested. "Must you go tonight? I've been feeling—" She halted in mid-word. Perhaps it wasn't really serious, after all. Dr. Trowbridge was an old man, and a general practitioner. He could be mistaken, and Bill must not be worried.

"Yes?" Bill prompted, a thought impatiently, as her silence lengthened.

"Oh, nothing. Just one of my silly premonitions, I guess. Go ahead and enjoy yourself. I know you'll make some valuable contacts at the convention."

It might have been midnight, possibly an hour later, when she woke in dreadful pain. It was worse than it have been in the afternoon—tearing, piercing, ripping like a red-hot bayonet. She clasped her arms across her stomach, hugging herself in blind agony.

Bill! His name was like a beacon to a storm-racked ship. Just to hear his voice would be an anodyne. Half blind with suffering, she groped her way across the room, dialed long distance.

"Mr. Jeffers—William Seffington Jeffers!" she gasped when the hotel answered.

A moment's agonizing wait. Then the telephone girl's high-pitched, nasal announcement: "I'm sorry—we have no one by that name registered."

The pain eased slowly, but she was too much shaken to sleep. Switching on the bedside lamp, she opened the evening paper, glanced through the club notices and turned to the amusement page. A child star's portrait smirked at her, there was a scene from a forthcoming movie, but like a compass needle swinging to the north her startled glance swept down the page to the halftone that was centered under the word "Charmer."

The picture was that of a woman beautiful in a well-tended way; a woman of high gloss and a hard finish: large eyes with long lashes, a straight and well-formed mouth chiseled in long curves. Her skin was flawless, her dark hair hung back from her face in a long bob that emphasized the good modeling of her head. Beneath the cut was the caption:

Ernestine McMurtie, star of "These Charming Ladies," now having its tryout at Hanneford. According to all indications both the charming Ernestine and the Charming Ladies are due for a long run on Broadway.

Ernestine . . . Hanneford . . . Watertown . . . Bill! The words clicked through her brain in series, like a telegraphic message. Hanneford was just ten miles from Watertown. The best hotel there was the Savage.

Hating herself, she ran almost headlong to the telephone, dialed long distance once more. It was mean, ignoble, disloyal and suspicious—but she had to know! Presently, the Hotel Savage's response: "Just a moment, please . . . Yes, there's a Mr. William Jeffers here, but he's not in his room. Shall we have him paged?"

"No, thank you." Marilyn hung up the phone and stumbled back to bed. No need to page him. As well as if she had been present in the flesh, she saw him . . . him and Ernestine.

In a little while the pain returned, and agony of body gave her some surcease from agony of heartbreak.

Three people stood beside her cot: Bill, Miss Masterson, the nurse, Dr. Van Raalte. The room was banked with flowers—"just as if I were already

187

gone," she thought bitterly. Early sunshine gilded everything. A bird, deceived by warm September weather into thinking summer still lingered, was twittering outside the window.

"Everything'll be all right, dear," Bill said heartily. "You see if it isn't."

"Of course, it will—it's just a simple little operation," seconded Miss Masterson with a smile that was bright and artificial.

"How do you feel, Mrs. Jeffers?" Dr. Van Raalte asked. He was a tall, lean man in his early forties, with prematurely gray hair brushed so sleekly that it shone almost like a skullcap of burnished pewter. Trained at Heidelberg and Vienna, he had brought home something of the Old World with him. His lean features, studious and unsmiling, had a hint of Prussian arrogance. He held himself as if he were in uniform and on parade. His tailoring and haberdashery had the trans-Atlantic perfection of Saville Row and Bond Street.

"In half an hour, if you please, Nurse," he told Miss Masterson, speaking with the sharp-clipped, cold precision of a drill master.

"Yes, Doctor—oh, you can't come in!" Miss Masterson ran toward the door. "No one else is allowed—"

"Oh, you can't keep me out, you simply mustn't. Mrs. Jeffers and I are old friends."

Arms filled with a bouquet of lilies, Ernestine McMurtie stepped into the room.

Her black sheer-crêpe redingote with the silver fox scarf draped across her shoulders, emphasized by contrast the ivory of her skin and enhanced the vivid black of her hair. She was poised and beautiful as she postured in the doorway—but she was not lovely. Something too closely akin to gloating malice shone in her eyes.

"Why, Ernestine!" Bill's heartiness of greeting almost hid his consternation and embarrassment. "It was kind of you to come—"

"See the lovely flowers Ernestine has brought, dear." He turned, smiling broadly toward the woman on the bed. "I'll get some water for them."

He leaned to take the lilies from the visitors, his back turned momentarily on his wife, and as he reached for the flowers his questing fingers found Ernestine's and clung to them, as if for strength.

Marilyn's great dark eyes seemed darker, deeper, and a small frown, as of sudden pain, brought her brows down. In the mirror of the dresser standing opposite her bed she had seen Bill's fingers seeking Ernestine's and finding them.

"Doctor," she asked in a whisper, "how much chance have I?"

He answered coolly, impersonally. "Not much more than one in a million, Mrs. Jeffers. You waited too long—"

"Doctor," she cut in, speaking softly, but with dreadful bitterness, "if—when—I die, will I be truly dead, or will I just seem so, with a consciousness of what goes on around me still remaining?"

He gave her a look hard and keen as one of his own scalpels, He, too, had seen the furtive handclasp.

"You need not give yourself uneasiness, madame. You will be completely blotted out."

Two hours later as he stripped his rubber gloves off he reverted to the language of his student days.

"*Herr Gott,* there's hardly enough left of her to bother about putting in the ground!"

"I'm taking charge of things for Mr. Jeffers," Ernestine told Miss Masterson. "A woman can handle such things so much better than a man. Have you a pair of scissors?"

"Scissors?" echoed the nurse.

"Yes, my dear, scissors. I want you to cut Mrs. Jeffer's hair. Cut it very short, please."

"Well," Miss Masterson prepared to carry out instructions, "all I can say is that if I had hair like that I'd want it buried with me. I never saw such fine, long silky—"

"That's just it," Ernestine broke in. "It's not to be buried with her. She's to be cremated. It would be a shame to burn that lovely hair, wouldn't it?"

"Yes'm," answered the nurse, as the shears cut through the gleaming coils of chestnut hair with the neat precision of a guillotine blade.

Ernestine McMurtie smiled at her reflection in the hotel dresser mirror. She was beautiful; she knew it, and the knowledge pleased her mightily. Her night robe was cut like an evening gown, sheer amber crêpe, sleeveless, almost backless, cut so low in front that it exposed the shadowed hollow between her breasts. It was belted at her slim waist with a tasseled golden cord, Grecian fashion.

On her bare feet she wore little gilded sandals whose wide, instep-straps made a pleasing contrast to the brilliant lacquer of her carefully kept nails. Across one slim bare arm she looped a braided length of hair—there must have been five feet of it, heavy as a ship's hawser, gleaming with the semi-iridescence of a chestnut fresh from the burr. She was thinking back twelve years, back to a scene in the powder room of this same hotel at the dance that followed the class play.

"I said I'd do it—and I did." Delighted laughter bubbled up between the words. "I promised that I'd crop that mane of hers some day. . . ."

She ran her hands along the smoothly plaited hair, kicked her sandals off and rose upon her gleaming-tipped toes to pirouette across the room.

"Stay there tonight," she tossed the heavy braid up on the shelf of the clothes closet. "Tomorrow I'll decide about you."

The coiled hair struck the back wall of the closet with a sound like that of a dropped coil of rope, partially unwound, and dropped a loose end over a clothes hook. Ernestine laughed again.

"I'm half a mind to hang you there all night, like an old gown," she said then shrugged bare shoulders as she closed the closet door. Why bother? She'd won all along the line. No need to rub it in. Not now, anyway.

She had been sleeping soundly, but all at once her eyes were open. Involuntarily she sat up in bed, in a state of semi-wakefulness. The room was heavy with rich, creamy, silky perfumed darkness that buried her completely as earth thrown in a grave. What was it? She was feeling it, physically, like a cool draft over face and arms and neck and breast, yet there was no sound, no hint of movement in the room. All the same, she knew that she was not alone.

191

Some deep instinct, some inner warder of the senses, was telling her there was someone, something, in the darkness with her. She sat waiting, breathless. It was so quiet she could hear the ticking of the tiny watch clasped to her left wrist and the click-click-clicker-click of the little traveling clock upon the dresser.

Something stepped—no, wafted!—toward the closet. Light, invisible, impalpable as air it was. It couldn't be a person, couldn't even be a thing, but that it was some sort of presence, some entity, she knew. Reason denied it clamorously. Instinct affirmed it, and mankind had its instincts a million years before it attained reason.

The closed door creaked softly, hardly audible, as if a stealthy hand were trying it, or a light wind blew on it.

"No, you don't!" she murmured as she flung the covers back and leaped from the bed. "Oh, no! I took it, and I'm going to keep it. You shan't have it!"

Automatically her hand strayed out and turned on the bedside lamp. Beside it lay a folded copy of the evening paper. She snatched it up, ripped it apart, crumpled it and thrust it crackling into the empty fireplace.

"You think you're going to take it to be burned with you? Oh, no! I'll burn it myself, right here and now, and you can't do a thing to stop me. *You're dead!*"

She was at the closet now, jerking back the door, reaching for the braid of hair that lay coiled on the shelf. Too high. She couldn't reach it. A hassock was the answer. She dragged the little slipper-stool across the room, mounted it, reached for the hair, seized it, dragged it toward her. . . .

The thing seemed imbued with sentience of its own. It resisted. She stood on tip-toe for a better grasp on it.

It came away so suddenly, she lost her balance, swaying backward, almost falling from the hassock. But only for an instant. Like a snake that holds its stroke until its victim is in easy reach, the loose end of the plaited hair lashed out. There was a double loop twined round her throat. The hassock, slipping on the polished floor, slid from beneath her.

She struggled with the clutching coil of hair. It might have been a hempen hangman's rope for all the effect that her frantic fingers had on it. She stretched her feet until they were continuations of her legs, like a ballet dancer's when she rises on her toes. They missed the floor by something like two inches, and she swung clear in a small, struggling arc.

Now she was thinking back twelve years again. Back to the scene in the powder room of this same hotel at the dance that followed the class play. ". . . I said I'd crop her mane some day, and she said some day she'd . . ."

The pounding in her ears increased its volume till it rumbled like the thunder of a thousand kettle-drums. And Ernestine ceased thinking.

Healer

by Mary Elizabeth Counselman

An eerie tale of a man who absorbed the pain of those who came to be healed . . .

It was a minor accident, but painful, and somewhat embarrassing.

Coming from the Deep South as I do, I was not accustomed to icy sidewalks. I was not dressed for below-zero weather, in fact, as I stepped out of the taxi that had carried me and my luggage from the airport. A new snow had fallen on the downtown streets of Minneapolis, freezing where it lay. And my heels were rubber-tapped. . . .

I fell, hard, on one knee. My handbag skidded away in one direction, my traveling case in another. It bounced open, its contents scattering across the sidewalk. Panties, bra — school-teacherish and severe. Liver pills. My extra dentures. Everything personal!

Trying to regain my feet, and slipping again to a jolting pratt-fall half-off the curb, I sat for a moment, keenly aware of the snow, to right gold-rimmed glassed hanging askew from one ear. A flush burned my face. Passersby were glancing back at me, snickering, but not stopping to offer help. *Don't get involved! The lady may be drunk . . . !*

Then, gratefully, I became aware of a hand under my armpit, helping me up.

"Easy, ma'am. . . ! You may have broken something . . ."

I glanced up into a face—a very nice-looking young hippy in jeans and a sloppy overcoat. His hair was shoulder length, his beard unkempt. But to me he was *Beautiful*.

"Thanks!" I gasped, clinging to him and gingerly trying my weight on the hurt leg. I winced—visibly, from his look of concern. "Sorry to be so much trouble. I'm here with the Teachers' Convention. Don't know anyone. . . . *Ooh!* I'm afraid I've . . . wrenched my knee . . ."

I glanced down, ruefully, at my torn nylon hose. Blood was running freely down my leg from the scraped knee, and the heel of my shoe had broken off. I wobbled, precariously, standing alone with an effort as my Good Samaritan rounded up my scattered belongings. He shut them in my traveling case; hung my handbag on my arm.

"Maybe I'd better get you to a doctor." He grinned solicitously. "Get that knee patched up, anyhow . . ." He looked about, frowning. "Let's see . . . What street is this? I'm from St. Paul; don't know the . . . But I think I noticed a sign just down the street. *Some* sort of medic . . ."

Taking my arm, he helped me limp a few yards further through the tide of hurrying, lunch-bound, pedestrians. He pointed. I peered through my glasses at a weather-worn sign swinging above a numbered doorway:

> *Dr. Wilbur Smithgall*
> *Empath*

"What's an empath?" I asked, clinging to the youth's arm and limping toward the frosted-glass door. "Something like an osteopath?"

"Damned if I know!" My young Galahad laughed. "Says *doctor,* though, so he ought to be able to give you first-aid anyhow—*whatever* he is!"

He half-carried, half-guided me into the warm, neat outer office, where a pretty assistant was toiling over some record-books. I collapsed into a chair as the young man explained, smiling:

"Lady here had a bad fall, out there on the ice. Can the doctor fix that knee for her?"

"Oh, yes. Yes, of course." The girl peered up at him briefly, then went on with her paper-work. "Bills, bills, bills," she muttered. "Oh, I *hate* the first of the month . . . !"

"You just have to mail 'em *out.*" My young gallant made a face at her. "Suppose you had to *pay* 'em!" He hesitated. "Say, just what *is* an empath? I mean—some kind of specialist, your boss is?"

"Yes," the girl said, briefly and briskly. "Do you have an appointment?" Blinking, as the youth looked at her with impatience, she nodded. "Oh!

196

Oh yes. You did say . . . the lady had a fall, outside. Well, I'm sure we can work her in, ah, *some* time this afternoon . . ."

I gave a little gasp, glaring around the perfectly empty waiting-room. "The doctor has another patient in there now. . . ?"

"No." The girl smiled at me briefly, soothingly, as at a fretful child. "He's . . . just resting. Accident-case this morning. It took a great deal out of him."

"Oh?" The young man lingered, hopefully, measuring the girl with admiring eyes. "That two-car thing at the intersection? Man, they really totaled that station-wagon . . . ! Nobody seriously hurt, I hope?"

"Almost." The pretty assistant gave a cheerful shrug. "Fortunately, Dr. Smithgall got to the man before the ambulance came. Otherwise, they might have . . . you know, amputated." She grimaced. "Leg was crushed, poor guy. *Mangled* . . . ! And fractured in three places."

"That drunk?" My youthful helper, frowned, puzzled. "But he . . . I saw him *walk away*! Cops had to go after him. Leaving the scene of an accident . . . . Man, I bet they put him *under* the pokey!"

"Yes," the girl nodded briskly. "He couldn't have walked *anywhere* though, if not for Dr. Smithgall. I mean, *ever again*! I certainly hope he has the decency to pay his bill . . . !" She bent over her paper-work again, muttering. "So many of them *don't*! And, without a license to practice, he *can't sue* . . . !"

I started. No license to practice? For the first time, I looked around at the office walls—usually graced with framed diplomas from the various medical colleges where the practicing physician had graduated. There were none. Over the girl's desk hung a large picture of St. Francis of Assissi and on another wall, a soulful-looking nun with bleeding wounds on her high forehead. I recognized Sister Theresa Meumann—the famed Stigmatic who bled from "scratches" like those made by Christ's crown-of-thorns. On a third wall was a simple, one-word motto, etched on an unpolished wooden board: *LOVE*. Glitter had been sprinkled on it. The letters caught a ray of sunlight through the door and twinkled out at me, benignly.

I frowned; got shakily to my feet.

"Your . . . Dr. Smithgall," I blurted. "Is he . . . some sort of *faith-healer*?" I glanced down at my injured knee, hesitating between bearing the pain (until I could find a *real* physician) and courting the possibility of an infection caused by a quack. There was even a chance my kneecap was cracked. Without a proper X-ray examination! "I . . . I . . . Perhaps I'd better come back later," I began, glancing helplessly toward the young man—who, I could see, had elected to hang around the pretty receptionist as long as possible. "Would . . . would you call a cab for me? My hotel. If I could just . . . ."

But, at that moment, the glazed-glass door to the Inner Sanctum swung open. A little man about five feet tall, stood there, with warm brown eyes and thinning blond hair, amazingly broad shoulders, and a quizzical but melting smile. He came out and took me by both hands. I stared down at him — awkwardly aware of my own towering five-feet-nine, which only seemed to "turn him on," as my students say.

"Come in, come *in*, madam!" he greeted me solicitously. "My!" "That's a bad-looking knee. Hurts, does it? Well-ll . . ." he crooned soothingly. "We'll have you fixed up in no time! Just lean on me. Tha-at's it! That's the way! Take it slow . . . !"

Before I knew what I was about, I was leaning on the little man in the crisp white jacket, limping into his office.

There was, I noted at once, no equipment in the room. No cabinets of shiny instruments; no X-ray machine. Nothing. The walls were painted a soft blue, and there was a deep, upholstered chair against one wall, with a footstool of the same blue-tinted leather. Nothing more. There were no pictures on the walls, but on the one opposite the windows was repeated, in large plastic letters, the word: *LOVE*.

I sat down, uneasily, in the deep chair, hoping this weird little medic was not going to put a more intimate interpretation on his slogan. But, to my old-maidish relief, his manner was kind but impersonal as he sat himself down, astraddle the footstool.

"Doctor . . . ?" I demanded. "Wh-what, exactly, *is* your, uh, speciality? What's an empath . . . ? . . . I don't believe I ever heard of . . ."

"Empath?" The warm brown eyes examined me keenly, from head to foot. "Never heard of *em-*

pathy? Oh, now, my dear lady! Surely you must have! Of course," he nodded thoughtfully, "we are rare. We genuine ones, I mean. Naturally, there are *pretenders*! But their cures are always, shall we say, accidental. No *organic* cures at all, really; they're just . . . well, psychosomatic. Auto-suggestion—it only works when the trauma was a mental one, rather than physical. That's the fallacy behind all these so-called "faith-healings." The ailment is always, originally, hysterical."

"But . . ." I drew myself up, firmly. "*Please*, doctor. Before you . . . er, begin treatment, I'd like to know just what an empath *is*! Something like an osteopath? You . . . manipulate the joints, or something?"

"Oh, no. No." The tiny man beamed at me, his large, brown eyes, friendly and full of compassion. "Are you frightened madam? Please don't be! I'm not going to *hurt* you. At *all* . . . ! On the contrary, as fathers say to their small sons just before a spanking: "This is going to hurt *me* worse than it does *you*!" He reached out gently, taking both my hands again in a firm, steady grip. "Now, now!" as I tried to pull away, startled. "You must *relax* . . . ! And *trust* me. That's essential."

"Wh-what are you going to do?" I asked. "What kind of . . . treatment do empaths . . . ?"

"Treatment?" He chuckled pleasantly. "No treatment—you wouldn't call it that medically speaking. Some might call it hypnosis—though it really isn't. It's . . . it's more . . . well, a transference of atoms."

"*Atoms* . . . ?" I jerked my hands out of his

grasp. "Now, really, er, doctor! I . . . I just came in to . . . to get my knee *bandaged* . . ." I peered at it; it was still bleeding, and beginning to throb now like a toothache. "Aren't you . . . going to X-ray? For a possible fracture?"

"No need." Dr. Smithgall beamed at me . . . "Empathic magnetism will simply . . . *draw out your injury*. Whatever its nature. A total empath, like myself, can *absord* pain, along with its source. Shall we try it now? Any time you're ready."

"I . . . don't quite . . . !" I gave him back my hands, somewhat warily. Trying not to let those intense brown eyes relax my vigilance again. This little man was some kind of *crackpot*! Certainly he was no physician, and I would do well to get out of here, I told myself. *Fast*! If only I could *walk*—

"Now!" he was saying quietly, calming me like a wild bird. "An empath? What *is* one? Well-ll . . . *Most* people, when you tell them something's hurting you—making you suffer—will say: "That's too bad! But it could be *worse*—it could be *me*! The brown eyes twinkled humorously. "Just . . . callous. Indifferent. "Don't tell me your troubles; tell 'em to the chaplain! Understand me?"

I nodded, lips compressed, grinning back at him in spite of myself.

"*Sympathetic* people," he went on lightly, "will say: "Oh, I'm so sorry! I'd like to help you, if I could . . . !" You understand? *If, if, if!*" He sighed, "*Empathetic* people, though the partial, empaths, that is—will *share* every pain you feel! A husband may even experience birth-pains when his wife is in labour. Mothers run a fever when their children are ill. Twins are empathetic, evern at a great distance—identical twins are especially . . . !

"Oh, nonsense," I broke in, laughing. "You're—As my high school students say, you're putting me on!"

"You're a teacher?" The little man's soft hands were still holding mine. I even fancied I felt a tiny *prickling* sensation from their touch, like static electricity. "Are you married? Such a fine figure of a woman! Of course you must be." His admiring glance made me blush.

"No, I'm . . ." My shrug was eloquent, slightly embittered. "My fiance just didn't come home from . . . Korea. End of sob-story!" I said crisply, drawing myself up erect in the deep-upholstered chair. "Are *you* an empathetic person? If you are," I drawled, "I'm sure you know this knee is *killing* me . . . !"

"I know," the doctor said gently—and I was puzzled to seen an expression of pain pass across his face like a moving shadow. "*Oh-h* . . . !" He drew in his breath sharply. "I . . . I believe you may have a torn ligament. Besides the . . . the surface wound . . . *Very* painful!"

He was gazing, almost dreamily, into my eyes as he spoke. Once again, the look of pain crumpled his features. His hands tightened their grip on mine. He winced. Grunted. And I saw his teeth bite into his lower lip as though to hold back an outcry.

At the same instant, my knee stopped hurting. It simply *stopped*. Astonished and relieved, I glanced down at the torn nylon, now stiff and brown with drying blood. There was a large tear in the fabric. And, through it, I could see the flesh of my exposed knee . . .

Healed flesh. Where the raw, skinned placed had been, there was now only a light reddish spot. Even as I looked at it, the inflammation faded to a healthy pink—as uninjured as the rest of my stockinged leg.

Then, with a small gasp, I noticed a dark red stain spreading across the white fabric of the little doctor's trousers—on the left leg, at the exact spot where my wound had been.

Dr. Smithgall glanced down at it with mild annoyance.

"Oh, *drat*!" he said lightly. "I should have rolled up my trouser before we began! Now I'll have to change them . . . ! Last clean pair, too!" he added, laughing. "That accident case this morning . . .! Bet I lost a *pint* of blood on that one. And—self-healing is so exhausting," he sighed. "I'm sorry you had to *wait* so long. But I must . . . *recharge my forces* after a healing."

I was staring at him now, as he rolled up his white pant's leg to examine, on his left knee, a scrape-injury identical to the one that had just vanished from mine. He poked at it gingerly, then closed his eyes as if in fierce concentration.

In about two minutes, the bleeding wound had disappeared . . .

If, indeed—I jolted myself upright in my chair—I had really *seen* such a wound on the doctor's bared knee! *Hypnotism*, hadn't he said? *Suggestion* . . .?? An experienced stage-hypnotist can make one "see" things that are simply "imaginary."

I stood up, furious at myself for no reason I could give a name. Had my knee-wound "disappeared?" *Or* had I ever *suffered* such an injury? True; my nylon was still torn and stained with dried blood—Or was it simply mud from the snowy gutter?

"Thank you—*Doctor*!" I said, somewhat waspishly. "How much do I owe you for the mesmerism?"

The little man chuckled, gently.

"So you don't believe your own eyes?" he drawled. "Well your reaction is . . . typical, I'm afraid. As yet, empaths aren't recognized by AMA! It's all too *simple* for the . . . trained scientific mind. Besides—The brown eyes were twinkling again humorously—"if the practice spread, quite a few physicians—and—surgeons, who are making a bundle now, would be . . . on relief.

"How *much*, please?" I fumbled in my purse, scornfully.

"Oh—five dollars." He shrugged. "It was a minor injury. I hardly felt a twinge . . . !" As I held out the bill, he waved me toward the outer-office door. "Pay my secretary, will you? I . . . I really don't have the time or strength to worry about . . . *fees*!" He frowned, somewhat ruefully. "My *wife*, though—she wishes I'd be a bit more *practical*! Or go into something that *pays* better. Like psychiatry—if I had the degrees for it."

I felt an unreasonable spasm of jealousy, all at once, as he spoke the word: *Wife*. In spite of my spinsterish asperity I had felt myself strangely at one with this odd little man. Almost, it seemed I had know him all my life! Closely. Warmly. *Intimately*—as I had never felt toward my long-dead fiance. Trustingly—without reservation. As I had found myself unable to respond to the fumbling advances of others. Why, it was as though I had *fallen in love*! At my age? Ridiculous! And with some weird little quack I had just met . . . ?

Fleeing from the sensation, which made me feel like a romantic old fool, I stalked out to pay my five dollars to the pretty secretary. She was trying, wearily, to fend off, the advances my persistent young "Boy Scout," and at the same time cope with a queralous blond, reeking of expensive perfume and swathed in mink. She was digging crossly into the doctor's till.

"Is *this* all you took in today?" She exploded. "That *fool*! If he'd give up this stupid *empath* kick, and *train* for something! Even take up chiropractic! "That Dr. Tuttle on Nineth has a *new Mercedes-Benz* . . . !"

"Yes, Mrs. Smithgall," the secretary was murmuring politely, with another glare at my youthful Galahad. "All*right*!" she hissed under her breath. "I'll *go* to the rock-concert with you! *Now* will you *get lost*?

"Sure! See you tonight, baby!" The youth waved at me, winked, and faded out quickly into the snowy street with an exuberant yell: *EE-YAH-HOO*!"

Grumbling, the mink-covered blond stalked out, with a fistful of cash—including my five-dollar bill.

I was about to leave, myself, when a middle-aged man with a wry, pasty face fell in out of the windy street. He was groaning and holding his stomach.

"*Oi!* Such *pain* I got! The doc—he's in? He'll take me?"

"Yes. Good afternoon, Mr. Finebaum," the secretary greeted him, rolling her eyes at me. "Oh, *no!*" she muttered under her breath. "Not an *ulcer* case . . . ! Poor Dr. Smithgall—he always gets sick to his stummick with ulcer cases . . . ! Honest, I don't see how he *stands* all their suffering!"

I snorted, and walked out briskly into the drifting snow.

Settled in my hotel room at last, I became more and more convinced that I had just been rooked by a clever little charlatan. Knee-injury! As I changed hose, dressing for dinner, I found not the slightest trace of a scab or scar on my healthy pink flesh. Obviously, I had *imagined* the wound! Shock can do strange things to one's mind—and I had certainly suffered a painful, jolting fall to that icy pavement. Small wonder I had been hallucinating!

Our banquet that evening was dull—chicken patties and a limp salad, with long, dreary talks about "evaluating the goals of teaching young hoodlums." I stifled a yawn and poked at my cherry cheesecake, again finding my thoughts drifting to the little doctor with the warm brown eyes.

Was there such a thing as an *empath*? I frowned. My dinner partner was an elderly psychoanalyst, retired, teaching now at some Western university. I peered at him; cleared my throat . . .

"Er . . . Could you give me some information,

Doctor? I . . . I . . . ran across the word *empath*. In, er, an article I was reading on the plane. Ever heard of such?"

The good professor squinted at me pleasantly over his pince-nez, sipping his coffee, one ear on the droning voice of the speaker.

"Empath?" he whispered, so as not annoy others seated at our long white-clothed table. "Oh yes. A *sensitive*. It's a very rare condition—neuro-psychotic, of course. "One who is super-sensitive to the suffering of others"—I think that's a fairly apt definition of the word. Zola was one, Emile Zola; that's why his books are so . . . perceptive! *Nana. J'Accuse*. Many artists are empaths, many composers. Wagner, I think—yes. He felt the suffering of humanity so keenly! And poor, epileptic Van Gogh—he even cut off his own ear, to punish himself for listening to gossip that had hurt a friend . . . ."

"No, no" I interrupted his pedantic little dissertation. "I mean, as a . . . a *medical* man. One who can . . . draw pain and injury *out* of another person. With just . . . oh, I suppose hypnosis, medical hypnosis. I've heard it can be used instead of anesthetics? For dental work, surgery, child-birth?"

The professor nodded. "Yes, indeed. It's used widely, nowadays, for patients who can't tolerate ether or drugs. Mesmer discovered the power. Freud used it, extensively, in hysteria cases . . ."

"No, that's not . . . not quite what I meant." I hesitated. "Tell me; do you believe a . . . a G.P. could simply *will an injury out of a hurt patient and into his own body*? A visible, physical injury . . . ? Like a cut? A simple fracture? A torn ligament? Or something like, say, a peptic ulcer?"

My dinner partner laughed, sipping his coffee and signaling a bored waiter for a refill.

"Now, *that*," he chuckled, "is a bit on the side of *voodoo*! Homeopathic magic? AMA would certainly frown on anyone who tried to present the idea as *practical medicine*!"

"That's what *he said . . .* !"

"Eh? *Who* said . . . ?"

"Er, the man who wrote the article," I evaded swiftly. "But, do you think such a thing is possible?"

"Anything is *possible*," The professor shrugged. "Heart-transplants — A century ago, that would have come under the heading of *science fiction*! And — space-medicine? Sending a man from weightlessness? Oh, yes. Yes. Anything is possible!"

I sat silent for the rest of the banquet, hardly aware of the speakers who rose, said their piece, and sat down again to a patter of applause.

Back in my hotel room, an hour later, I tried to watch T.V. Tried to read; to marshall my scattered notes on the various talks I had heard on new teaching-methods. But the face of little Dr. Smithgall kept rising, vividly, in front of me. Those brown eyes — tender, compassionate, discreetly flirtatious. My chill heart began to beat faster. What, day-dreaming heaven — knows it — I was almost irritated by a timid knock on my room door.

"Yes? It's not locked . . . come on in!"

One of the high school delegates entered — a

mousy little woman from Iowa, of about forty. She was pale, ill-looking, holding her head.

"Oh, *dear!*" I'm afraid I'm going to have one of my *migraines*. They . . . they knock me out for *days* when they hit me. Do you have anything stronger than aspirin? Any pain-killers? Without a prescription, I can't get . . . ."

"After-dinner speakers *always* give *me* a migraine!" I sympathized, and fumbled in my traveling case. "Here; these should do it. Don't take more than one!"

"Oh, *thank* you! If I can just . . . get some rest . . . !

She skittered out, leaving my to wonder why I had not kept one of the capsules for myself, in case my knee began to throb again in the night. Although, it felt fine at the moment. Had it *ever* really *hurt?* I had certainly fallen with all my weight on it, fallen hard, to the frozen pavement. At the very least, there should be a bruise. But there was none.

Crossly, I read myself to sleep with Burdett's Principles of Classroom Psychology . . . and drifted into a silly Sex-dream about little Dr. Smithgall. His arms were around me, holding me. We were kissing, and he was murmuring, over and over, in my ear: "Love! *That's all it really is, my dear—Love. The strongest force on earth!*"

I awoke, flushing, trying to remember how John had looked in his uniform as he boarded that troop train, the last time I ever saw him. He was tall, muscular, Garry-Cooperish . . . . But the memory had Dr. Smithgall's face! To save me, I could not conjure up the remembered features of my lost fiance.

"Ridiculous!" I snapped at myself, aloud in the empty hotel room. "You're acting like a lovesick teenager! And you're old enough to know better!"

I was phoning for a room-service breakfast of coffee and a poached egg next morning, when there was another timid knock on my door. It was the mousy little delegate from Iowa, still suffering from her migraine headache.

"Do you suppose there'd be . . . a hotel doctor? She moaned "I . . . I can't see to *dial the desk*, even! These attacks leave me blind as a bat. And nauseated . . ." She gagged; stumbling into my bathroom.

On an instant—and not because of any real sympathy for my fellow-delegate—I thought of a doctor she *could* consult. I had to see him again. *Had* to! And this was an excellent excuse . . .

If I saw him again, I told myself sensibly, maybe I would come to my senses. And act like an adult, forty-two-year-old English teacher attending a professional convention!

A taxi whisked us across town and deposited us in front of the glass-doored office with the small sign swinging in the wind: *Empath. Dr. Wilbur Smithgall* . . . I was furious at the way my heart skipped a beat at sight of his mere name on his shingle!

But, in the waiting-room, the pretty secretary sleepily assured us that the "doctor" could take my friend at once. Would I like to go in with her? Yes. Yes, I *would*—since she was blinded by her migraine, and needed someone to lead her.

The little doctor beamed up at me, at once, with his heart in his melting brown eyes.

"I was *praying* I'd see you again!" he whispered. "I . . . I've never *had* a patient with such . . . *instant empathy* as we established. Must be *love!*" The dark eyes twinkled. "I . . . I almost phoned you last night. My secretary mentioned the name of your hotel . . . How's your knee injury?"

"I never did *have* a knee-injury!" I snapped, taking refuge in rudeness. "All this is . . . utter nonsense! *Empathetic magnetism* . . . ! That's just a claptrap phrase you . . . you . . . invented!"

Dr. Smithgall winked, smiling up at me in a way that made my pulse jump. Then, briskly efficient, he turned to my fellow-delegate, already seated in the deep-upholstered chair.

"A migraine?" he murmured soothingly. "My secretary says you have them recurrently . . . ? Well, now, we'll get rid of *this* one in a *hurry!*"

I stood back, jealously watching as he took my friend by both hands and gazed into her clouded eyes. Perversely, I felt a sharp headache myself—from the desire to have him hold *my* hands and "heal" *me* instead! But—, "Hypnotism?" It was certainly not a thing of "eye-power." His present patient could not *see* those melting, compelling brown eyes! She could only hear his soft voice; feel his strong hands holding hers, *willing* her pain into himself.

And—less than two minutes later, the delegate from Iowa blinked and smiled. At the same instant, little Dr. Smithgall swayed. He moaned, pressing fingertips to temples, open mouth squared in sudden agony.

"Why, it's . . . it's *gone*!" My friend gasped in relief. "These attacks usually last a week or more! And I'm just *helpless* . . ." She looked from the doctor's face to mine. "It's a miracle! Oh, *thank you* for bringing me here! He's . . . just *wonderful*! But—what did he *do*? She stared from one of us to the other. "Some sort of . . . ? Like Oral Roberts? Or Tyrone Power, in the movie of the Somerset Maugham novel, *The Razor's Edge* . . . ? Thought-force?'

"Something like that," my little doctor was murmuring now. His face was slowly becoming relaxed, no longer contorted by—*Ridiculous, I told myself sternly*!—the pain of my friend's migraine, which he had drained off into his *own* head. And was now "willing" away . . . .

The Iowa teacher bustled out into the waiting-room, to pay her bill and chatter a bit, in wonder, with the pretty receptionist. The good-looking hippy was back again, I saw—waving at him through the door. Naughtily, I wished him luck with his "make-out."

Then I lingered a moment in the inner office, awkwardly. Trying desperately to think of something to say to Dr. Smithgall in farewell. *Oh, no—not good-bye—*!

There was no need for words, though. The melting brown eyes surveyed my tall, gawky figure in a severe two-piece suit, as thought I had been Rachel Welsh—in a brief bikini. *You're beautiful*! the eyes said. *You're Diana, and Venus, and Helen of Troy . . .* !

One of his soft hands closed around my fingers. And, once again, I felt a surge of vigor and well-being pass between, erasing my weariness from a night of insomnia. Though I saw my exhaustion pass from me into Dr. Smithgall's face, like a brief weakness. It was gone almost at once, and he beamed up at me.

"When can I see you again? Will you be here all week for the Convention?" he whispered. "Would you . . . just walk in the park with me? Over there, across from the office . . . ? I . . . I know I shouldn't ask, but—late this afternoon? Feed the swans, or something? By the lake . . . ?"

Shyly I nodded, wordless, and hurried out after my friend.

The rest of the day, with its interminable meetings and group-conferences, had a dream-like quality. I know I glanced at my pendant watch a hundred times, fretting at the slow way the hands were moving toward "late-this-afternoon." *How* late? He had not said . . .

But, at four-thirty, I was climbing out of a cab in the park. Strolling along the lakefront. Looking eagerly around.

Across the square, there was some kind of commotion. I moved closer, joining a small crowd that had gathered on the corner. And at once I learned the origin of the excitement. Some hoodlums had smashed a store-window; stolen some merchandise—a portable TV set, some clothing, a tape-recorder.

Plodding along on his beat, the cop assigned to this area had caught them red-handed. The youths had fled, dropping their booty and exchanging gunfire with the officer. They had escaped, but the cop had suffered a bullet-wound in the left shoulder.

Someone had noticed the "doctor" sign over a nearby door, and helped him inside. As I drifted past Dr. Smithgall's office, peering in, I saw him usher the middle-aged officer into his Inner Sanctum — calmly, pleasantly ordering onlookers about their own business.

I waited, torn between going inside and returning to the park to wait. Feeling foolish, I decided on the latter course. Inside, I could see the young hippy — again pressing his suit with the pretty receptionist. How those two youngsters would laugh if they knew a middle-aged old maid like myself was suffering from the same malady!

With a shrug, I walked briskly across the park to catch a cab on the corner beyond the doctor's office. He was not coming. I had been foolishly romantic to think he would . . . !

Then, suddenly, I saw him walking toward me. Hurrying. Almost *running*.

"*Oh-h!*" he panted, looking up at me in the dusk. "I thought I'd *never* finish with that police officer! His clavicle was shattered from the bullet . . . Took me some time to . . . recharge? "After I'd healed him. Bone injuries — they're harder, of course . . ."

He sank on a nearby bench, seizing my hand abruptly and pressing it to his lips. I tried to pull it away, but a strange, sweet weakness assailed me. I sat down beside him, very close, and let him take my other hand as well.

"You *love* me . . . ?" The brown eyes burned into mine suddenly. "Oh, you *do*! I'm sure of it! I . . . I felt it from the first minute . . . !" The little man sighed gustily. "Nobody . . . ever really *loved* me before. Not *enough*."

I sat shyly, dumbly, trying to pull my eyes away from his spelling gaze. My head began to swim. Tiny prickles in my hands were like static electricity passing from his hands to mine, and back again, as swiftly as an AC charge.

"*Yes!*" whispered Dr. Smithgall. "I sensed it! *You're* an empath, too—and just don't know it! I was certain this morning when you brought that other teacher in for treatment. You liked her—and so you briefly *empathized* with her! When I saw you rubbing your forehead, I knew you were *partially absorbing her migraine headache*! Just as I was! *You're a total empath—like me*! You're what I've been *looking* for! If . . . if only I could make you *love* me, really empathize with me . . . ! Then I could *reverse* the process of—of . . . healing!"

He stood up suddenly, dropping my hands. Smiling in a new, determined way. I saw his eyes—not warm and tender, but hard and shining with triumph.

"*Thank you*, my dear!" he whispered softly. "Now I . . . I can go home! To . . . to *her*!" His face contorted with frustration. "To my *wife*! I don't know *how* an intelligent man can get *hooked* on a woman like that—a mean, frigid little *gold-digger*! I've given her everything. Worked my . . . my empathy to the last *bone*, to buy her

215

anything she could possibly want! But I . . . I . . . can't *last* like I used to. This damned *black-lung fever*! I absorbed it from a coal-miner! Thought it was just a *cough*! He was breathing hard, gasping for breath. I smoked too much; always have. There's such nervous tension in my type of work. "And—with a *wife like mine*! What a *nympho*!"

He was breathing, suddenly, with more ease. Backing away from me now. Nodding exuberantly.

At the same moment, I felt an odd constriction in my lungs. I tugged at my collar, panting. Finding it harder and harder to draw a deep breath . . . .

"Yes! *Yes!*" My little healer nodded eagerly. "You've *absorbed* my illness! It's *gone* . . . !" He drew a long, satisfied breath of the soft evening air. "*Aahh*! *Thank* you, dear lady! I . . . I really do feel like a cad and a *bounder*, though. Taking advantage of . . . a over-romantic maiden-lady like . . . *Ooh!*" He clutched at his stomach suddenly. "That damned cop had enteritis! I'll be on a rice diet for *days* now . . . ! But that's curable. emphysema just—*isn't*. Not yet . . . Sorry! Hope you don't sufter *too* much . . . !"

He turned, cheerfully whistling, and strode away across the park. Back to his greedy sexpot-wife . . . .

I stared after him, breathing hard. Trying to get myself together. To laugh. To take a hard, face-on look at myself for being such a *fool*! An awkward, unglamorous old-maid school-teacher? "Over-romantic." His word stung my pride to the quick.

Was I, then, so unlovable?

But—Kenneth Peabody, our new chemistry teacher, had not seemed to think of me as a over-romantic old-maid. I smiled remembering the way he kept pulling out my chair for me, seating me gallantly at our faculty meetings. And lingering in the hall between classes, making some excuse to chat. About anything and everything . . . .

I had not let myself respond to his shy overtures. There could never be anything between us, I had told myself firmly. Except . . . a very painful farewell, in a few months. I could, perhaps, go on teaching for a year at the longest, my family physician had told me sadly . . . .

But not now! Now I could live again! Perhaps even love again! Kenneth had such nice manners. And a sincere way of . . . .

I began to relax—aware of that dull, nagging pain that had been gnawing at my vitals for months. It was fading, diminishing. Disappearing. As the surgery and the cobalt treatments had never made it recede. Why, I was hardly feeling it at all now . . . !

Glancing after Dr. Smithgall's retreating figure, I saw him double up suddenly, clutching his stomach. *Enteritis?* He would soon know. Emphysema was treatable. But . . . .

I sighed, and shook my head with deep pity.

Perhaps *someone* would come up soon with a cure for stomach cancer, I thought, hopefully. For his sake. Just any day now, surely! Before poor Dr. Smithgall . . . .

With a sigh, I strolled slowly back to my hotel, to send a picture postcard off to Kenneth Peabody saying: *Wish you were here* . . . .

The House Without Mirrors
by David H. Keller, M.D.

From the Casebook of Adam Lazarus, Doctor of Souls

Dr. David H. Keller, M.D., was a psychiatrist who specialised in stories whose horror was based upon the terrible urges and flaws within the human mind. His first story appeared in these pages in the issue of July, 1928. It was entitled "The Little Husbands," and from that date over the next fifteen years, he had some fifteen appearances in the Unique Magazine. His most famous story is probably "The Thing in the Cellar," from the issue of March, 1932; but his best and most unforgettable tale is "The Golden Bough," which was published in the issue of November, 1942. Like most authors, Dr. Keller died leaving behind him a body of unpublished manuscripts; among these is a sequence of tales which have never previously been published until now, and this is the first of them all. His stories are notable, if for nothing else, for the chillingly quiet understatement with which they probe the secret recesses of the human mind and soul. These tales of the Doctor of Souls, in particular, are remarkable for the mild language in which they reveal the recesses of the human condition. One could wish, indeed, that more authors of horror fiction possessed a doctorate in the science of the mind . . .

Since Dr. James Wilson, my niece's husband, had almost entirely taken over my medical practice, I was able to enjoy the quiet life of semi-retirement in North Shore and for some time had enjoyed a comfortably vagabond existence. Every day when the weather was pleasant I went for a long ride, pausing now and then to gossip with my neighbors. It was a pleasure to realize that I knew practically all the good folks in our little community.

Occassionally I passed Mr. Lowell walking through the countryside. He came to the store every Monday morning for the mail, but otherwise seldom, if ever, visited the village. His greetings were always courteous and dignified, but during the years I spent in the seaside town there had never been any indication that he would welcome conversation.

Therefore it was a distinct surprise when he walked over to my side one day, rubbed the horse's nose, patted my bulldog, Lady, and actually began to talk with me.

"I have just had the pleasure of reading your last book, Dr. Lazarus. You seem to be singularly fortunate in your ability to understand the inner problems of your patients. And I understand that you have endeared yourself to just about everyone in North Shore."

"Thanks for a very kind compliment, Mr. Lowell," I said. "You have discerned what many others have failed to see: I am more interested in the *souls* of my patients than I am in their bodies, and perhaps in my efforts to make them happier I have enabled them to forget their often purely imaginary symptoms."

After a few more general remarks, we parted and each went his way.

"What do you know about Mr. Lowell?" I asked Caleb Watkins that afternoon as we sat in his store. "We have frequently passed each other, but today he talked to me for the first time. I know considerable about most of my neighbors, but practically nothing about him. Apparently he has lived in North Shore for many years without ever becoming a vital part of the community."

"Ethan Lowell is our only citizen who is really wealthy," Watkins replied. "He is not only rich, but very much of a gentleman. Here is as much of his story as I know:

"One day, years ago, our sleepy town was set agog by the news that the old Blanchard house had been sold. It had been empty since Horace Blanchard died, as no one around here could afford to buy it. Then several wagonloads of furniture arrived from Portland. A man and his wife soon followed, put in a stock of food and fuel and began to set the house to rights for the new owner. We heard that a Mr. Lowell and his bride were on their way from Boston and would spend their honeymoon inside the high brick walls, which, you know, completely surround the place.

"I forgot that I was a grown man, and acted like a boy. When a coach was driven slowly down Main Street I took a short cut and climbed the large elm near the main gate to the Blanchard place. I saw a fashionably dressed young man, wearing a high beaver hat, step from the coach and assist a little lady to the ground. She fluttered into the house like a butterfly. After several trunks were unloaded the coach drove away, probably back to Portland."

"You are positively poetic, Watkins. I'll have to remember that phrase 'fluttered like a butterfly.' What happened then?"

"After that no one saw the little lady. That is, almost no one, though a few weeks after their arrival I again climbed the elm and watched them playing croquet on the lawn. After that I climbed no more. I realized that they were entitled to their privacy.

"Lowell started to take long walks into the country every pleasant day. He would bow to all the ladies he met and after learning the names of the men always exchanged formal greetings. The maid who had helped open the house seemed to be in complete charge. She bought all supplies, but, when I delivered them, her husband took the bundles at the gate, which otherwise was always closed. Lowell rarely came to town. All their bills

222

were paid promptly. Occasionally they received a mite of mail, and once in a while Mr. Lowell sent a package to Boston.

"Some of our women called, but were told by the man at the gate that Mrs. Lowell was not receiving company. Naturally, no one called a second time. Gossip spread like wildfire, burned fiercely and then died for lack of fuel."

"You ought to write a book, Watkins. Your account of this affair is positively fascinating," I said, smiling.

"When I was young I wanted to write; but being a husband and postmaster and storekeeper took up too much of my time. However, let's get back to the Lowells. As the years passed, thick mosses grew on the brick wall. At one corner an acorn sprouted on top of the wall, found some nourishment in the rotten mortar and finally sent its roots to earth. That tree is now well over six inches in diameter. For some reason of his own, Lowell never had it cut down.

"He continued to take his solitary walks, but we knew little more about him and his fluttering bride than we did the day they came to North Shore."

"You have left a lot untold."

"That is because I know nothing more. If you row up to a stately derelict on the Sargasso Sea and notice a large 'No Admission' sign hanging from the rail, you make no effort to go aboard. Not if you adhere to the code of North Shore."

"That's true. At the same time, there's a mystery about Mr. Lowell and his wife which I would like very much to solve."

"Perhaps you will, some day."

A week later Mr. Lowell astounded me by actually paying me a visit. He laid his high, old-fashioned beaver hat on the marble table in my office and sat down, stiff and erect, his hands clasped about a gold-headed cane held between his knees.

"There are no mirrors in my house," he said unexpectedly.

I waited, and he repeated the statement.

"You have said that twice," I remarked calmly. "Can you explain why it is necessary to dwell upon this fact?"

"Yes. Even as a child my wife had an intense antipathy to mirrors. When we became engaged and I started to prepare the Blanchard house for our home, she made me promise that there should be nothing in it wherein she might see her face."

There was a peculiar hesitancy in his choice of words, as though he was having difficulty in expressing himself. I let him talk without interruption, feeling that he would finally tell me the reason for his visit.

"This is a queer story, Doctor. I doubt if you have ever heard one like it. I was very much in love with Rose when we were married and I still love her—but our life has been very strange. I mean, our life together. I have not minded the isolation. Being a writer I live largely in dreamland. Perhaps you have read some of my books, not knowing they were mine, as I use a penname. Writing, however, is only of secondary importance, as my only purpose in living is to make my wife happy.

"We had a quiet wedding. Neither of us have any near relatives, so we have been very much alone, before and after our marriage. We were very content and happy as we drove to our new home. We wanted it to be a home to love in rather than just a house to live in. Our servants have been faithful, our wants few, and our finances ample. For all these reasons the little lady and I have been very happy. The first night we spent in our new home she elicited a promise from me that we would not leave it for a week but simply live there with the world shut out by the brick wall. So for a week we lived alone and admitted no one. On fine days we played croquet and on wet days we played at housekeeping; but always we played the game of love. Afternoons were spent in the garden, long evenings in the parlour. It was summertime in nature but spring in our hearts.

"On the seventh day of our marriage I dressed with more than usual care, believing that my wife might consider it an anniversary. She did not appear for breakfast; but at noon she entered the parlor, beautiful in her wedding finery. Although her eyes were open it seemed, somehow, that she was not aware of her surroundings. As I rose to greet her, she began to recite her wedding vows. To humor her, I recited my responses. When we finished she lifted her face as if for the first nuptial kiss. She shyly told me that she was glad the months of waiting were over and at last we were happily married.

"Since I thought she was playing a little game, I humored her. After dinner we sat on a stone bench in the garden and, as we sat there, she asked that for one week we live alone, with the world shut out by the brick wall. That was thirty-nine years ago. This will be hard for you to believe, but every seventh day we have repeated the wedding ceremony and every time it seems to her that we are just married. After I realized that she expected the ceremony repeated each week I always prepared for it, shaved more carefully and wore my wedding suit.

"During all these years I studied her carefully, and I became convinced of a few facts: she was not playing a game; she simply could not remember our wedding for more than six days. During the sixth night's sleep and on the seventh day all she could think of was that it was at last her wedding day. She has flutterd through life, happy and utterly unable to realize that her existence was anything more than a succession of honeymoons of one week's duration. She immediately forgot all previous events in the ensuing week of pleasure. I thought a child might help her, but no shooting star has ever deigned to visit our home.

"These years have changed her, as they have me, but she has never realized it. You see, each week she thinks she is a bride, and a bride is always young; besides—she has never seen her face.

"That was the way we lived till yesterday.

"As usual I was waiting for her in the parlor. I rose to stand with her before the imaginary minister, when she suddenly turned and stared at me, aghast. Indignantly, she told me that I was an imposter, an old man trying to act as proxy for her fiance, who was a handsome young man.

"Sobbing, heartbroken, she ran to her room. Since then she has refused to see me. You may imagine how I feel. I am a rudderless ship in a storm-swept sea. Lifetime habits cannot so easily be broken. We have lived a perpetual honeymoon. Now she treats me as a stranger and an old man. True, I am old and time has changed me. She also is changed—but this she cannot realize, as there are no mirrors in our home."

Without answering, I went to my bedroom, took a handmirror from the dresser, put it in my pocket and returned to the office.

"In that very rare antipathy to mirrors," I explained to him, "I believe we have both the cause and the cure of your wife's peculiar illness. Suppose, without further discussion, we test my theory."

When we reached the old Blanchard house I advised Mr. Lowell to conceal himself behind a large screen so that he might hear the conversation without being seen. He asked the aged housekeeper to bring Mrs. Lowell to the parlor. In a few minutes the servant returned, escorting a little lady with silvery hair, who, as she fluttered in, reminded me of nothing so much as a beautiful moth.

"I understand you have come to help me, and I am so glad," she said. "You will bring him to me, won't you? We were to be married yesterday at noon; but when I came down to meet him, an old man was there who insisted that he was my husband to be. The very idea of such a thing—December marrying May! Please find him for me, so we may live our young lives together. I have been waiting in my room with the unwavering faith that my true love would soon come to me."

"So you have never been married?"

"Of course not! We have been engaged only a year. The very idea of thinking that I had married before!" and her flashing eyes bespoke her indignation.

"Are you comfortable in that chair?"

"Yes, thank you. It is my favorite."

"Now listen to me most carefully. It is true that Mr. Lowell is elderly, but you too have aged with the years. I ask you to come out of your dream-life and face the world as it actually is. You, Mrs. Lowell, are the wife he has so devotedly cared for during all these long years."

Her eyes flamed and she sprang to her feet in rage. "You are a wicked man to say that. Surely you don't expect me to believe you? I wanted you to find Mr. Lowell. Instead you tell me I am old and the wife of an old man. I know that I am young. *I am young*! How can I be old, when I expect to marry Mr. Lowell as soon as he comes to claim me as his bride?" She burst into tears.

Without a word I offered her the mirror. She took it and held it before her with shaking hands. Then she looked into it—and saw. Slowly, through the tears, there came a look of understanding.

* * * * *

Eventually she joined her husband in slow walks around the edge of the town. At my suggestion some of the ladies called on them. His publisher arranged for a short visit to Boston. Occasionally I spent an evening with them, playing whist. Shy at first, they gradually became a real part of North Shore. Though she was never completely at her ease, their lives soon were almost normal.

I told my niece their story, believing that if she knew the details she might be of some help in their readjustment. I said that in my opinion they had lost many precious years; but perhaps my niece was right when she stated that it would be a better world if all married folks would do as they had done—live in a perpetual honeymoon.

Dreams in the House of Weir

by Lin Carter

"The hooting sounds are closer to the house tonight, and Elaine has glimpsed something huge and white squirming through the shrubbery under the walls . . ."

The following pages from the Journal of Hareton Paine were found amongst his papers, and may shed some light upon the mystery surrounding his suicide.

EXTRACTS FROM THE JOURNAL OF HARETON PAINE

February 16th, 1931:

No progress was accomplished on the *Chauraspan-chasika* today, due to virtually continuous street-noise and frequent interruptions from neighboring flats and the accursed telephone. The technical difficulties of trying to translate the complexities of the Sanskrit *schlokas* into decent English verse are, of themselves, quite enough to deter any but the most indefatigueable of scholars, but the almost incessant noise and requirements of domestic life render the deed not only impossible but an absurdity. I have taken to sleeping (or *attempting* to sleep!) during the day, reserving the nocturnal hours for my literary labors, which is a bit rough on poor Elaine. I begin to discover that a flat in Belgrave is not the place to work; these surroundings are intrinsically inhospitable, if not actively hostile, to scholarship. I must have solitude, and quiet, in order to concentrate. Bryce dropped in this forenoon and received my "whining" with a sympathetic ear; he suggests I let a place in the country for eight weeks or so, something remote and woodsy, devoid alike of close neighbors and, if at all possible, that infernal machine, the telephone. Candidly, it sounds like heaven, but doubt if my slender purse could afford such luxuries. However, at his insistence, I did speak with an estate agent who listened to a description of my needs, and promised to ring me back if he could find suitable accomodations among his listings. I feel rather dubious about the whole matter, and question whether I can afford the sort of peace and quiet I require; and then there is the problem of poor Elaine's condition. At any rate, the fellow did not call, so there's an end to it, most likely.

February 20th:

Wharton, the estate agent, rang me up this morning with several listings which more or less met my principal requirements. One of these caught my interest, a place called Delaware House, up in the north country. It was the name of the place which appealed to me, as Elaine has relatives living in the American state of the same name. Further questioning elicited several interesting facts. It is a large, mostly empty stone house some miles out on the moors from the nearest village, built in the Thirteenth Century by a Norman baronet, one Sir Ranulf de la Weir (hence the name of the place, simplified over the years), on Saxon ruins believed to have been continuously occupied from the Eighth Century. If I remember my walking-tours through that part of the country on holidays and vacations, no more somber and desolate surroundings are likely to be found. The downstairs rooms are still furnished, Wharton affirms, and village shops are near enough for weekly deliveries. It certainly sounds promising, I must admit. Elaine suggests I take a run up this weekend and look the house over. I am tempted to do just that, as the rental seems surprisingly moderate.

February 26th:

We arrived early this afternoon at Weirton Station, books, clothes, papers, files and miscellaneous personal articles all bundled into a battered old steamer-trunk. The village was small, the houses dingy and dilapidated, and the natives seem sullen and close-mouthed, and eyed us mistrustfully, muttering amongst themselves. As we wish little contact with them at best, however, this may all to the good. At least we shall have no interruptions from visitors.

Wharton's local man, whose name I failed to catch, met us at the station, bundled us into his roadster, and drove us over the moors to Delaware House. At first and even second glance, the house appears to wear a forbidding, even sinister, look, squatting motionlessly amidst the dreary flat desolation of the moors, a somber and ugly pile of age-darkened stone. It is build in the pure Norman style, the cold angular walls unsoftened by ornamentation, spare and gaunt and lean. You can see it brooding over the level waste kilometers off. As we drove nearer it grew in size under a cold, wet, heavy grey sky, until it seems to dominate the entire landscape. I could see Elane found it oppressive and disconcerting—in truth, the place does look grim and inhospitable—so I kept up a cheerful running conversation, mostly one-sided, knowing she would relax once she saw the interior.

And, of course, she did. The rooms are huge and of immense extent, with lofty, vaulted ceilings, and rather dark and chilly. But they are snug enough, and dry as a bone. The interior of the house was "modernized," a bit, under the early Tudors, at least to the extent of panelling up the naked interior walls, covering the rough stone with quaint carved oak panels, now black with age. And the furniture, which is ancient enough to qualify as

233

antique, is solid and comfortable enough, while the drapery, bedding and towelling, although musty from long disuse, are clean and usable.

I pointed out these features to Elaine, who still seemed a bit dubious. The kitchen — huge enough to feed an army, and high-ceilinged, with smoke-blackened rafters — was equipped with an old iron range, and pots and pans of pewter, and old china. For heating, well, there is a huge yawning fireplace in every room, and Wharton's man has had a copious supply of firewood cut and drawn, stacked neatly in the shed. There are even indoor bathroom facilities! Oh, we shall be comfortable enough here, as I assured Elaine.

March 1st:

Settling in, nicely. Delaware House is less somber and hostile than it seems — first impressions are usually bad impressions, or however the old apothegm has it! Architecturally, the house is an extremely interesting and unusual, and portions of it predate even the Saxon period, for there seems to have been a structure of one kind or another on this plot of ground from time immemorial. Wharton's man waxed voluble on its history while showing us around the enormous pile; the foundations are soldered stone-to-stone with molten lead in the ancient Roman manner, and the stonework in the crypt is considered Pictish by the vicar (who is by way of being the local expert on antiquarian matters), if not displaying traces of Phoenician.

I listened to this without further comment that

the usual polite, social noises; but, if it is actually true, it means that this site has been continuously inhabited by man for considerably more than two dozen centuries. Hard to take this sort of thing seriously, but, still, stranger things have been known to exist in this queerly desolate region of Britian.

Elaine seems subdued but comfortable. Dire and foreboding although this country seems at first exposure, the utter and deathly silence of the moors is most appealing. Believe I can begin my long-delayed work on the Sanskrit tomorrow morning.

March 2nd:

Rose bright and early after a deep, refreshing sleep which drained all of the tensions and nervousness induced by city-life from my being, and left my mind clear and receptive.

The beds are really quite comfortable, as is all of the furniture, although it must be veritably ancient. The absense of the telephone is sheerly a blessing; however, it is a pity that the house of the de la Weirs was never wired for electricity. Candlelabra or lanterns do little to lessen the dense gloom of the old house, where the shadows seem to lie thick, like layer after layer of dust of darkness, settled over generations and centuries.

Still and all, the lack of interruption and noise is marvelous. The unutterable silence of this house would be positively oppressive to anyone less morbidly sensitive to sound than I, and Elaine, although she says little and never voices a syllable of complaint, must feel it. Today I at least made a sizable start on my work, armed with a photostatic copy of the Sanskrit text, and my armful of glossaries, concordances, dictionaries, and, of course, the text of the Powys-Mathers translation. No interruptions of any sort occurred to break my concentration, although after some hours I did become gradually aware of a faint, distant hooting as of marsh-fowl. Over supper, Elaine mentioned glimpsing something in the underbrush near the house; the knee-high shrubbery grows right up to the outer walls, I should perhaps mention here, so if any wildlife inhabit the moor we are in an uncomfortable proximity to it. Nothing to worry about, of course, but Elaine seemed a bit jumpy and insisted on my closing the tall, narrow windows.

March 3rd:

A bit off my feed today, after rather an uncomfortable night. Bad dreams or something like that; indigestion, probably. Didn't quite feel up to tackling thorny old Chauras today, so wasted the morning poking through what remains of the de la Weir library. The family died out in the Eighteenth Century, I understand, and most of the collection was sold off to satisfy the creditors when the cadet line inherited the property, but recent owners or tenants have left a modest few shelves of odds and ends. Some popular novels, a few of those trashy romances women insist on reading, odd volumes of the Lake poets, and some intersting old Gothic romances from the following of Walpole and Mrs. Radcliffe. Grisly titles they have: *Buckets o' Blood* and *Varney the Vampire* and one that particularly caught my eye, with the entrancing title of *Horrid Mysteries*. Any more of this brand of literature, and I would suspect Weir House (as I have come to think of it) as being the original Northanger Abbey!

March 4th:

Accomplished little today. Hooting or honking of distant marsh-fowl kept breaking my concentration, and the gloominess of the huge, echoing hall I have chosen for my work-room made me queerly uncomfortable. The day was grey and overcast, the wind wet and chill, the piercing dankness penetrating through the dim window-panes.

Elaine says she does not like it here. When I pressed her for her reasons, she could give voice to none. But there is something about the old gaunt stone house lost in the immensity of the cold, windy moors that depresses her.

March 7th:

I have not been keeping up my Journal, must remember to do so. Have been sleeping badly—terrible dreams, which I can never remember upon waking. The work is not going good. I am aware of a curious inability to concentrate, and keep starting up from the pages as if I half-heard a distant voice calling me.

The hooting sounds are closer to the house than ever, and Elaine has glimpsed something white squirming through the shrubbery under the walls.

March 8th:

Last night I had a most peculiar dream which, upon awakening, I set down on the notepad I keep beside my huge, canopied bed. I shall copy the dream in my Journal here, as I can still make out my hurried scribble.

I was in a room I have never seen before, with gleaming metal walls and floor, and queerly-angled niches cut in the walls, holding stacks of plates or tablets. There was a nine-sided window in the wall, but from the position in which I was sitting I could not see it clearly.

I was at a lectern or stand, also fashioned of glistening metal, perusing an ancient book written in a language not remotely similar to any writing I have ever seen before—not cuneiform or heiroglyphics, not Mayan pictoglyphs or Arabic cursives, and certainly not Sanskrit. If anything, it looked like Chinese ideographs, but only vaguely.

The illumination was garish and livid, and emanated from a source unseen. Lost in the columns of strange charactery, my attention seemed to wander. Only my arms were within the range of my vision, and they were cloaked in some heavy, woven fibre which seemed metallic. I could not see my hands, but my arms moved oddly, with a boneless and sinuous grace suggestive of more joints than the human arm possesses.

Suddenly something caught my attention and I half-turned towards the window. It was, as I have said, nine-sided, and through it I caught a dizzying glimpse of a strange, unearthly landscape, all steep black crags cleft with vertiginous chasms. Beyond the rocky heights soared bizarre metal towers, and beyond them—incredibly—a weird sky lit by *five* multicolored suns.

Then, quite suddenly, I awoke to find myself trembling violently, my night-clothes soaked through with cold perspiration.

What does it mean?

March 10th:

Another of those unutterably bizarre dreams. I was again within the metal chamber, studying with feverish intensity a set of enormous metal plates inscribed in angular, vaguely runic, symbols. This time I seemed more "deeply" settled into my dream-body. I was even aware of its name— Kzoora, as nearly as I can reproduce the phonemes with my earthly tongue. I even knew what language was inscribed upon the metal plates—the language of the Nug-Soth.

Rising from my seat, which was a prism-shaped metal crystalloid, I paced the chamber restlessly with an odd, fluid gait. I could hear the rasp of the hem of my robes of woven metal as they brushed the flooring, and the click and clatter of my shoes against the steely tiles. Or was it the clashing of hooves that I heard, or the scraping of claws? I ask this, because it seemed to me in the dream that my nether limbs were curiously articulated, with more joints than are found in human limbs, and . . . yes, now I recall the sensation! . . . *that I possessed more limbs than are normal.*

Returning to my prism, I again focussed my perception upon the metallic plates. They were, I dimly knew, the Tablets of Nhing. And it seemed to me that it was my task to search the Tablets for spells which would hold at bay the frightful Dholes (although what this strange term might signify, I do not know). But I was aware, as Kzoora, that I was but one of a vast cultus of wizards bound to the worship of the premier divinity of this world, a goddess named Shub-Niggurath the Mighty Mother, prisoned here innumerable eons ago by the Elder Gods, her foes.

The Dholes were her servitors, I knew, even as we were her worshippers; but Dholes have certain . . . *habits* . . . which make them fearsome neighbors. Hence it was that those of my race, the Nug-Soth, who inhabit the surface of this planet strive endlessly to pen the terrible Dholes in those enormous and noxious burrows which they have tunneled beneath the crust of the planet. This world, by the way, is called Yaddith, and revolves about one of the many-colored suns, an orb of emerald radiance known to the astronomers of this earth as Deneb. The other suns are of various hues: one is the rusty dark crimson of drying blood, another a stark, livid blue-white sun, and there are two more whose colors are not within the spectrum of visible light known to my earthly eyes, and which are thus hues I can neither name nor describe.

Under the searing rays of the five suns the Nug-Soth and their ghastly neighbors had long striven in contention. But over recent eons the Dholes had grown in size as they had grown in strength, until by now their subterranean burrows threatened the foundations of our metal cities. And, with puzzling and inexplicable defection of one of our most potent archimages, a certain Zkauba, our barriers of magical force which held the ghastly Dholes pent in their fetid warrens were perilously weakened.

These morsels of information were apparent to me as if they floated upon the surface of my Kzoora-mind: absorbed in his perusal of the Tablets of Nhing, he was idly aware of them without thinking about them, as you or I are continuously aware of our identities and addresses and modes of occupation, without having to deliberately recall them to mind.

The dream ended quite suddenly. It seemed to me that the structure in which the metal-walled chamber of Kzoora was situated *shuddered* as to waves of seismic disturbance. Curious objects of unknown purpose fell clattering to the floor, and Kzoora came swiftly to his feet with, again, that odd articulation that seemed multi-jointed. As he did so, he turned and, from the corner of my vision, I observed his reflection in a pane of silvery metal. The peaked hood of his metallic robes fell back, exposing a visage of such horrible inhumanity—a proboscis like that of a tapir, and rugose, with seven red eyes, and a squamous body bipedal and human-like in design, but essentially insectoid in its several clawed limbs—that my earth-self recoiled in revulsion, and I awoke screaming, shaking like a leaf in the gale, and drenched in icy perspiration.

If these uncanny and disturbing nightmares persist, I shall have to seek an opiate from an apothecary in the village. But, please God, let them end . . .

March 11th:

I went for a long walk on the moors during the late afternoon, my mental processes too numbed by the lack of normal, healthy slumber, and driven forth from the gloomy old house by a restless agitation of body and spirit. The gorse and heather which cloth the hillocks are of dull shades of rust and purple, and dark, brackish pools lie hidden underfoot. There is something about this part of the north country which breeds ill-health; even the air seems stagnant and vitiated, as if intermixed with some poisonous miasma breathed from the pores of the earth . . .

For days I have been concerned by Elaine's pallor and lassitude. Her whining complaints get on my nerves, which are already frayed by those weird dreams which torment me nightly, and I become increasingly impatient and annoyed by her listless manner. Returning to the house, I caught her reading an odd little book, curled in her dressing gown on the window-seat. I inquired (I think a bit too harshly) what book it was; easily distraught, she fled from the room as if, for some reason, frightened of me, the book falling from her hand. I took it up and examined it.

It was a manuscript, written in a fine Spencerian hand, the leaves sewn together with scarlet thread. The title-page bore this inscription in hand-lettering: *Visions from Yaddith*, and the name of Ariel Prescott. I bore the slim folio into my workshop with excitement and surmise. I had thought that strange name "Yaddith" to have originated in my dream-disturbed brain, but here it was, affixed as title to this odd little hand-made volume. And there was one other element in this discovery which contributed to my excitement. When I had been at Cambridge, the decadent verse of Ariel Prescott had enjoyed a mild vogue among the undergraduates—those of them given to sampling hashish and studying occultism and Theosophy, at any rate. I had looked into her work and found it to be puerile pseudo-Swinburne, seasoned with the dark perversities of *Maldoror*.

What I held in my hand might well be an authentic manuscript by the poetess, who had, I vaguely recollected, died raving in a madhouse. I opened the folio and read a passage at random:

My nine claws trace inexplicable hieroglyphics acid-etched in perdurable metal.
Through odd-angled apertures pour diverse solar colors in five distinct luminosities.

> Crouched on my prism, I ponder cantrips to hold
>   at bay the bleached and viscous swine-snouted
>   worms.
> On Nython and Mthura, my brethren barter for
>   more potent ensorcellments.
> For lack of these, must the Nug-Soth perish in the
>   foundering of intricate metal cities?
> Alas, the mother remains indifferent as to which of
>   the races of her minions triumph!

I cannot describe the eerie effect these strange verses had upon me. So much of the poem seemed to tally with the details of my most recent dream, that I felt my blood run cold and my scalp tingle and crawl. *For the paw-like hand I had glimpsed in the metal mirror had borne nine claws . . . and the suns in the sky had numbered five.*

A shrill scream roused me from my tranced fascination with the little volume. A moment later, Elaine staggered into the room, panting of some apparition she had seen at the window; she virtually fell into my arms. I demanded exasperatedly what she had seen.

"A face . . . huge and white and bloated," she faltered. "With tiny eyes and a snout like a pig's."

I had little patience with her deliriums. "Some local farmer's hog has broken loose and went rooting amongst the bushes," I said scathingly. "Surely, that is nothing to make a grown woman scream like a banshee."

"But . . . it was so *huge!*"

Changing the subject, I brusquely inquired

244

where she had procured the little volume she had been reading when I had entered from my stroll on the moors. She said she had found it jammed behind some old books on the top shelf. I made her show me the place, but found nothing of further interest.

I must remember to ask in the village if Ariel Prescott had ever lived in the House of Weir.

March 14:

Doubtless because of my perusal of those weird verses in the little book Elaine had discovered hidden in the library, my dreams were again of the city of bizarre metal towers and dizzy black crags and labyrinthine streets of intricately-fashioned metal, under the burning rays of the five suns. It seemed to me that I squatted in a row of my fellow Nug-Soth as we hearkened to the thought-waves of our hierophant, Buo, the Arch-Ancient, him who was first among the servitors of the Mighty Mother.

These mental projections exhorted us to redouble our endeavors, for the monstrous Dholes had, only three day-fractions ago, broken through into the birth-crypts beneath the Ziggurat Z-12, to feast on the larvae of our young in a certain manner which was hideously indescribable. At this horrible news all of those ranked with me in the great ampitheatre became fearfully agitated, and raised a clamor of conflicting thought-impulses about which the dominant pulsations of him who was the prime servant of Shub-Niggurath soared: We must venture forth again in the light-beam envelopes, to plead stronger sorceries from the denizens of worlds yet farther off than any heretofore visited, that was the import of Buo's thought-message.

At that, we stilled timorously. Did the Arch-Ancient think to dispatch us to trans-galactic Stronti, or the triple star Nython, or Kythamil, or even fear-haunted Shaggai itself?

Even as we trepidated, the surface of the planet shuddered under our nether limbs, and black cracks appeared in the sheeting of the metallic pave. *Lä! Shub-Niggurath!* we prayed, our mind-radiations in flawless unison, as when we focussed our pulsations together to sustain the barriers which held the Dholes in their grisly depths.

And again I woke screaming, drenched in perspiration. To still my perturbed mind I groped on the bedside table for something to read, thinking to calm myself. I found the *Visions from Yaddith* pamphlet, and opened it to the following passage:

Sheathed in bent light, we drift to Kythamil or Kath.
The fungoid intelligences of Nzoorl repulse our entreaties.
Even should we migrate to a world remote from this,
The snouted worms can track us through our dreams
Which call like beacons through the eldrich dark . . .

I cast the vile pamphlet from me, shivering uncontrollably.

March 17:

My only friend and, to some extent, intellectual equal in the sordid little village is, as I have earlier recorded, the local vicar, Dr. Minge. He prides himself on his knowledge of the vicinity, and assured me that "Ariel Prescott"—the name was a pseudonym, it seems—did indeed once reside at the house Elaine and I now rent. When I mentioned finding the manuscript, he waxed voluble, if not enthusiastic, and informed me that the poetess had published her *Visions from Yaddith* in a small booklet issued from Charnel House Publishers in London in 1927, shortly before her mental derrangement grew so noticeable that she had to be confined in Oakdeane.

He also informed me that her surviving family had all known copies of the booklet hastily bought up and burnt, for some reason, before hurriedly moving out of Weir. Which meant that my manuscript was perhaps one of the only known copies of the text to exist . . .

On my way home from the village, crossing the moors, I heard again that sound of honking or hooting which we now heard nightly, and thought I saw one of those hogs which poor, sick Elaine is always seeing in the shrubbery. It was albino-white, and its fat sides seemed to *glisten* curiously; also, it seemed extraordinarily huge for a hog, but the swinish snout was unmistakable.

By the time I had gotten up to where I had thought I saw the monstrously swollen hog, it had gone off. Nor did I find tracks of its hooves, although the earth was moist and oddly beslimed: nothing but a broad, shallow groove as might be left by a heavy body either slithering or being dragged through the underbrush—odd, how these morbid fancies fill my mind these days! Those damnable dreams, no doubt—

And suddenly my flesh crawled and my throat went dry—absurd, and for no discernible reason. Just a thought that had flashed through my recollection—a line from that vile little volume of insane scribblings—

The snouted worms can track us through our dreams.

That night, drugged with a powerful opiate procured from the village apothecary, I slept heavily. And there were no dreams.

March 19:

Something strange happened today. I was on the roof, searching for dislodged tiles, for water or slime had been seeping into certain of the upper chambers, causing a particularly nasty stench. The day was leaden and grey, with dull light filtering through motionless, overhanging clouds. All was still as the proverbial grave, when I became aware of that annoying hooting or honking I had once ascribed to marsh-fowl. We had heard it oft of late, weirdly distorted to a deeper timbre—doubtless due to the fog which has risen nightly from the moors.

Now I heard the irritating sound again, but louder and closer than ever before. The deep bass notes of it were like the grunting of foghorns—no fowl that ever lived could voice such ominous tones!

Peering over the ancient battlements, I saw something slithering through the dry bushes that grew close around the base of the walls; whatever it was, it seemed *of an abnormal length*, unless it was several creatures in a row. Again, I caught a glimpse of something albino white, bleached and glistening, and for some reason the breath caught in my throat and I felt the sick clamminess of fear. *Then suddenly the white thing reared up against the wall of the house, and I saw that it had no limbs, no limbs at all, and the—size of the thing!—*

The next moment I found myself crouching behind the battlements, dizzy and shaking. I had momentarily blacked out—I, who had never fainted in my life! I crawled to my knees and peered over the edge, but there was nothing at all to be seen below that was unusual. And no trace whatsoever of the horribly immense, sluglike thing I had seen, or fancied I had seen . . .

In a moment or two, my head cleared. I realized, of course, that I had seen nothing: I had merely hallucinated the entire episode during my swoon. I forced a laugh at my gullibility, but my laughter sounded false even to my ears . . . and why was I trembling?

March 21:

Another of those accursed dreams I have come to dread almost nightly. Again Kzoora squatted on his prism, perusing the Tablets of Nhing; but unlike my previous dream-visits to Yaddith, none of the several suns were aloft. Instead, the nighted sky was lit by uncanny aurorae—trembling curtains of vaporous colors, among them nine unfamiliar to my earthly eyes.

It seemed that I was even more deeply settled into the sentience of the wizard Kzoora than on my previous visits. I understood that these queer, uncouth runes held the key to the planes of existance, and that by means of them could barriers be erected or the pathways made clear. For there are gates between the dimensions of space, and strange paths that exist between them; it was by this mode that the minions of Shub-Niggurath negotiated the universe in their light-beam envelopes, and—

My hand shakes upon the page: almost am I loath to trace here the next thought-current that drifted through the intelligence of Kzoora. But record it I must.

Others beyond the Nug-Soth may tread the paths between the planes, and among these are the horrid Dholes. And the runes which, even at that moment, the insect-creature was pondering, exposed to my shuddering consciousness a final, shocking revelation before which at this hour my soul sickens: for all intelligence has this mystery, that the mind is fragmented, with many sides—like the facets of a crystalloid. I was able to enter the mind of Kzoora, because the mind of the wizard was one facet of the many-sided mind, another part of which was my earthly self, Hareton Paine. And once one facet of the many-sided mind has entered another mental facet, though the gulfs traversed in dream be wide and very vast, *the Dholes can follow the tracks and trace you to your lair.*

And now at last I know the peril which broods here on these empty moors. And the white, squirming things we have glimpsed in the shrubbery — the hooting, honking, abominably swollen glistening things — are not hogs . . .

Later:

They are all around the house now, making the night hideous with their baying. We have taken refuge in the upper storeys, but even through locked and bolted doors we can hear the splintering of timbers and the shattering of tall windows before thrusting swinish snouts. *This* was the horror that drove Ariel Prescott mad . . . and am I any the more sane?

I have oiled and loaded my old army revolver, but there is little that hot lead can do to injure shapes of flesh that can travel through the very planes.

At least, they will not feed upon Elaine — sucking the life-essence from her flesh with those obscene, quivering snouts. For she lies at my feet, shot through the heart by my own gun.

In a moment, I will terminate my own existance; how merciful an end is death, an endless sleep in which there are no . . . *dreams*.

I curse the day I ever came to the House of Weir. The damnable thing should be torn down, stone by stone, and the site purified by fire. God alone knows how long ago the psychic linkage between this montrous pile of stones squatting amidst the moor and far, nightmarish Yaddith was established. And only God knows what huge, unthinkable and atrocious Act was done on this plot of ground ages ago, that makes it the nexus of evil contagion from alien spheres.

Not long to go now; even the stone walls shudder to the monstrous weight pressing upon them—

The window!—Merciful God, that FACE! Can anything that lives be so huge—

(*At this point the Journal breaks off and was never resumed.*)

*

FROM THE STATEMENT OF POLICE INSPECTOR FORSTER

. . . entering, found considerable damage to the doors and windows on the first floor, but no sign of theft or vandalism. The deceased was discovered on the fifth storey of the house, dead from a self-inflicted gunshot wound through the right temple. Near the body lay that of a young woman, later identified as wife of the deceased.

Could find no damage to the room, but the large window directly facing the two bodies had been smashed from the outside, as if by a powerful blow. Traces of peculiar slime on the woodwork of the broken window have defied analysis by police forensic laboratories.

No other signs of violence, other than the cause of death, were found on either of the bodies, but they are peculiarly *shrunken* and depleted, as though something had been drained out of them. Forensic experts are unable to account for this condition.

Recommend that the crime be assigned to the work of unknown vandals, and the case be placed in inactive files.

Statement ends

Continued from page 7

When *Weird Tales* finally ceased publication with its 279th consecutive issue, that dated September, 1954, it was a lone survivor of that great golden age of the pulp magazines. And when "the Unique Magazine," as it is sometimes called, was briefly revived in 1973 in time to celebrate its first half-century, it was a living legend from a fabulous, bygone era.

And now *Weird Tales* lives again, newly incarnated as a "paperback periodical" which is scheduled to appear twice a year, at least in the beginning.

Welcome to our *second* half-century!

This magazine made its first appearance on the newstands of America with the issue of March, 1923. It was published out of Indianapolis, by J. C. Henneberger, who also published *College Humor* which had been founded three years before and had quickly become a popular symbol of the "Roaring Twenties."

Mr. Henneberger, hoping to enlarge his young publishing empire, planned to bring out two new magazines of fiction, *Detective Tales* and *Weird Tales,* and he employed men based in Chicago to edit them: Edwin Baird, the mystery writer, and a music critic and writer named Farnsworth Wright, who served in the capacity of "first reader" of manuscript submissions. For the first issue of *Weird Tales,* Mr. Baird succeeded in finding a remarkable story—"Ooze," by Anthony Rud, which has since been anthologized many, many times — and a story by the pulp adventure story writer, Otis Adelbert Kline, a friend of Mr. Henneberger's.

Since Mr. Baird was only to edit the first thirteen issues of *Weird Tales,* his memory has very largely been eclipsed by the far lengthier editorial reign of his successor, Farnsworth Wright. It is a popular misconception that Mr. Wright discovered all of the great *Weird Tales* writers, but this is certainly untrue. Considering his brief time at the helm of the Unique Magazine, it is much to Edwin Baird's credit that he was able to attract to the fold such exciting new talents as Clark Ashton Smith, H. P. Lovecraft, Seabury Quinn, Frank Owen, Henry S. Whitehead and Greye la Spina.

Shortly before *Weird Tales* moved its editorial offices to a more convenient and central location in Chicago, Mr. Baird was replaced by Farnsworth Wright, who had contributed three stories to the early issues of the magazine before succeeding to the editorial chair. Farnsworth Wright was to edit *Weird Tales* for the next sixteen years and it was during this period that the Unique Magazine achieved its astonishing peak of success. Farnsworth Wright discovered and first printed such *Weird Tales* notables as Frank Belknap Long, E. Hoffman Price, Arthur J. Burks, Nictzin Dyalhis, H. Warner Munn, Robert E. Howard, August Derleth, Edmond Hamilton, Donald Wandrei, Manly Wade Wellman, Carl Jacobi, C. L. Moore, Robert Bloch and Henry Kuttner.

Mr Wright seems to have possessed the genius of

a true editor. Before long, this first of all the fantastic fiction magazines in the world (which appeared on the stands three full years before *Amazing Stories,* the first science fiction magazine, was launched) had become a prestige publication and to appear in its pages was a genuine honor. Writers from abroad, whose names are not generally associated with American pulp magazines, flocked to contribute to its pages—authors as distinguished as E. F. Benson, Algernon Blackwood, Gustave Meyrink (author of *The Golem*), S. Fowler Wright, and Gaston Leroux, who wrote the famous weird classic *The Phantom of the Opera,* thrice filmed. These were original contributions, by the way, and not just reprints.

And writers who had begun their careers under the auspices of other magazines were also attracted to the prestigious *Weird Tales:* A. Merritt, Murray Leinster, Jack Williamson, David H. Keller, and others. Mr. Wright's most celebrated editorial feat was to recognize the nascent talent in a brief short-story submitted by a fourteen-year-old boy named Thomas Lanier Williams, whose very first story he published; very much later, under the pseudonym of Tennessee Williams, that teenaged *Weird Tales* fan was to develop into one of the most distinguished playwrights of the American theatre. What is less-well-known, is that another of Wright's discoveries, the poetess Leah Bodine Drake, who contributed to the Unique Magazine for many years, also won, like Tennessee Williams, a Pulitzer Prize of her own.

In time, the Unique Magazine was sold by J. C. Henneberger to a new publisher based in New York City. It moved its editorial offices to a building in Manhattan—the famous "9 Rockefeller Plaza" address of my boyhood—and continued under the editorship of Farnsworth Wright, whose health by this time was failing.

Before very long, Mr. Wright retired and was replaced by a new editor (or editrix), Dorothy McIlwraith, a diminutive blonde Scotswoman with an impish sense of humor, who had been working as associate editor of *Short Stories*, another magazine issued by the new publisher.

And now *Weird Tales* had a new publisher as well, in the person of Lamont Buchannon. I was buying *Weird Tales* at the newsstand in my hometown in Florida in those days, and those two names are very familiar to me from the contents page masthead of every issue.

From the beginning, *Weird Tales* had specialized in finding new talent to brighten its pages. People you'd never dream had ever appeared in *Weird Tales* appeared in *Weird Tales*—mystery writers, later to become very famous, like Phyllis A. Whitney, John D. MacDonald and William P. McGivern; science fiction authors like Frederik Pohl, Damon Knight, Isaac Asimov, Robert A. Heinlein and Lester del Rey.

And so, for the last fourteen years of the first and greatest phase of its long life, *Weird Tales* under its new editor continued to discover, promote and encourage new talent. It is to the credit of Miss McIlwraith that she printed the first stories of such writers as Fritz Leiber, Ray Bradbury, Allison V. Harding, Stephen Grendon (which was actually a pseudonym for August Derleth, although this did not become known until very much later), and H. Russell Wakefield.

Weird Tales' third editor also attracted to the pages of the Unique Magazine the stellar talents of Theodore Sturgeon, who, although a discovery of John W. Campbell, Jr., the distinguished editor of *Astounding Science Fiction,* flourished in the pages of *Weird Tales* and contributed thereto some of his most memorable stories. And Dorothy McIlwraith became one of the first editors in America to recognize the unusual genius of the then-little-known British master of the macabre, William Hope Hodgson, whose brilliant tale "The Hog" she captured for *Weird Tales.*

Unfortunately, time was running out for the first and most famous of all fantasy magazines. Many of its greatest writers, like Robert E. Howard and H. P. Lovecraft, were dead . . . so many others had moved on to other magazines or more lucrative genres, such as C. L. Moore, Henry Kuttner, and Robert Bloch, then at work writing scripts in Hollywood for television and the movies . . . and so many other fantasy and science fiction magazines had arisen to crowd the now limited market.

Never in the healthiest financial state even at its peak, *Weird Tales* was losing money heavily during its last years. In September, 1953, the magazine converted to the popular new digest size, in a last-ditch effort to compete on the newsstands with the host of new fantasy and science fiction pulps. It was probably a case of too little and too late, unfortunately, for the issue of September, 1954, *Weird Tales* ended the first phase of its long and truly extraordinary career.

I can think of no other magazine in history which exerted quite the same sort of influence which *Weird Tales* exerted over the genre it shaped and perfected, and the authors who contributed to it so devotedly over the years. For example, the hard-cover publishing firm of Arkham House was founded by two *Weird Tales* writers, August Derleth and Donald Wandrei, for the express purpose of preserving in the dignity of bookform the best work of the more talented contributors to the magazine; and, forty years later, Arkham House is still at work doing just that. And there can have been very few fiction magazines in the history of publishing who have had as many of their stories dramatized on radio, television and in the movies.

As mentioned earlier, all rights to *Weird Tales* were purchased after its demise by Leo Margulies, the former publisher of such magazines as *Startling Stories, Thrilling Wonder Stories* and *Captain Future,* and the second phase in the unusual history of this magazine began. At first, Mr. Margulies simply mined back issues of the Unique Magazine for its best stories, which he republished in such paperback anthologies as *Weird Tales* (1964) and *Worlds of Weird* (1965), from Pyramid Books. Some years later, however, Mr. Margulies decided to revive the Unique Magazine in time to celebrate its fiftieth anniversary, and four issues were published during 1973 and 1974, under the capable editorial guidance of the distinguished anthologist and historian of the pulp era, Mr. Sam Moskowitz.

This second phase in the history of *Weird Tales* closed with the final issue, which was dated Summer, 1974.

And now we begin the third phase in the remarkable history of this extraordinary magazine. Since its revival in magazine form was unsuccessful, my publishers and I have concluded that the pulp magazine era is truly at an end and that such periodicals simply cannot compete in the marketplace with the enormously popular paperback book. It has, therefore, been decided to revive *Weird Tales* as a "paperback periodical," which will appear twice a year, continuing the old Volume-and-Number series from the last published issue.

Since the demise of the Margulies/Moskowitz magazine, all rights to the title and logo of *Weird Tales* have been purchased by Robert Weinberg, whose work in reprinting forgotten stories from the old pulps has earned him a high reputation among the buffs, as has his magazine, *The Weird Tales Collector*. By arrangement with Mr. Weinberg, we are able to launch this new series of *Weird Tales*.

But we need your help!

Whether you are an old-time reader of the original magazine, or a newcomer who has never seen an issue till now, it is only with your encouragement, your enthusiasm, your support, that the new *Weird Tales* can survive at all. Buy the magazine—read it—talk about it to your friends—collect every issue. In the long run, it is the readership alone that makes or breaks a magazine.

Won't you join your support and enthusiasm to our own, and come along for the ride as we launch forth into the *second* half-century of the most unusual magazine ever published?

Please do . . .

Lin Carter: Editor

RAY BRADBURY, one of *Weird Tales'* **most distinguished discoveries, writes from Los Angeles:**

I began to submit short stories to *Weird Tales* in the late '30's, heavily influenced by such sterling writers as Robert Bloch and Henry Kuttner. Throughout my high school years in Los Angeles I read *Weird Tales* at the local drug story—I couldn't afford to buy it. One of the few copies I ever truly purchased had a fine Virgil Finlay nude lady on the cover; my mother promptly tore the cover off and burned it. Her motives, to this day, have remained mysterious to me.

Anyway, by the time I was 22 and still selling newspapers on a Los Angeles street corner (supporting myself that way while trying to learn to write), I took a short story to Henry Kuttner. He read it, criticized it, and, when I couldn't write a proper ending to the story myself, he sat down and typed out a finale. I sent the story, "The Candle," out. *Weird Tales* bought it and published it in 1942. Kuttner's ending still remains on the story. I salute his friendly ghost.

From then on, I began to sell four or five short stories a year to *Weird Tales,* most of which went into my first collection, *Dark Carnival,* published by August Derleth's Arkham House in 1947. But, long before my appearance in *Weird Tales,* I had influenced its artistic makeup. In June, 1939, I had traveled across the United States on a Greyhound bus, bringing with me a dozen or so Hannes Bok drawings and paintings. I visited Farnsworth Wright in his offices, and he immediately commissioned Bok to paint a cover for *Weird.* I returned home on the bus in triumph, delighted that I had brought Bok and my favorite magazine together.

There, briefly, you have it. Poor years; happy years; years that influenced and helped me permanently. *Weird Tales* truly started me along the way. I am glad to be appearing here again, with some old friends.

ROBERT BLOCH, another fine author whose first work appeared in this magazine, writes from California:

Frankly, I can't remember just when it was that I wrote my first letter to The Eyrie—and will most certainly strangle anyone who tries to remember for me.

But as of this moment I'm experiencing a feeling of *déjà vu* for which I am most grateful. And the notion of once again reading a brand new issue of

"The Unique Magazine" conjures up a *vu* that is *déjà* indeed.

Seriously, the prospect of WT's resurrection is quite exciting. And most appropriate. If ghosts can become *revenants*, then surely *Weird Tales* ought to be able to come back and haunt our nightmares once again. As one who has always preferred Dracula unstaked, Larry Talbot at his most hirsute, and the Phantom of the Opera minus his mask, I rejoice in WT's return.

Congratulations, and warmest best wishes!

THEODORE STURGEON, another of *Weird Tales'* **most famous alumni, writes to wish us good luck:**

Few things in this life could make me happier than the revival of *Weird Tales*. I recognize, of course, that modern production and distribution compel its appearance as a paperback; but wouldn't it be great if it could appear with raggedy edges and absorbent paper and smeary ink and that special smell—and come out every month at 25¢? Ah, well—I always *was* a fantasist!

I understand that you are determined to make the new magazine as much like the old one as can humanly be done. I hope that this means that we'll see some of the great names of the past in the book, people who have the same thrilled nostalgia that I feel as I write this; people who have come a long way since those wonderful early days and who would like to return, with love, some of that welcome and encouragement the old magazine gave them.

I hope, too, that it continues to discover new talent, the young, fresh, skewed, inspired writers whose wonderful work no one else will look at.

As soon as I can pry myself loose from some of my too-many projects, you can expect a story from me. Meanwhile, all congratulations and best wishes to you for this much-wanted, much overdue rebirth.

SAM MOSKOWITZ, the respected pulp era historian and our immediate predecessor in this editorial chair, writes from Newark, New Jersey:

I was delighted to learn the news of your ascendency to the prestigious editorial throne of *Weird Tales*. Particularly so, since I know that you have the love for that unique magazine that will inspire that extra effort required to put it over.

A few of the old authors are left that might contribute, some new ones have developed that like the old tradition and, most importantly, there are many major authors around that like the idea of contributing to an old prestige publication, to be associated with a name that means more than money.

I ghost edited for Leo Margulies the Pyramid paperbacks *Weird Tales* (1964) and *Worlds of Weird* (1965), which were intended to be a series, with covers and some interiors by Virgil Finlay. They apparently did not do well enough to justify continuing the series (though both went into three printings with Jove substituting the Margaret Brundage cover from the October, 1933 *Weird Tales* of a girl with a bat headdress and partial mask replacing the original Finlay of a glowing man in a graveyard. We will probably never know whether or not it sold better, because the paperback line was sold to Berkley/Putnam before returns were in on that edition.

Probably the most unique thing about *Worlds of Weird* was my introduction, an essay on Clark Henneberger, founder and original publisher of the magazine. Farnsworth Wright, as editor, had become such a legendary figure that hardly anyone had ever bothered to ask who the publisher was. I got my information for that essay, incidentally, from Clark Henneberger himself, who was then still alive and with whom I not only exchanged several letters but also had several luncheons.

I twice talked Leo Margulies out of reviving the magazine, once in 1958 and again in the sixties, because I thought he would lose his shirt. When he did revive it briefly, in 1973–74, I resisted the idea of making it all reprints from *Weird Tales,* and suggested reprints of stories so out-of-the-way as to be virtually new, since hardly anyone had ever read them or could be expected to remember them, and to continue the magazine in this manner until a new string of contributors could be developed. Actually, the magazine, while it was losing money on its last revival, had a relatively short distance to go to break even and, with a publisher with more financial reserve, could easily have gone into the black with a few more issues. I don't think the odds are against you in that respect now.

Every best wish for success!

I swam until the afternoon was gone, and later walked into the town. Darkness was falling as I entered, and I found in the dingy streets foolish, tinsel tokens of lives which were not even conscious of the great, gloom-shrouded thing lying so close — vapid marionettes perched on the lip of the ocean-chasm, oblivious to what lay above them and about, in the grandeur of the multitudinous stars and the leagues of the night ocean. I walked along the gloomy shore as I went back to the bare little house, sending the beams of my flashlight out upon the naked, impenetrable void. And I felt an indescribable emotion born of the mighty, moving waters and the perception of my own smallness near a realm immense, the black borders of the earthly deep, the nighted deep, wherein shapes moved in darkness beyond my vision or comprehension.

Complete in the next issue, a remarkable
lost novelette only recently discovered—

THE NIGHT OCEAN
by H. P. Lovecraft and Robert H. Barlow

———— Also ————

FEAR
by Joseph Payne Brennan

**THE DESCENT
INTO THE ABYSS**
by Clark Ashton Smith

THE SOMBRUS TOWER
by Tanith Lee

TRICK OR TREAT
by Ramsey Campbell

THE LAMASHTU AMULET
by Mary Elizabeth Counselman

THE SURVIVALIST SERIES
by Jerry Ahern

#1: TOTAL WAR   (960, $2.50)
The first in the shocking series that follows the unrelenting search for
ex-CIA covert operations officer John Thomas Rourke to locate his
missing family—after the button is pressed, the missiles launched and
the multimegaton bombs unleashed . . .

#2: THE NIGHTMARE BEGINS   (810, $2.50)
After WW III, the United States is just a memory. But ex-CIA covert
operations officer Rourke hasn't forgotten his family. While hiding
from the Soviet occupation forces, he adheres to his search!

#3: THE QUEST   (851, $2.50)
Not even a deadly game of intrigue within the Soviet High Command,
the formation of the American "resistance" and a highly placed
traitor in the new U.S. government can deter Rourke from continuing
his desperate search for his family.

#4: THE DOOMSAYER   (893, $2.50)
The most massive earthquake in history is only hours away, and
Communist-Cuban troops, Soviet-Cuban rivalry, and a traitor in the
inner circle of U.S. II block Rourke's path. But he must go on—he is
THE SURVIVALIST.

#5: THE WEB   (1145, $2.50)
Blizzards rage around Rourke as he picks up the trail of his family and
is forced to take shelter in a strangely quiet Tennessee valley town.
Things seem too normal here, as if no one has heard of the War; but
the quiet isn't going to last for long!

*Available wherever paperbacks are sold, or order direct from the
Publisher. Send cover price plus 50¢ per copy for mailing and handling to
Zebra Books, 475 Park Avenue South, New York, N.Y. 10016 DO NOT
SEND CASH.*

MORE FANTASTIC READING FROM ZEBRA!

GONJI #1: DEATHWIND OF VEDUN   (1006, $3.25)
by T. C. Rypel
Cast out from his Japanese homeland, Gonji journeys across barbaric
Europe in quest of Vedun, the distant city in the loftiest peaks of the
Alps. Brandishing his swords with fury and skill, he is determined to
conquer his hardships and fulfill his destiny!

GONJI #2: SAMURAI STEEL   (1072, $3.25)
by T. C. Rypel
His journey to Vedun is ended, but Gonji's most treacherous battle
ever is about to begin. The invincible King Klann has occupied Vedun
with his hordes of murderous soldiers—and plotted the samurai's
destruction!

GONJI #3: SAMURAI COMBAT   (1191, $3.50)
by T. C. Rypel
King Klann and the malevolent sorcerer Mord have vanquished the
city of Vedun and lay in wait to snare the legendary warrior Gonji. But
Gonji dares not waiver—for to falter would seal the destruction of
Vedun with the crushing fury of SAMURAI COMBAT!

SURVIVORS   (1071, $3.25)
by John Nahmlos
It would take more than courage and skill, more than ammo and guns,
for Colonel Jack Dawson to survive the advancing nuclear war. It was
the ultimate test—protecting his loved ones, defending his country,
and rebuilding a civilization out of the ashes of war-ravaged America!

THE SWORD OF HACHIMAN   (1104, $3.50)
by Lynn Guest
Destiny returned the powerful sword of Hachiman to mighty Samurai
warrior Yoshitsune so he could avenge his father's brutal death. Only
he was unaware his most perilous enemy would be his own flesh and
blood!

*Available wherever paperbacks are sold, or order direct from the
Publisher. Send cover price plus 50¢ per copy for mailing and handling to
Zebra Books, 475 Park Avenue South, New York, N.Y. 10016 DO NOT
SEND CASH.*

THE HOTTEST SERIES IN THE WEST CONTINUES!

GUNN #14: THE BUFF RUNNERS   (1093, $2.25)
Gunn runs into two hell-raising sisters caught in the middle of a buffalo hunter's feud. He hires out his sharpshooting skills—and doubles their fun!

GUNN #15: DRYGULCHED   (1142, $2.25)
When Gunn agrees to look after a dying man's two lovely daughters, he finds himself having to solve a poaching problem too. And he's going to have to bring peace to the mountains—before he can get any himself!

GUNN #16: WYOMING WANTON   (1196, $2.25)
Wrongly accused of murder, Gunn needs a place to lay low and plan his proof of innocence. And—when the next body turns up—pretty Mary is his only alibi. But will she lay her reputation on the line for Gunn?

BACK IN STOCK!

GUNN #1: DAWN OF REVENGE   (1149, $2.25)

GUNN #2: MEXICAN SHOWDOWN   (1150, $2.25)

GUNN #3: DEATH'S HEAD TRAIL   (1182, 2.25)

GUNN #4: BLOOD JUSTICE   (1183, $2.25)